THE ONION EXPRESS

STORY OF MYSTERY

BRAD MCCLURE

Bloomington, IN Milton Keynes, UK

authorHOUSE

AuthorHouse™
1663 Liberty Drive, Suite 200
Bloomington, IN 47403
www.authorhouse.com
Phone: 1-800-839-8640

AuthorHouse™ UK Ltd.
500 Avebury Boulevard
Central Milton Keynes, MK9 2BE
www.authorhouse.co.uk
Phone: 08001974150

First published by AuthorHouse 3/16/2006

ISBN: 1-4259-1626-0 (sc)

Library of Congress Control Number: 2006901619

Printed in the United States of America
Bloomington, Indiana

This book is printed on acid-free paper.

DEDICATION

To:

Steve and Jennifer

Without your support and special talents,
writing would not be nearly so fun!

Thank you!

SPECIAL THANKS

To: You, My Readers

I write on the premise that casual reading ought
not to be a laborious task but rather it should
provide you with a sense of familiarity filled
to the brim with life, fun and adventure.

Your feedback supports that ideal.

Thank you to all!

BOOKS BY BRAD MCCLURE:

DESIGNATED DUMPEE

UPS & DOWNS

THE ONION EXPRESS

PRELUDE

The nearly sixty-year-old world-renowned restaurant and bar was already fully engulfed in flames when the first, of what would be several, local engine companies arrived to battle the four-alarm blaze. The fire had taken off and moved swiftly through the old structure. Even the first passers-by and early gathering spectators could feel the heat of the rising flames from the other side of the boulevard, some eighty-feet away, before the first siren had been heard approaching the scene.

From its beginning island residents frequented the popular bar often to enjoy its casual ambiance, maybe to listen to favorite local musicians, and of course, to enjoy the restaurant's local main dishes. Many of the tourists came to taste the bar's famous Mai Tais made from blended fine rums and juices squeezed from locally grown fruit.

The mesmerized, growing crowd watched in awe as the flames spread quickly inside the open-air dining area. The fire seemed to be leaping toward and teasing the oversized ceiling fans where the rising heat was forcing the blades to turn lazily as if on low speed. Looking deeper within the restaurant, observers could also see flames reflected by the great collection of antique beer and wine mirrors mounted inside the fully rounded bar located in the center of the restaurant. The famous bar itself, where so many people (probably millions) had seated themselves over its lifespan was burning intensely too. The fire's fury, aided by the many coats of lacquer the bar had received over so many years, continued to spread quickly. Also fueling the fire were hundreds of pieces of fine, hand-made rattan furnishings, which made a quick and easy meal for the ravenous flames sweeping through the entire scene.

The firefighters, knowing the restaurant was lost, placed their main concentration on and worked frantically toward protecting the adjacent hotel from the burning restaurant. The nearest parts of the hotel to the restaurant were the connecting breezeway and a few guest rooms. The fire's smoke and the firemen's high-pressured hoses now streaming in water from several different vantage points were ruining those parts of the connected structures.

From above the restaurant's kitchen, flames could be seen rising through the roof while occasional small explosions, presumably from small propane tanks and alcohol produced startled looks and groans from the still growing number of on-lookers, as well as from the firefighters involved in the battle.

Some six hours later the flames were fully extinguished, except for a few localized hot spots, which were being dealt with individually by the remaining firefighters left to perform the mop-up. The aftermath of the fire included a no longer existent local icon, *The Onion Express,* and a hotel so damaged by smoke and water that the insurance company would list it as a total loss.

It wasn't until the next day, when the ashes and burnt debris were sufficiently cooled that fire investigators combing the scene, found the ashen remains of two men in a tiny office that had only been accessible from the kitchen. The men, listed as missing by their worried families, were the restaurant manager and the night-shift supervisor. Because the remains were only charred bones and ash, it would not be until several months later that people would realize that the fate of the two restaurant employees had been sealed well before the first flame had come into view.

Characters

Family

Jack Bryce	Main Character
Veronica	Jack's Wife
Warren	Youngest Son
Patrick	Oldest Son
Ashley	Oldest Daughter
Marie	Youngest Daughter
Pogo	Fox Terrier
Ralph	Labrador Puppy
Aunt Jenny	Kid's Aunt

Onion Express Staff & Family

Tommy	Limo Driver
Kainoa Kapuulaa	Owner
Kappy Kapuulaa	Owner's Father
Pua Kapuulaa	Owner's Wife
Mark Malone	Manager
John Chu	Cook
Luanne	

Lahaina Police

Lieutenant Hai Ho	Homicide Detective

MAUI SCENES AND PEOPLE

Kahului Airport	Maui Airport
Maui Banker's Club	Restaurant
Honolua Bay	Snorkel Spot
Richard Hatcher	Stevedore
Jude Makala	Developer
Blaze	Runs Cockfights
Cigar Face	Works Cockfights
Lou	Assailant
Kimo & Paolo	Father & Son
Mary	Mary's Fish Market

FRIENDS & NEIGHBORS

Lt. Jim Alverez	Jack's friend
Geoff	Marie's boyfriend
Kathy	Warren's Girlfriend
Ally	Patrick's girlfriend
Rusty	Ashley's boyfriend
Vickie	Alverez's Wife
Gene & Marilyn	Jack's neighbor
Art & Chris	Soccer Coaches
Dr. Paklan	Town Doctor
Pablo	Poker Buddy
Cowboy	Poker Buddy
Matt-Man	Poker Buddy
Streaks	Poker Buddy
Jack Ass Jim	Poker Buddy
Big Dave	Poker Buddy
Sly-guy	Poker Buddy

CHAPTER 1........
THE ARRIVAL

Because Veronica is not very keen on heights, I had the window seat for the entire flight. Therefore, Veronica stepped out first, making room for me to squeeze into the already crowded aircraft aisle directly in front of her. Once there, and after stretching to get the kinks out from our four and a half hour flight, I reached into the opened overhead storage compartment to retrieve our two carry-on bags. The trek through the plane, following the other passengers toward the door, was stuffy, very slow and typical of unloading from a large tourist-filled passenger plane. I compare egress from an airplane as similar to cattle being prodded through a narrow chute. In cases like this flight of mostly tourists, the prodding came from the front and the rear. Whether it's being goosed in the rear by an in infant's car seat, or being hit in the groin by a swinging travel bag, the results are the same…airplane egress is truly one of life's little inconveniences.

As we reached the plane's opening, the sky was amazingly bright blue and it was dotted with infrequent small white puffy clouds along the horizon. When I stepped off the plane and onto the top of the portable ramp, the impact of the heat and humidity was immediate and the sun's warmth felt great.

Remaining at the top of the platform, I moved aside so that Veronica could join me for the temporary and somewhat perched view of the airport tarmac. After stepping on to the top of the ramp too, she reacted to the warmth and clean Hawaiian air with an approving smile.

"I can't believe we are here Jack," she said.

"Yeah, isn't it great?" I said as the line of people moved and we began following them down the stairs, onto the asphalt. "Can you believe it? I am going to be living here for the next six months and you and the kids will be able to come over as soon as the school year is over."

Veronica replied, "This is so awesome Jack. I can't believe you are going to actually live on Maui."

"Yeah it's great. The letter said someone would meet us in the baggage area so let's keep watch for a sign with our name on it."

We followed the other passengers into the covered and somewhat crowded baggage claim area as if we were again, part of a great herd of cattle following some unknown leader that was far ahead and well out of sight.

Kahului Airport is probably small by most international airport standards but the staff keeps the planes, passengers and baggage well organized and moving. Just as we arrived at the carousel, I could hear the motors starting up to drive the large conveyors responsible for moving our bags. Now the herd tried squeezing toward the conveyors as though it were a huge feed trough with everyone trying to get in close. Once there, luggage is plucked from the moving trough when recognized by their respective owners. Since the area was totally jammed with people, we decided to settle Veronica outside of the crowded baggage lines with our carryon cases while I wormed and maneuvered my way through the masses to retrieve our single but very large and very heavy suitcase.

On my way back to the carousel, I was moving in and out of traffic, trying to maneuver as the artful dodger, when I accidentally ran smack into the backside of an enormous man. In fact, when we collided, I bounced off him like a pinball while he didn't seem to budge at all. As I gathered my composure to offer a sincere apology the man turned, smiled a huge smile and asked, "You okay brudah?"

"Yes, thank you. Sorry about that," I smiled back.

"It's okay brudah."

The gentle giant with the large friendly smile was obviously a native to the islands and I guessed he was at least six foot four and definitely more than 300 pounds of solid mass. It would have taken more than two of my arms to match the girth of one of his biceps. As I moved around him, I noticed his colorful Hawaiian shirt, khaki pants and comfortable looking but more than casual leather sandals. I also noticed that he was holding a sign between his two large hands. As I got around him, I looked again only to discover the sign he was holding spelled Bryce.

"Excuse me?" I said regaining his attention. "But, my name is Bryce. Jack Bryce. Are you here for my wife and me?"

The grinning man looked at his sign to confirm Bryce and then looked at me. "Ahh, sure brudah. You Mr. Bryce den I am here for you. But I don't see your wife or your bags."

I explained to him that Veronica was not far away and that I was trying to recover our one large and very heavy suitcase from the baggage carousel.

"Ahh. You show me your bag ticket number and I go get it for you."

When I pointed out the bag, the giant gently parted the people in his way picking up the ninety-five pound bag with one hand like it was a purse or something. I envisioned the gentle giant in the weights section of some gym performing weightlifting exhibitions.

When he returned with the bag, his smile was still as huge as when I first bumped into him. "My name is Thomas but everyone, they just call me Tommy. Is that okay with you?"

"Okay. Well thanks, Tommy. People just call me Jack."

"Okay brudah. We go get Mrs. Bryce now and I drive you to your place. Okay?"

"Okay," I replied.

Tommy followed me out to where Veronica was waiting with the two small bags and I thought she was going to strain her neck when I introduced her to Tommy. After the introduction, Tommy reached out taking up the two smaller bags with his free hand and led us to a dark blue limousine, a Lincoln Continental, where he placed the bags in a spacious trunk and then opened the door for Veronica. Once she was inside, he left me standing at the open car door and said, "Okay. We gonna go now."

All I could do was to say "okay" and then I climbed in next to Veronica pulling the door closed behind me.

Tommy, smiling and seemingly very friendly, remained mostly quiet unless Veronica or I asked a specific question. One question I had was, "Where are we going Tommy?"

Picking up an envelope off the front seat and handing it back to us he said, "We going to take the road past Lahaina and go straight up to Kahana. The company has a real nice place for you der. I already delivered your other things der yesterday. Your place is on the tenth floor and has a very nice view of Molokai." Tommy was referring to some personal belongings that Veronica and I had packed and shipped in advance of our arrival.

"What can you tell me about the *Onion Express,*" I asked of our friendly giant.

"Da' *Onion Express*? You here for da' *Onion Express*? Da' *Onion Express* burned down more den four months ago. The place for, for everybody who go der, is shaka bruddah. So you da' big kahuna who is gonna fix up da' place?"

"Well I'm supposed to be the Project Manager who is going to help rebuild it. By the way what is shaka?"

"Shaka?" The big man turned and grinned his biggest smile yet. Shaka is olelo for excellent."

"Olelo?" I asked.

"Oh sorry bruddah. Olelo mean language in Hawaiian. So, dat's great that you are going to fix da' place. Lots of da' tourists stay der in the hotel, but it is also a favorite place for locals because dey go to the restaurant and bar for the food and da music. Man dey got some of the best sounds on da' island. So if you gonna go der and be da big kahuna den you gonna be everybody's brah."

"What's a brah Tommy?" Veronica chimed in.

"Oh! Brah? Well brah is good. A brah is a pal. Everybody going to like you and be your brah because you are going to fix up der favorite place."

"Sounds like fun, Tommy. I'm looking forward to getting started as soon as I can."

Just as we pulled into the left hand turn lane to enter the Kahana area Veronica asked, "How did it get its name?"

Tommy smiled and responded, "You ever eat Maui onion? Well at da' *Onion Express* they do things with da' sweet Maui onion that make them mo' beta den anywhere else. Dat's one of the reasons da' locals go der so much.

CHAPTER 2........
MAKALOPUA

Tommy pulled us into what seemed like the covered entrance of a hotel lobby. "This is da' place where you gonna stay," he said helping Veronica out of the limo. With that, he led us into the open-air lobby area where he introduced us to a young and very pretty lady whose name was Daisy. "This is not like a real hotel, except for if you need anything, you just ask Daisy and she take care of you. You have no worries okay. Da' Company, dey gonna take care of everything okay. Now I take you to your place and den I come back to get your bags."

We followed Tommy past two small-connected ponds and as I looked closely, I could see a number of turtles in varying positions. The pond area was also decorated with tropical foliage, lava rocks and the blue lined ponds themselves.

Arriving at the elevator, we followed Tommy inside and rode up to the tenth floor where we exited the elevator into another open-air breezeway, and I do mean breezeway. It was afternoon now and the trade winds had picked up to the point that Veronica was struggling to keep her dress down, and Tommy was holding on to his hat as he marched us toward the company-provided accommodation.

About halfway down the breezeway Tommy produced a key from his pocket, opened a screen door and then unlocked the front door, to what was going to be our new home while on the island. Tommy held the screen door open against the strong breeze while I followed Veronica inside. I stepped in alongside Veronica and the two of us stood there, side-by-side, with our mouths wide open staring at an incredible view of the ocean, with the island of Molokai in the background.

"Makalapua hey! Makalapua mean beautiful," said Tommy and then he disappeared, presumably to retrieve our bags.

"Absolutely!" I said.

"It is stunning and wonderful!" Veronica added. "You are going to love this place Jack."

"Well, you are going to be in and out of here too."

"I'm here for five days Jack and then maybe some more time later. You are going to be here every day and have this incredible view. I can't wait to see what this is like at sunset. We do see the sunset right?"

I looked out at the horizon gauging the view before answering. "Yep, I think from this view we will see the sun set into the ocean right about there every night," I said while pointing off to our right and into the western horizon just beyond the fully furnished patio outside the living room area.

We began to take notice of how bright and cheery the place had been decorated. The comfortable looking couch had a light-colored floral design, and the walls were decorated with three wooden-framed, glass-covered pictures of brilliant and finely detailed orchids. The glass-topped coffee table contained a book of Maui, and a pair of high-powered binoculars. The kitchen was on the small side but it was complete with all the amenities needed and there was a breakfast bar with four stools. Out from the breakfast bar there was a rattan dining set for six, which had a large basket of fresh fruit and a card in the middle.

I followed Veronica down a short hallway that led first to a full bathroom, which had an exterior wall and window along the breezeway, and then into the bedrooms. Next was a huge double door hall closet, complete with standard items such as an iron, ironing board, a laundry basket as well as cleaning tools and supplies. To my pleasant surprise, it also included three complete sets of snorkel equipment including nice facemasks, fins and snorkels. There were boogie boards stacked tightly into one corner.

The first bedroom, located along the exterior wall, had a long, screened, sliding window. The room had two twin beds, two small oak dressers, mirrored sliding closet doors and nightstands with lamps for each of the twin beds.

Along the way, Veronica pointed out how neat and convenient everything was located and that when the kids and she were to return for a visit, there would be room for all of them and their things.

I moved to the master bedroom located across the hall from the bedroom with the twin beds. I whistled as I entered, and Veronica followed saying, "Oh my God! This is incredible." The master bedroom included a beautifully covered, cherry wood, four-poster, king sized bed with matching nightstands. I was drawn to the view and private deck overlooking the ocean and beach off the master bedroom, but turned my attention back to Veronica when she got totally excited about the lamps on the nightstands.

"Jack. These are real Tiffany lamps on the nightstands. They are gorgeous! These are really beautiful."

I responded with, "Check out the view and the private deck."

"You don't understand Jack. These lamps are worth thousands of dollars each."

"Well then, I guess we are going to need to be careful around them. Look out there, we have a glass table and chairs on our deck, just like at home, and there is another pair of binoculars here too."

Veronica remained focused on the Tiffany lamps. "Jack, you don't understand about the lamps."

"Yes I do. They are very expensive and we'll need to be careful," I said moving out to the deck and picking up the binoculars to look through them.

"Men are so different. You would rather look through those binoculars at boats in the ocean than to take in the beauty of things like these gorgeous lamps."

What I was looking at was some bikini clad beautiful young women tanning themselves on the beach. Boats were the farthest thing from my mind. "Oh, I understand beauty honey, and to guys boats can be beautiful too."

Just then, from right behind my left ear Veronica said, "Yes, I can see the kind of boats you are looking at Jack."

Thank God Tommy came into the master bedroom just then, and we both turned our focus on him.

"You gotta good place huh brudah?" said the gentle giant.

"It's beautiful Tommy," replied Veronica.

"Yes, this is going to be great. It's very nice." Turning my focus back to the reason I was there I asked, "How will I get to work in the morning?"

"The boss, Mr. Kapuulaa, he say I should pick you up tomorrow and bring you to his office so I be downstairs at 7:30 in da morning to give you a ride. Okay brudah?"

"Sure Tommy. I'll be there waiting for you."

"You no have to wait. I have da' girl call you when I get here."

I knew I would be there when he arrived but just said, "Sure."

Then Tommy reached into his pocket and pulled out a set of car keys. "I guess dis for you den Mrs. Bryce. Dees keys go to da' red convertible Mustang in da' parking lot. You find it okay because I think it is da' only one down der."

Veronica took the keys offering thanks and surprise that she would have a car for tomorrow while I would be at work.

Tommy said, "I gotta go now because my missus wait for me to pick her up. You read da' note from Mr. Kapuulaa?"

"Not yet Tommy, but thanks for all of your help," I said while trying to hand him a twenty dollar bill.

Tommy held up both hands saying, "No. No, tank you brudah. Mr. Kapuulaa, he pay me plenty good and I'm not supposed to take tips. I gotta go now so see you tomorrow," he said matter-of-factly, then turned and walked out of the condominium.

Veronica began to unpack while I took a minute to look at the note from Mr. Kapuulaa, which read:

Welcome Jack,

I hope that both you and Mrs. Bryce will find your accommodations acceptable.

Tomorrow morning Tommy will pick you up at 7:30 AM in the loading zone adjacent to the lobby area. He will take you to the office trailer at the construction site where I look forward to finally meeting with you in person. In case you arrive before I can get there, please introduce yourself to Luanne. If acceptable, Luanne will provide you administrative support while you manage the construction project.

Until then,

Kainoa

Working together, Veronica and I had all of our things unpacked and put away in less that an hour. After we had finished, we donned shorts, slipped our flip-flops on and then rode the elevator down to ground level where we immediately headed to the beach adjacent to our building. There, we took off the flip-flops and waded into the warm clear ocean water.

At home, Veronica and I love going to the beach. We like the fall and winter months at the beach best because there is less fog, traffic and people. We pretty much love all the beaches and frequent everything from Manresa to San Gregorio. We have a secret and favorite beach not too far from Año Nuevo where, when there is a good minus tide, you can walk along gorgeous tide pools for what seems forever. At our secret beach, we often find the young bull elephant seals that are too immature to mate, just lounging around the beach or in amongst the dunes. They are great to see, but we go to great lengths to provide them plenty of clearance and not get in their way. Being chased by a two-ton irritated and horny young male elephant seal is scary as hell to say the very least.

After dipping our toes in the ocean, we headed across the parking lot and into a nearby pizza and pub restaurant where we had, of course, Hawaiian pizza and Primo beer. It was fantastic!

Sipping my beer, thinking about where I was and smiling at my wife, I thought to myself, *Makalapua.* (Beautiful)

Chapter 3.........
The Onion Express

Tommy picked me up right on time and it seemed I was going to learn to be part of the Maui morning commute. Traffic was bumper-to-bumper starting the minute we got on Highway 30, Honoapiilani Highway.

It took about 25 minutes to go the approximately seven miles between our place, on the beach in Kahana, to the construction site of the new *Onion Express*. Tommy dropped me off curbside and told me to just have Luanne call if I needed to go anywhere, and then he sped away.

Inside the trailer, I first noticed that all of the windows were open, allowing for a gentle cross breeze, which was rustling the curtains. As I took another step inside, an attractive, brightly dressed, middle-aged woman with short, dark hair moved to greet me. "You must be Mr. Bryce. My name is Luanne and I will be your Administrative Assistant."

"Please to meet you Luanne. You can call me Jack. Is Mr. Kapuulaa here yet?"

"No, but he called and said he is running a few minutes late and that he will be here shortly. Apparently, there is a lot of traffic coming this way from the Heliport. Is there anything I can do for you Jack? Coffee?"

"Sure. Coffee would be great but only if you will join me," I smiled.

"Okay. Follow me."

Luanne led me into what seemed to be a small conference room, which included a side table that contained a coffee maker and a bowl of fresh fruit.

"Heliport?" I asked Luanne.

"Oh. Kainoa. Mr. Kapuulaa arrives from Molokai by helicopter when he comes to work on Maui. He has businesses on Molokai, Maui, and the Big Island, so he mostly travels by air in his own helicopter. "

"So which of the islands does he live on?"

"His home is on Molokai where he raises his own cattle and makes his own dairy products. And here on Maui, Mr. Kapuulaa has his own onion farm, which is located on the upper slope of Haleakala. Haleakala is a dormant volcano in case you didn't know. For some reason the volcanic soil there helps create what is now one of Maui's most famous crops. Before the Hotel and the Onion Express restaurant burned down we only served onions from Mr. Kapuulaa's onion farm."

With a fresh cup of Kona coffee in hand, Luanne led me through the office trailer, which was standard for construction projects. As she led me into the bathroom, I could not help but to check, with my foot, if there was any give in the floor. Typical of these portable offices, I found the floor to have more give than the floor in the other rooms. I'd had a previous experience in an office trailer fire, where my only way out was to dig through the water damaged and weakened particle board flooring using the sink faucet as a tool to dig and pry my way out.

I set up my laptop and quickly sent out a message to just about everyone I knew with my new home number, office number, FAX plus Luanne's name and number. I had already decided Luanne was going to work out fine.

Kainoa Kapuulaa was a much younger man than I had envisioned. I never fail to be amazed with how wrong I can be when imagining the features of the person I'm talking to on the phone or even e-mailing. They always turn out to be so different than what I had imagined, or expected to see. Anyhow, the man approaching me had a rugged look, dark complexion, short jet black hair and a boyish smile that I'm sure most women would think charming. His clothes were crisp, coordinated and obviously tailored to fit. Somehow, I felt a kinship for this man I was finally meeting after two months of long distance communication.

Luanne darted over to make the introduction as I moved to greet my new employer. "Mr. Bryce, I'd like you to meet the owner of *The Onion Express*, Mr. Kapuulaa," she said with a hand gesture meant to okay our handshake.

"Please everyone, just call me Jack. When someone says Mr. Bryce I think they are talking to my father," I said as we shook hands.

"And likewise Jack. Please call me Kai."

"It's a pleasure to finally meet you Kai, and I want to thank you for the great condominium. It is spectacular. And my wife loves it there. She got really excited about those beautiful Tiffany lamps in the bedroom too."

14

"That's fine Jack and if you need anything for the place, just let Luanne know. By the way, it was my wife who decorated the place. When she ran across those lamps, she simply had to have them. I'll let her know how much they are appreciated. Now let's talk some business."

We moved to the meeting room where Kainoa pulled out an existing set of drawings and spread them on the table. "Jack, you have a big job to do. I would like it done in the fastest time possible. I've reviewed your notes on the plans you with our architects and I have approved and ordered each of your recommended changes. We figured you already saved us over thirty thousand in construction costs by reworking the utility drops and environmental controls as you suggested. A percentage of those and each additional approved savings you achieve will be added to your bonus so long as you continue to be on time and stay under budget."

"Thank you Kai. I'll do my best to get the job done on time."

"That's fine Jack, I'm sure you are going to do a great job. But there are some things I'm sure the insurance company didn't tell you. And that is actually why I'm here."

The tone in Kainoa's voice turned somber and the big smile disappeared.

"Jack, I'm not always the most popular man on these islands. There are certain business groups that don't like me growing produce, meat and dairy products to supply my own restaurants and other businesses. There are many suppliers and direct competitors, who would love to see me fail.

Don't get me wrong though Jack. I do have lots of family and friends. However, some people out there would rather not see me rebuild. Some of the other hotels and restaurants have noticed increased sales since this place burned down, and they are not anxious to lose that new business. You are aware that the place burned down under suspicious conditions, aren't you?"

"That answer would be a no Mr. Kapuulaa. I think the insurance company neglected to tell me about that little detail."

"Well, there was no hard evidence found but the fire department investigators and the insurance people were never able to identify the exact cause of the fire. The police report leaves it as 'Suspicious Origination'. Anyhow, I am sorry you didn't know all the details and if you want out of this project, you can go ahead and stay in the condo for a few days on me and we will call it even. What do you think?"

"What do I think? Hmm, I think we'd better not tell my wife about this," I said with a wink and a smile.

"So then, you are going to stay on the project?" Kai asked, studying me closely.

"Well, I'm here, I like the project, the weather, the water and that condominium is spectacular. Plus, although my wife is going home in a few days, she and the rest of the family have it all figured out to come spend time in Maui as soon as school lets out. Besides Kai, if anyone out there is upset about this project, they are likely upset with you. They don't even know me."

"Great! I am glad you are going to stay. I liked you from the first time we talked and I have a good feeling about you Jack. I think everything is going to work out fine."

"Me too." I replied. However, my brain was asking me what in the hell was I getting myself into...again?

"I've set up a one o'clock meeting with heads of each of the subcontractors. They are all anxious to meet with you and get this project moving. Unfortunately, I have to be in Hilo at that time but you can handle it. Besides, I'd probably just be in the way anyhow."

I saw Kai to his brand new silver Audi TT. After he drove off, I wandered the construction site, envisioning the old hotel and restaurant, and comparing them to the new design. It seemed both the new hotel and the restaurant were to be upgrades compared to the previous landmark and icon. The new look will be larger in scale, more rooms than before and the round shaped restaurant will be attached to the hotel, plus the roof on the restaurant is designed to look like the top half of an onion. As I thought about the onion look of the restaurant, my personal opinion was that it was going to look strange, if not down right tacky. However, if that was what the owner wanted then I would make sure that is what he got.

As I viewed the entire scene, it became clear to me that *The Onion Express* was a long way from Boulder Creek, California.

CHAPTER 4...........
LIFE ON MAUI

The afternoon contractor's meeting went extremely well. As I became acquainted with each of the sub-contractors, it was easy to understand how and why Kainoa had chosen them...they were all relatives. As I greeted each person, every one of him or her explained to me his or her relation to Kainoa. Some of them were related by marriage, a couple of them were nephews, and some were distant cousins. No matter what relationship they had with Kainoa though, they each seemed knowledgeable in their trade and all were helu 'ekahi, number one!

During the meeting, we made all the tactical arrangements for locations, needed utility hook-ups, portable toilets and staging areas for materials. Per Kainoa's request, the area was to be cordoned off by solid wood fencing instead of chain link and there were to be pedestrian view holes every forty-five feet for those people who just have to take a look.

As the meeting began to break up, each person approached offering handshakes and "a hui hoa " and "Alaka'I". After everyone had left I returned to the office and asked Luanne what ahui hoa and Alaka'I meant.

"A hui hoa means until we meet again Jack. And Alaka'I means leader. It means they all liked you and they are looking to you as the overall leader. It seems you have their respect."

Remembering a word Tommy had used the day before I responded to Luanne with, "That's shaka!" Luanne smiled.

Instead of calling Tommy for a ride, Veronica came by to see the construction site and get the work number where I could be located. After meeting Luanne, reviewing the drawing's and commenting on the onion top roof with an, "Oh, that's interesting," (meaning she was skeptical), we left the site together. Veronica was looking *very* sexy behind the wheel of the topless, bright red, convertible Mustang.

"Where are we going?" I asked.

"Well," she said reaching into the back seat and handing me my swimming trunks, "I thought maybe after your first day on the job you might like to go for a swim and do some snorkeling."

"Has anyone told you they love you today?" I said with appreciation.

"The answer is yes of course. People tell me they love me all of the time!" she said reaching over, placing her free hand on my thigh and laughing.

"So honey…where exactly are we going?"

"We are going to go right past Kahana along Highway 30 and up to a little spot known as Honolua Bay. Apparently the beach there is small and very rocky, but there is a huge reef close in and the snorkeling is supposed to be awesome."

The traffic thinned out after Napali and then we pretty much had the road to ourselves. Since there were no other cars, I took the opportunity to wriggle out of my work clothes and into my swimsuit and the tank top t-shirt. "What are you grinning at?" I asked Veronica when I caught her with an ear-to-ear smile on her face.

"Well Jack, I was just thinking to myself, yesterday morning we were in Boulder Creek, where it was cold and pouring down rain. And now, here we are, one day later, and I am in Hawaii driving with the top down in a sporty red convertible, and there is a half-naked, good looking man, changing his clothes in the front seat, right next to me. Life is very good!" She said, still grinning from ear-to-ear.

We arrived at Honolua Bay where there were about a dozen other cars parked along the narrow road, which outlined the tiny bay. We put the top up, grabbed the snorkel gear, a couple of beach towels, locked the car and headed off down the dirt trail toward the ocean waters.

The scenery along the well-worn walking trail included thick jungle like undergrowth on our left, some dry rocky streambeds crisscrossing the main trail and a beautiful, huge Banyan tree on our right. The tree was enormous and well worth the drive and the short walk, all by itself. From the striking huge, lush green canopy to the wondrous and amazing root system the tree was spectacular. The roots seemingly sprang straight up from the ground, like small individual trunks, in at least twenty-five different locations for this particular tree. I've heard there is a single Banyan tree in Calcutta that spans over four full acres. I was going to have to add the Banyan tree to my list of favorite things, which will always have at the top, the giant Redwoods that cover the mountains and valleys of the California Central Coast.

"I'd like to come back here with our camera and take a picture of this incredible Banyan tree for our friends back home," I said to Veronica.

"Just a minute," Veronica replied. Then, from her small backpack, she pulled out her Pentax IQZoom140 that I had given her for Christmas about five or six years ago.

With the pictures taken, we continued on the trail toward the beach passing a few people who were going the other way, back towards the road. Finally, we broke out onto the mostly rock covered beach, where there were a few families with small kids, and the stunning Pacific Ocean, showing a few dotted heads and snorkels on the horizon.

We carefully made our way across the rocky terrain, finally picking a spot about twenty-feet from the water's edge to stow our gear and get ready for entering the water. Having done this before, we carried our swim fins to the water to put them on. The advantage of putting our fins on in the water is that the flippers don't get filled with sand, and you don't have to clamor over the jagged rocks looking like the creature from the Black Lagoon. The disadvantage of putting my fins on in the water is of course, just being clumsy me!

For Veronica, putting her fins on seems to go rather smoothly. For me it is a much larger task. Sitting in the water, it seems that I not only defeat the reason of going to the water by still getting sand in my fins but the small and gentle rolling waves were too much for me to contend with. I would no sooner get a fin just about on one foot, than a small wave would roll me over as if I was some sort of a small-beached whale. Then the damn thing would come off again causing me to scramble to grab it before the surf took it out to sea. The awkward scene repeated itself about four or five times in a row before Veronica finally said, "Bring your fins over here to put them on."

To my chagrin, Veronica pointed to an underwater rock where I could sit out of the way of the rolling waves, and put my fins on sand-free. How is it that some of us can live in such complex and challenging business environments, but fail at the little things miserably and feel like complete inept asses?

Finally, all ready to venture out, we waded backwards into deeper water. Once we were swimming, I was much more at ease, and feeling less like an idiot. Despite my lack of coordination for putting on those damn fins, I am actually pretty fair in the water. I can swim for miles, I have mastered most strokes, can float freely for hours and hours, and I have a good lung capacity, allowing me to stay underwater for a good two and half minutes.

Almost immediately, there was a school of two hundred or more black and gray fish circling us and nibbling at the bubbles of air attached to our legs. Not wanting to feel like a feast for piranhas, we swam quickly to get away. As we moved into the deeper water, and in and out amongst the large reef, the scenery was spectacular. Triggerfish, Angelfish, Clown fish, the state fish, which is called a Humuhumunukunukuapua, and lots of others I can't name, were everywhere.

We continued to explore the left side of the bay, swimming in and out of the small canyons that lay within the extensive reef. Veronica, forever adventuresome, led the way and often waited for me while I tended to dive deeper at times. Veronica was first to spy the rising green sea turtle, and she signaled for me to follow, which I did happily.

The turtle, which was probably used to people frequenting the area, swam lazily along the surface taking in new air. We gave the turtle plenty of room and watched as the huge shelled lumbering sea turtle took a final breath and began his decent to the bottom of the reef. Veronica continued swimming near the surface but I decided to follow this big boy toward the bottom, just to glimpse where he might typically hide himself. Staying behind the big green turtle, near the bottom of the reef, an eel suddenly popped up just to my right startling me. The open jawed, and somewhat angry looking eel, had been in a small cavern in the coral that I hadn't seen. He came out threatening me for being too close to his home. Although eels are not particularly dangerous, unless provoked, this eel was close enough to give me a startle sending me topside pronto. When I came up right next to Veronica, she gave a small laugh…"Didn't expect that to happen, did you?" she said teasingly.

"No and I'm thinking about checking my suit 'cause he scared the crap out of me!"

We continued exploring the amazing underwater world, and before too long we looked back and noticed, we were quite a ways out from the rocky beach where we had started. We were exploring the farthest edge of the reef where it fell off like a steep cliff into what looked like thirty to forty feet of water, when Veronica motioned me for another pow-wow on the surface. "Look Jack, there are people snorkeling on the other side of the bay!"

Before I could comment, Veronica was off heading across the bay toward the cliffs and the people on the other side.

When we left the shallower reef area, the water immediately deepened and the ocean bottom terrain changed to flat and sandy. Although we continued to snorkel across the small bay, there wasn't much to see, except a few anchor tracks in the sand and an occasional flounder scooting across the open bottom. We swam about halfway across the bay when I got my first glimpse of the long shadowy figure moving rhythmically beneath us. Veronica obviously hadn't seen what I had, so I grabbed her leg, stopping her forward progress and setting us up for a topside chat.

"What's up?" she asked after removing her snorkel.

"I think we're not alone," I said pointing toward the bottom.

We put our snorkels back in place, to look around the water beneath us. Sure enough, there was a shark, a big tiger shark was my guess, and it was slowly but deliberately circling below us. Veronica tugged at my arm and signaled she wanted to talk again.

"What should we do?" she asked with more than a little concern.

Although we have both done some snorkeling before, neither of us is very experienced with the ocean or its inhabitants. "I'm thinking we should continue on our way to the other side and into the protection of the shallow reef. But, we need to keep a close on eye on that guy."

As we continued the trek, keeping more than one eye on the big shark below, we only got about another forty feet or so when I noticed that the shark had come up about halfway from the bottom and that it had started tightening its circle beneath us. I grabbed Veronica's arm to signal for another topside parlay, and the unexpected touch scared the hell out of her.

"Honey, I'm thinking that we had better cut back on our swimming movements because the amount of kicking and splashing we are doing seems to be drawing him closer to us. Let's keep moving ourselves toward the reef, but maybe we should slow it down so that we are almost just treading waster and see if that will help him lose interest in us," I said trying not to sound like I was scared. However, the thought of becoming some critter's dinner had already crossed my mind and I was not real thrilled with the idea.

We took up a back-to-back position with me facing the open seas and Veronica facing toward the shoreline, which I figured to be about three hundred yards away. Just as I was putting my mask back on, I spotted a commotion about one hundred yards out in front of me.

I could see that there was a school of big fish headed our way and, before I could say anything to Veronica, the school moved in on us, as if they had been purposely aiming directly for us.

Just then, about twenty yards to my right, two dolphins came fully out of the water as if to say hi, we're here, and then suddenly there were dozens of them all around us and we could even hear their chatter underwater.

I could hardly believe what my eyes were telling me, and I was totally blown away by what happened in the water next. It seemed as though the dolphins were busily harassing the tiger shark, which had been stalking Veronica and me. The shark, being alone and outnumbered, decided we were not worth the effort so he moved away swiftly, with a gang of dolphins on his tail, back out toward the open and deeper waters. Veronica and I watched the entire event of driving the shark off. It was truly amazing. It seemed as if the dolphins had realized our predicament and that they had come to rescue us from the menacing shark.

"Did you see what those dolphins did?" I asked Veronica excitedly. "It was so awesome the way they drove that shark away!"

"God Jack! I was so scared and then those dolphins came out of nowhere. How terrific was that?"

The dolphins seemed intent on staying with us a little longer. In fact, we felt as though they were gently guiding us toward the protection of the reef and the shallower water. We continued to watch with amazement as the dolphins seemingly put on a personal show for our enjoyment.

From what we could tell, there must have been more than a hundred dolphins surrounding us. Several of them came in close eyeing us and provided chatter, as if scolding us for having been in the wrong place at the wrong time. In addition, they gave us one heck of a show! The obviously friendly and fun loving mammals were doing acrobatics above and below. They were leaping high out of the water and performing tricks as if professionally trained at Marine World, and Veronica and I knew this was something very special to be experiencing first hand. Below us, they seemed to be playing chase games amongst themselves and they seemed to be having a great deal of fun with us and with each other. The show lasted nearly twenty minutes, and as we neared the reef, they began to disappear almost as fast as they had arrived. Both Veronica and I watched with appreciation and extreme gratefulness until the last dolphin was out of sight. With the dolphins back out into the deeper ocean, other swimmers and people on the beach came up to us, excitedly talking about our encounter and how unusual it was for dolphins to come into the little bay.

For the entire ride back to the condominium, we could only talk of the dolphins, our rescue from the menacing shark and the show of a lifetime, to which we felt privileged and would likely never see again.

The tiny bay had automatically become a favorite spot for the both of us forever. From the minute Veronica had picked me up at work, we had truly enjoyed each other's company.

Back at the condominium, we continued our great day together. After she put together a wonderful salad, Veronica joined me as I grilled fresh mahi-mahi, some vinaigrette marinated asparagus and new potatoes on one of the communal barbecues near the swimming pool. Later that night we went to bed, leaving our ocean view sliding door and drapes fully open, letting the cool of the evening and the sounds of the gentle ocean waves lull us into a good night's sleep. For sure, life on Maui was feeling good!

CHAPTER 5......
ONE IS A LONELY NUMBER

For each of her remaining mornings on the island, Veronica drove me to work. In the evening, we continued exploring, touring and playing in the beautiful warm water and on the beaches of Maui. Before leaving to return to Boulder Creek and the kids, who were staying with their Aunt Jenny, Veronica made sure the condominium was well stocked with healthy foods and that I had all the essentials like toilet paper and laundry soap. To my surprise, she had also brought and put some family photos around the condominium. It was a nice touch considering the family was going to be separated off and on for the next several months. The last time the family had been separated was after the '89 Loma Prieta earthquake that totaled our home. At that time, our kids were still pretty young, and Veronica and the kids stayed with her mother while I camped out at the house or stayed at my mother's. Anyhow, lengthy apart times are not a normal situation, or a particular desire for either of us. Nevertheless, we all do what we must in order to make our way through this world.

On our last night we went to dinner at one of Maui's fancier restaurants. We managed to consume an entire bottle of wine (we chose a familiar brand grown by a Santa Cruz Mountain vintner we know), coconut shrimp appetizers, and two terrific meals whose presentations looked so good that we hated to mess up the plates by eating the food.

After dinner, we walked up and down the beach adjacent to our condominium. We were feeling totally relaxed, dressed in comfortable shorts, light airy shirts and walking barefoot. The ocean waters shimmered and danced with reflected light from the full moon, which was high in the sky and slightly to the east. The island of Molokai lay outlined as a huge darkened shadow dotted with tiny lights and across from the sparkling waters in our view. Eventually, we sat down on the still warm sand, where we made small talk, until we finally ended up in each other's arms, laughing and giggling like two high school kids on a date. Later, in the privacy of our moon lit room, we made love as if there were no tomorrow, which was true for the time being. This was our last chance to be together for the next five weeks. The plan we made together was for me to return home for a long Memorial Day weekend in Boulder Creek and then, when school was out, the family would join me on Maui as part of their summer vacation.

In the morning I drove Veronica to the airport, where I escorted her as far as I was allowed to go, which was the security gate. There, we stepped aside to say our goodbyes with lots of hugs and kisses, and then I watched as she disappeared into the crowded terminal. I waited there until her plane boarded. From afar, I watched as she slowly climbed the ramp, waved one last goodbye in my direction from the top of the ramp, and then stepped inside the plane for her trip home. As the plane took off and then flew out of sight, I began the trek back to the condominium, with a sinking and empty feeling of being alone.

Somehow, being alone now, even though I was surrounded by freeway traffic, reminded me of a time when I had been alone in Vietnam. When I had first arrived in Southeast Asia I got picked to volunteer, which is what happens when no one steps forward, to augment the base's security forces. At our base, they called us augie doggies and we pulled guard duty on the perimeter when the APs (Air Force Police) were short handed or if the Intel people thought we might be attacked. Anyhow, the first time I had to play that role I was stuck in a covered pit in the ground at dusk. Within an hour, because it was a moonless night, my surroundings were pitch black and I literally could not see my hand in front of my face. At first, I felt really alone, but it was just for a little while because as I started hearing noises in the jungle I was too scared to feel lonely for very long. Obviously, I got through the night, but I'll always remember that initial feeling of being totally alone.

Anyhow, I arrived back at the condominium and the feeling inside the condo was one of emptiness, without my wife or family there. So, I called Aunt Jenny's to let her and the kids know that Veronica had left on time, but the real reason I called was to talk to the kids because I just plain missed them.

That night, after Veronica called to say she had arrived safely back in Boulder Creek, I watched the moonlight sparkle on calm seas while sitting on the veranda, drinking a glass of wine and enjoying the warm tropical evening. When I finally went to bed I fell asleep quickly and slept soundly

CHAPTER 6......
THE REAL PROJECT BEGINS

The next morning, rising earlier than normal, I filled my to-go cup with freshly made hot coffee, and then made my way to the job site, thinking I was going to be a bit early. This turned out, not to be the case. Two backhoe crews were already hard at work excavating trenches needed for utility systems. The crews were laying new pipe for water, gas, and sewer lines, and then filling and compacting the trenches with laborers utilizing powered whackers or what others might call tampers. I wondered whether the early morning noise would disturb the neighbors. Then I realized the surrounding area is commercial property and with no residences for several blocks.

I put on a pot of coffee for Luanne, and whoever else might drop by, and then I went over to the sub-contactor's trailer. The one that was responsible for laying the underground utilities. Talking with the supervisor there, I learned of our first tactical problem. It seemed that they were using some surplus material from their yard instead of what we ordered. The material for our job, he informed me, was still on a barge waiting to move to Maui for off-loading before it could be trucked over to our site. I got the contact name and number of the shippers and went back to my trailer to see what I could find out about why our material had not been delivered or off-loaded from the barge.

The information I received from the conversation turned out to be an ear-full of bad news regarding the unexpected shipping delay. At first, the shipping person claimed that he was not aware of any delays and said that everything had left from Oahu on schedule. I replied, "If the shipment were on schedule as you say, you and I wouldn't be having this conversation." At that, the shipping person promised to run down the cause of the delay and get back to me as soon as possible. But I wasn't having any of that either.

"You already told our sub-contractor that you would look into the delay yesterday. However, he has not received any information or explanations back from you. And like I said, that was yesterday. I want you to tell me, right now, the real reason why we didn't receive our material on time," I persisted.

"Your material is already there on da' barge in da' harbor Mr. Bryce, but you are on a low priority for unloading," the Hawaiian voice finally replied with a more truthful response.

"What do you mean we are a low priority? Who sets the priorities and what is his number?" I demanded.

"Hey pah, I don't make da' rules okay. So, der is no need to be angry wit me. We get your materials to you, soon as we can, okay?"

"No, it is not okay! Please give me the name of the person in charge," I said not wanting to let go of the issue.

The voice on the end of the line said, "hang-on for a minute brudah." Then he put me on hold.

Finally, someone with an English accent identifying himself as Richard came on the line. "I understand there is a problem with getting some construction materials to your job site there on Maui. I want to explain that unfortunately we have a huge shipment of perishables that we are unloading and putting into the dispatch trucks for fast delivery at this very moment. I can only promise to you that your materials will be of off-loaded and trucked to your site not later than tomorrow."

"Thank you for your honesty, Richard. I am assuming then, that I have your word on this new delivery date and that we will receive the entire shipment tomorrow. Please tell me, what time should we expect the shipment to arrive?" I pressed.

"Well Mr. Bryce we will do our utmost to get the load to you tomorrow as a matter of priority. It will likely arrive not later than midday. Will that be satisfactory?"

"Okay Richard. I'll expect the material to arrive by noon tomorrow." I took down the number for Richard's direct line and let the conversation end amicably.

I no sooner got off the phone than a person, wearing a city decaled hardhat, entered the trailer along with Luanne. I offered both persons coffee and I got a grateful "Thank you" from Luanne and a "No thanks" from the visitor who turned out to be a City of Lahaina Buildings Inspector.

"How can I help you?" I asked the inspector.

The inspector explained that he was there to view and approve the pipe installation and afterward, the soil compaction. Soil compaction testing is a standard and very necessary test to protect public safety. Without proper soil compaction, building foundations, bridges, dams and roads could be subject to failure or even collapse, because non-compacted soil may sink under the heavy loads.

With the City Inspector checked in, I grabbed a cup of coffee and settled myself at my desk to organize and approve project paperwork. I had only been situated for a few minutes when the phone on my desk began to ring. "Jack Bryce. How can I help you?"

"You already are! What's happening with my new hotel and restaurant?"

"Hey Kai! Everything is okay here."

"Just okay? I detect some frustration. Is there a problem?" Kainoa asked.

"Just a little problem with receiving material but no delays yet," I explained.

"Let me guess. Is there a bottleneck at the docks?"

"Yes. However, your cousin used some of his personal piping inventory as a means of working around the problem, at least for the moment. I personally talked to the folks at the dock this morning and they are promising on-site delivery not later than noon tomorrow."

"I am not at all surprised by this delay tactic," Kainoa explained to me with a sigh indicating his frustration too. "The stevedores and the teamsters have a very strong union and they are very much aligned with the other unions on the islands. The hotel employee unions have tried several times to obtain a foothold in my hotel businesses, but they have had no success. Anyhow, most of my competitors do employ union workers, and that is part of the problem too. Like I said to you the other day, there are a lot of people around here who would rather not see me rebuild *The Onion Express*."

It was while speaking with Kai that I began to understand the nature of *the real project*. Not only did I need to manage the overall construction project for *The Onion Express*, but in order to be successful, I was going to need to manage Kainoa's enemies as well.

Chapter 7........
No Mo' Delays

The next two weeks of work saw the completion of installing all the underground utilities. The mains and connecting laterals for the gas, water, electrical, sewer, and storm systems, had finished being installed, compacted, and stubbed up to above foundation levels. The grease trap system for the kitchen was already laid out; however, the grease trap itself would need to be installed later.

Richard, who directed the stevedores and teamsters work schedules and priorities for the docks, had delivered that next day as promised. Now I had new concerns for the next stage of materials due in from the mainland. The expected material, custom formed steel framing pieces were a key to completing the construction project on time. Any delays on the steel could have a domino effect on the rest of the construction.

Due to their huge size, the steel frame pieces had to be installed into heavily reinforced drilled piers as part of the foundation footing. Heavy-duty wooden forms were then hand constructed in order to support each steel-framing piece in position until the concrete footings hardened enough to support the heavy framing members and the load that would be attached to them. Anyhow, as I learned from my sub-contractors, there are only so many trucks on the island of Maui, and their use is usually reserved well in advance. Missing your concrete pour date meant you might wait weeks for another available date. And missing the steel frame delivery date could make that a bad reality.

I had already contacted the steel suppliers and confirmed that our order had gone out on time from the mainland. That meant the only delay between the steel leaving the Port of Oakland and arriving in Hawaii was either if the ship broke down at sea or if it sunk. And, if that were to happen, the whole world would have known about it.

With that knowledge in place, I began contacting Richard, directly, inquiring and prepping him for a timely delivery. "No problem bloke. I'll have them to you on time as I assured you before," he replied with his thick English accent.

The day the ship arrived at the dock I was on the phone with Richard. "Yes, yes. I'm looking at your steel right now. It is already unloaded and we will barge it over to Maui tonight. The truckers will have it to you bright and early in the morning."

The next morning, I arrived early and contacted Richard again. "How's that delivery coming?" I asked.

"I was just going to call you. Your steel is still sitting here. The boat assigned to tow your barge had to be redirected for another one that broke down."

"So then it's coming later today, right?" I asked trying to contain my anger until I had the full story.

"I'm afraid that will be impossible. The broken boat dropped its driveshaft into the Pacific and it will be at least a week before we can get a replacement."

"Well the other boat can get it to me by Friday right? I need to get that steel set before my concrete pour on Monday." At this point I envisioned added overtime costs for crane operators, laborers, carpenters and of course the iron workers who weld and attach the steel frames.

The reply set my blood to boiling, "No, I'm afraid it will be next week sometime bloke. I know it's a bit difficult on you old man, but there is simply no other choice I'm afraid."

"How late is your office open over there?" I asked applying a nasty tone.

"We're in the office until 5:00 PM. But I as I told you old man, it will do you absolutely no good to make the trip. Besides, it is already 2:30 PM and I doubt you would be able to get a flight that fast."

Tommy and I were at the heliport when Kainoa touched down in his helicopter. We climbed onboard without shutting down the engine. At 4:35 PM Kainoa, Tommy and I walked into Richard's office.

Tommy stood stoically behind Kainoa and I and I started the conversation. "Richard, I'm Jack Bryce and this is Kainoa..." but I didn't get a chance to finish my introduction.

"I'm well aware of who Mr. Kapuulaa is Mr. Bryce," Richard said not looking at me but rather looking directly into the eyes of Kainoa. "And I assure you there is nothing that can be done to get your material to your construction site before next week. You presume that Mr. Kapuulaa's presence here, just because he has money and power, will somehow change the situation and I assure you it will not."

Kainoa took a step forward towards Richard's desk, while reaching inside his coat and pulling out his checkbook.

Richard began again, "your money won't..."

It was Kainoa's turn to cut him off, "I'm not the one presuming too much Mr. Uh…oh I see it there on your desk, Mr. Hatcher. I'm just here to pay my account. Now how much is that barge rental?"

Then a young dockworker burst into the office excitedly explaining that one of the barges in the bay was being towed away…by someone else's boat!

"That would be my boat, towing your barge, filled with my material," Kainoa said without much emotion. "Now Mr. Hatcher, what do I owe you for the use of your barge?"

I just stood there silently, next to Tommy, with my arms folded across my chest, trying very hard not to laugh aloud. I really liked how Kai had handled the whole situation. There was no muss or fuss for Kainoa, it was just business. The man had class, plus he had style. He did not feel like he needed to flaunt his power and wealth. Instead, he used it effectively and with a great deal of wisdom.

The next morning, with a cup of coffee in my hand, I watched as our load of steel started arriving at the site by an array of different trucks, including a three-ton flatbed from Kainoa's onion farm. Kai, along with Tommy, came by to see that all had arrived safely.

"Well, the good news is that you got your material on time. The bad news is that it took $10,000 from that $30,000 you saved from your design changes. So, for now, you are still $20,000 under budget," Kai said with a big smile.

Tommy chided in too, and he rather summed up the whole ordeal when he said, "*No mo delays* from dat guy!"

CHAPTER 8......
A REALLY GOOD MAN

With an entire day lost due to the steel framing delivery delay, I went ahead and authorized overtime for the weekend to insure that the steel frames would be in place for the Tuesday concrete pour. We all got an early start with the overtime crew already hard at work when the morning sun rose from the east. I made a point of being involved as each mainframe member was located which often meant pushing, shoving and prying the crane suspended steel pieces to where they needed to go. At about 11:00 AM I had pizza and soft drinks brought in for everyone and after a short break, everyone got right back to doing the job for which they were hired. By 3:00 PM we had set about fifty percent of the steel members and I called it a day, figuring we had all of Sunday and Monday to finish installing the remaining steel.

I told Veronica when I got back to the condo, the first thing I did was to walk into the master bath, strip bare, put my grotesque and stinky clothes in a clothes basket, and climb in the shower. At first I showered with hot water to get clean and then I gradually moved the lever to cooler water so as to cool off. Following the shower, I put on my shorts, going commando for the moment, and threw on an unbuttoned Hawaiian shirt. Next, I grabbed the basket filled with a week's worth of dirty laundry and, adding two bottles of cold Primo beer to the top of the pile, I headed down the breezeway and took the elevator to the first floor laundry room. It must have taken all of three minutes to start the laundry in a washer and get to the beach where I planted myself in the sand and took a hit on my first beer. As I sat there in the warm sand, I decided that if one had to do laundry, that sitting on a warm tropical sandy beach surrounded by families playing in the water and watching bikini clad ladies casually walk by, it really wasn't that much of a chore.

I finished both beers and got back to the laundry room just in time to see my wash load finish. Then I moved it all into a dryer before heading upstairs to make a call home to Veronica.

"Whatcha doing beautiful lady?" I asked when Veronica picked up the phone.

"Hi honey!" Veronica said excitedly. "I didn't expect to hear from you until tonight but I was just thinking about you."

"You were thinking about me too? That's great honey! I was thinking about you too babe. I was just down on the beach waiting for my laundry to come out of the washer. I kept seeing all these beautiful women walking by, and I began to miss you so much that I came upstairs to call you. So, why were you thinking of me?"

"Well, I just got in from the rainy outside where I was cleaning the gutters and chopping some kindling, and while I was doing that I was thinking of you the entire time too."

"Ha ha...that was a funny one Babe! " I said sarcastically.

"I really was thinking about you and how it is Saturday and that we should be going to the flea market or Año Nuevo or just doing something together. You know how I am when you are gone. It's hard for me to sleep at night. When you are not here, I hear every little noise all night long. It's like I'm on guard duty or something when you are not around."

"I'm sorry that I can't be there for you honey, and I'm sorry that you don't sleep well. But, if it is any consolation for you, I don't sleep well without you either. In fact Babe, I find myself waking up at night because I'm not hearing you breath or because I can't reach out and touch you."

It took forty minutes for my clothes to dry in the dryer but Veronica and I talked for over an hour with only a couple of breaks which was when I got to say hi to Warren and Marie.

On Sunday, with everything well under control at the job site, I left work just after lunch. For the rest of the weekend, I just stayed around the condominium and never drove anywhere. Typically, I do some long walks, like to the open-air Farmer's Market, and I'll do some light jogging (morning and evening) for as far as the beach would let me travel. During the late afternoon, I latched on to one of the boogie boards and took it out to where the surfers were catching waves. I was afraid I might get a few sneers for being out there but that turned out not to be the case as everyone was very friendly and open to me sharing the waves with them.

I managed to catch a few good rides and talk with the wave riders about everything other than work. Therefore, overall, it was a good day, very relaxing, albeit a bit short.

On Monday I arrived at work at the usual time to find that Luanne had beaten me in and that the coffee was already brewed. Next, I checked in with the steel workers, who were already hard at work setting the remaining steel frame members. I also checked in with the carpenters who were busily framing for the first foundation pour on Tuesday. I was good with what everybody was doing and I returned to the trailer to a make a few calls. The most important people needing contacting were the City Building Inspector to let him know we were ready for another inspection, and then to the cement plant to ensure that our scheduled pour was all set. The call to the inspector went well and I ensured we were scheduled for his visit on Tuesday. However, when I called the concrete plant, it was a completely different story.

I about choked to death on my coffee when the cement plant related they had me down for fourteen yards of concrete instead of the hundred forty that had been ordered. "Just a minute please," I asked the dispatcher. "Luanne!" I hollered. "How much concrete did you order?" I asked her from the other room.

"Hundred and forty yards Jack," she replied. "I have the fax order and receipt right here, would you like me to bring them in?"

"Yes, please. Right away. I've got the cement plant on the phone and they show only fourteen yards for tomorrow."

I went back to the other line and the person I had put on hold. I explained that I had a copy of the fax order in my hand, with the fax delivery confirmation, and that it clearly called for one hundred and forty yards.

"I can resend everything right now," I explained.

"I'm not sure what went wrong Mr. Bryce, but right now I've got you for fourteen yards tomorrow, and all of my other trucks are already booked. I can see what I can do to squeeze in a few more yards, but I can't get you anywhere near the one-forty."

"Who do you have the other trucks going to?" I asked as politely as I could.

"Most of them are going to a new housing tract on the other side of the island."

"Excuse me but a typical house foundation takes about three to four yards. How many foundations do they need to pour in one day?" I asked with a lot of extra sarcasm.

"I don't know Mr. Bryce. It's a big union job and we are committed to them."

"Ahh, I see. I don't suppose your drivers are union are they?"

"Why yes they are Mr. Bryce and we do a lot of work with the unions."

"Listen son, I was a union member once myself and I have no problems with unions in general. In fact, I think they provide a great service for the workers. However, I do have problems with people who use the union as a tool to hurt others. I'd like to talk to the project manager at that housing site and see if I can work something out. May I have that name and number please?"

"Sorry, Mr. Bryce, but I can't give out that kind of information. Your fourteen yards of concrete will be there at 8:00 AM. Have a good day, sir!"

"I'm really sorry to bother you Kai, but I've got another problem here." I explained how our order had somehow been messed up, even though we had documented proof of our order. I also explained that without the full one hundred and forty yards of cement that the project would suffer serious delays.

"Not to worry Jack, I'll fly on over there and we'll see if we can't get to the bottom of what is going on and who is causing me all of these problems."

About twenty minutes later, I got a call from Kainoa who was airborne in his helicopter, somewhere over the ocean waters between Maui and Molokai.

"Sure I can meet you over at the heliport Kai. I'll leave right now," I said replying to Kainoa's request.

"Okay Jack, we'll take your car. I want to check out that housing construction that the cement plant person was talking about. I want to try and see who the builders and owners are and…hold on a minute Jack…what the heck is this Bob? …. If it's not yours and it's not mine, then whose is it?" Kai had interrupted our conversation but I could still hear him talking to his pilot, Bob, over the open cell phone.

"…What do you think it is? …. I've never seen it before either… Looks to me like it is some kind of a toolbox …here; let me open it up…"

I heard a crackle over the cell phone and then I heard an explosion from inside my office trailer. I immediately ran outside looking toward the ocean and the island of Molokai. What I saw was a huge cloud of black smoke and smoldering fragments of the aircraft were still visible as they streamed downward toward the ocean waters and Maui beaches below.

My stomach knotted and for an instant, I felt as though I was going to be sick, but then I quickly got my act together. I ran back inside the office trailer where I dialed 911.

Work stopped at the project as soon as I shared the sad news of what had happened to Kainoa and his pilot. Luanne couldn't stop crying but she wound up staying at her desk for the rest of the day, as did I.

Within an hour of the explosion, the local police were inside the trailer interviewing and recording me as I described the day's events and Kainoa's last conversation. I think that serious crime is pretty rare here and it seemed that no one was eager to list the incident as a homicide; however, the facts were clear. Kainoa had obviously found something out of place in the helicopter. They found something in the cockpit that resembled a toolbox, and neither he nor the pilot had a clue as to where it came from or why it was there. Opening the unidentified box must have triggered a bomb that almost disintegrated the tiny craft in mid air.

The police asked that I stay on the island for at least the next few days and I related that would not be a problem. In a show of respect for Kainoa and his family, the project shut down for the remainder of the week. I was not sure if the project would ever be restarted.

Having gone back to the empty condominium, Kainoa's condominium which his wife had decorated so nicely, my feelings were a mixed bag of sorrow for Kainoa and his family, anger at whoever might be responsible for taking the two lives and despair because I had no clue as to what was going to happen next.

"How ya doing babe?"

"I'm fine. It finally quit raining as of last night and the skies are clear today. How about over there? It must be about lunch time?"

What had happened and, true to form, and one of the reasons I love her so much, she helped me out of my state of confusion and despair when she stated, "Jack, your job now is to be there for that family. Kainoa's wife is going to need your help with rebuilding the restaurant and hotel. Even if she decides not to continue, she is going to need you to shutdown the project, don't you think?"

"You're right honey and thanks. I'll stick around until they tell me I'm not needed anymore."

"I've got two people who have hinted they would like to visit and maybe spend a few days with you in Hawaii."

"Really, who's that? Our neighbors?"

"Both Jim Alverez and Majid have provided some pretty hefty hints. I think they were mentioning it to me first because they don't want to bother you while you are working. "

"Heck Babe, I think it would be great to see them and to spend some time with them. Plus there is plenty of room here for them to stay, at least until you and the kids come over. I'm going to give each of them a call and invite them to spend some time with me in Maui."

After I hung up the phone with Veronica, I reflected on the day's events and Kainoa himself, the man I had come to like so well. Kainoa, it seemed to me, was one of those rare breeds. He had a lot of class, was very gutsy and direct in his approach to life, and he didn't flaunt his wealth. I truly believed that Kainoa and I would have become steadfast friends. Kainoa was a really good and rare kind of a man who was going to be mourned and missed by me, and many people for a long time to come.

CHAPTER 8......
PUA (FLOWER)

The first time I met Pua, Kainoa's wife, was at the funeral service held for Kainoa, near his home on the island of Molokai. My first impression of Pua was that she was a very attractive native Hawaiian woman who had just a hint of graying hair showing in the front. Her stature seemed to be one of a guarded but confident woman with a lot of class. She was being very polite to the many new faces, like myself, whom she was meeting for the first time. When Tommy and Luanne first introduced me to Pua, I did feel as though my name had drawn her extra attention, and that I had been immediately sized up as we were shaking hands.

I offered her my sincere condolence for her loss. She thanked me graciously and then stated that she would be coming by the project "within a few days."

Kainoa's memorial service drew a huge crowd, and was easily the biggest funeral service and reception that I had ever attended. There was somewhere between three to four hundred people in attendance. All of the contractors from the project were there, plus Tommy,

Tommy's wife and children, and Luanne so I didn't feel too alone or out of place.

I had noticed an elderly man near Pua, whom I correctly guessed to be, due to the similarity of his looks, as Kainoa's father. Apparently Kainoa's mother had passed away a year before after having fought a long bought with cancer. Luanne thought it was important that I meet him too and she made a point of taking me to him for an introduction.

"I am truly sorry for the loss of your son, Mr. Kapuulaa."

"Thank you very much for coming here today Mr. Bryce. Kainoa often spoke well of you and the excellent job you are doing to rebuild *The Onion Express*."

"Kainoa was a good man sir. I had a great deal of respect for him."

"Well, thank you for your kind words Mr. Bryce. I would like, if it is convenient for you, to stop by the construction site early next week."

"Of course Mr. Kapuulaa. I will look forward to meeting with you. And again, sir, your son was a fine and well-respected man."

During the funeral service, I sat with Luanne. Afterward, at the reception, I mingled between the Project's contractors and spent time with Tommy and his family.

It was while I was eating next to Tommy and his wife that I mentioned how both Kainoa's wife and father had said they would be dropping by the job site within the next few days.

Upon hearing that Tommy said, "Maybe that's not so good Jack."

"What do you mean Tommy?"

"Well maybe I should not say too much because I do work for all of dem, but I like you too. So maybe I should just say that with

Kainoa gone people are confused about who is gonna be da big Kahuna," he explained.

"I assumed that would be Kainoa's wife, Pua."

"*Da Onion Express* had been a family business since da beginning. Papa Kapuulaa, he gave da business to Kai about ten o' twelve years ago."

"Oh, so the business is really Mr. Kapuulaa's?"

"Well, I'm not so sure. Ya see, Papa, he don't care all dat much for Pua. And Pua, she don't care too much for Papa. Everybody here is waiting to see who is going to be da big Kahuna now dat Kainoa is gone."

"I see," I replied to Tommy. "But why is it bad for the project?"

"Well, Papa Kapuulaa, he want to build and run it just like befo' and Pua, she has different ideas. Sometimes she says she want to re-build and den sell da place, and sometime she say mo better to build it different so to bring mo rich tourists instead of da locals."

"I got the sense from Kainoa that he was trying to do both."

"Dats right brudah. Kainoa, he was a very smart man. He don't want no trouble so he was gonna try to make everybody happy."

For the remainder of the day, and even during the return boat trip back to Maui, I continued to think about what may be laying ahead for me with regards to interactions with the Kapuulaa family. Eventually I concluded that for me it shouldn't really matter who was going to be the Big Kahuna. My job was to rebuild *The Onion Express* per design and to do it in the most efficient way possible.

Although I had no preference, at least at this point, as to who might be providing my marching orders, my suspicion leaned toward Pua. Our exchange had been brief, but it seemed she bore an intensity and determination about her that said she was in control. Generally speaking I respect people who exhibit personal confidence. In fact, that was one of the traits that had attracted me to Veronica.

Getting to know and understand Pua, I surmised to no one in particular, would be an interesting experience for anyone.

CHAPTER 9......
IT'S A WONDERFUL LIFE

There were two messages on the recorder when I got back to the tenth floor condominium after Kainoa's funeral service. The first message was from Ashley who stated she had something to talk about and wondered if I might call her after 10:00 PM California time.

The second message was from my good friend Jim Alverez. "Hey Jack, I just got off the phone with your beautiful wife and she said that it would be all right with you to have visitors so, I was hoping it would be okay if Vickie and I stay with you for a few days. I've got some comp time coming for the extra hours I've been working, and I'm hoping that maybe next week would be all right with you. Anyhow, call me as soon as you are able and let me know so I can work on booking our flights, okay Jack? And, oh yeah, if you got any free time, I figured the three of us could charter a boat and try for some of those world class blue marlin they have out there. Call me soon buddy!"

I flashed back to a scene, during the Steelhead run on the San Lorenzo River only a few months back. My friend Jim was sitting in the middle of the stream after having slipped and fallen. I recalled seeing the embarrassed and surprised expression on Jim's face, while he was sitting in the cold winter water, and I chuckled to myself.

The two phone messages from home had lifted me from the more somber mood I had just been in, thinking about and feeling the tragic loss of my new friend and boss, Kainoa. I grabbed an ice cold Bacardi and changed out of the clothes I had worn to the funeral and into a pair of comfortable shorts and an unbuttoned Tommy Hilfiger, dark blue Hawaiian shirt. Next, I grabbed my cell phone and stepped out onto the deck off the living room to make my call while enjoying my view of the ocean, Molokai, and the people-dotted beach below.

It seemed as if Jim was wanting to put his life as a Police Lieutenant and investigative detective on hold so that he could spend some serious time with his girlfriend, Vickie, with whom he had been going out for nearly six months now. When I got off the phone with him, we were all settled on the dates of his visit and we only needed confirming flight numbers and times so that I would know when to pick them up from Kahului Airport.

When we eventually hung up, I was not sure who was more excited about the impending visit, Jim for the chance to get away with his lady, or me just because Jim had become one of my closest friends.

I kicked back on the chaise lounge and started to think about *things* in general. A management class I had attended, while working at PharmaLabs several years ago, had suggested it was sometimes beneficial to stop where you were and ask yourself, "Where are my feet?" In this case, I was taking into consideration my island paradise, the job at hand, and what events had recently transpired. There seemed to be an obvious attempt, by someone or some persons yet unknown, to disrupt and possibly even prevent the re-construction of *The Onion Express* to the point of blowing up the owner and his helicopter pilot. In addition, there was now a question, at least in my mind, as to whether or not the fire that had destroyed the landmark restaurant and hotel had been an act of arson.

If it were an act of arson, then it would seem my feet were in the middle of a murder scene where four persons had died. The dead included the two restaurant workers who perished in the flames of the burning restaurant, and now Kainoa and his pilot. Too, I was still faced with re-constructing an apparently unwanted, by someone or some persons, restaurant, without knowing exactly who was going to be providing the approvals, or signing the checks. Finally, I decided that I should worry about where my feet were tomorrow, and I went back inside to grab another Bacardi before calling home to see what the family was doing.

"Hello?" Veronica answered on the second ring.

"My name is Lester Brumbaker of Amalgamated Census and I wonder if I might have a few minutes of your time this evening," I said trying to disguise my voice by filling both cheeks with hard candy.

"Well, I am cooking dinner but I guess I can answer a few questions while I'm doing that. Go ahead."

"That is just fine and I'll try not to take up too much of your time. Since you are cooking dinner may I ask if you are single or if this is a family residence?"

"Family of six," Veronica replied.

"Six? That is a very nice-sized family. Then I'm assuming there is a mister. Do both of you work?"

"Yes, we both work."

"Now some of these questions may get a little a personal and I hope you won't mind. How would you rate your marital life? One being the highest and five being lowest."

"I guess I would have to give it a three."

"Only a three? Well I guess that is okay. May I ask why it isn't higher?"

"Well, my husband is off working in Hawaii right now and I'm a bit lonely."

"I see. How long has he been away?"

"Almost a month now and I'm getting a little more frustrated every day, if you know what I mean."

"Err, a yes, I can imagine."

"So Lester, are you a married man?"

"Why yes I am, but my wife is also away."

"Well Lester, right now, I'm standing in front of the stove wearing shorts, no panties and a bikini top. And, I'm not sure if it is the heat from the stove or talking to you that is making me so hot!"

"Do you often talk this way to strangers over the phone?" I mumbled with my mouth still of hard candy.

"Oh yes! Whenever my husband is away, or even if he is just out in the garage, I try to find a man such as you to talk with. Is that okay?"

"Well I guess there is no harm in that. May I ask where your children are?"

"They won't be home for another hour Lester. So, it's just me and you on the phone and do you know what I'm thinking now?"

"Uh, no I don't," I replied with great interest and trying not laugh aloud.

"Well right now I'm thinking that if my husband were home I'd tie him to the bed and have my way with him in every way possible until just before the kids got home. Do you think he would like that Lester?"

"I think I can say, without any doubt that your husband would definitely like to be there for that!" With that, I spit out what was left of the candy and we both laughed aloud. Next we brought each other up to date with what was happening in Boulder Creek and Maui. In the background, while listening to my beautiful and fun loving wife, I could hear Louis Armstrong signing <u>What a Wonderful World</u> and I couldn't help but think…yes it is.

At 7:00 PM my alarm went off and I called Ashley at her apartment on campus at UC Davis. "Hi Pumpkin. What 's up?" I said trying not to sound too groggy.

"Daddy, I thought you would like to know that finals are over and I got one A+, two A minuses, and two Bs. Pretty good huh?"

"That's great Baby! Well done. I'm really happy for you and proud too."

We talked a while longer about things in general including her job at the school and changing boyfriends, which is fine by me as I think a young woman, just as a young man, needs to experience other people before settling down. Anyhow, we talked for nearly an hour before she finally said, "Well it's almost 11:00 PM here and I have to get ready to start the new semester tomorrow. So goodbye Daddy and I love you."

"Love you too sweetie and I can't wait to see you when school lets out." After hanging up with my daughter I thought back to my conversation with Veronica and Louis Armstrong playing on the radio in the background and agreed again…it's a wonderful world.

CHAPTER 10......
WHO'S GOT THE HELM?

Arriving at work the next morning, I was greeted by Luanne who had arrived early. "So what's on our agenda this morning?" I asked her while pouring myself a cup of hot coffee.

"Well let's see...there is one message from Kainoa's father that he will be by this morning. There's another note from Pua that she will be here, in Lahaina, at twelve, and that you should meet her for lunch at the Maui Banker's Club. And, there is another message here from the cement plant saying they have had a cancellation and that they could start bringing us our concrete early in the morning on Wednesday."

"That's good news! Anything else?"

"Just one more from a Lieutenant Ho, who would like you to call him this as soon as possible."

"Ah, well it sounds like it should be an interesting day. Are all of the contractors back to work too?"

"Yes, and they are excited about the concrete coming on Wednesday."

"Hmmm. Word gets out fast around this place. Am I the last person to know about the concrete?"

"Just about."

After calling and confirming with the cement plant myself, I spent the next hour and a half in the contractor's trailer, reviewing drawings and ensuring that we were still ready for the concrete pour. In fact, I was still in the trailer when Tommy walked in to inform me that Palakapola Kapuulaa, Kainoa's father, was waiting for me in my office.

"Good morning sir," I said while shaking hands with the older gentleman. Over the years I've learned that I can tell a lot from shaking hands. The elderly Mr. Kapuulaa, who I guessed to be approaching 80, had rough but strong hands, indicating that this man knew how to work and that the work had built character and added strength to his grasp. In addition, the eye-to-eye contact let me know that I was dealing with a man who expected response and attention. "How can I help you Mr. Kapuulaa?"

"Well Jack, first I wanted to thank you again for your kind words regarding my son. And I also came by so that maybe we could talk about the hotel and restaurant. You know, of course, *The Onion Express* has been a part of our family a long time, and it is important to everyone that it continues to live to our tradition."

"Of course, Mr. Kapuulaa. We will all miss Kainoa. As for *The Onion Express* I will continue, assuming the family still wants me to rebuild the hotel and restaurant as designed."

"We do want you to continue Jack. Like I said the other day, my son thought very highly of you, and we would like you to finish the job."

"That's fine, sir. I do have a question though. Often, during construction like this, things like changes to design, or the need for additional funding are required. I'm wondering who, in your family, will be providing authority?"

The elderly man looked at me, studying me for just a minute, and then he broke into a huge smile as he answered my question. "I see that you are already aware of the, shall we call them, *challenges* within my family Jack. Well, it is a valid question needing answering." Again, the elderly Kapuulaa studied me before answering. "Let me see if I can answer your question as politically correct as it was asked. My daughter-in-law is a headstrong woman with ideas of her own. Let's just say her desires toward *The Onion Express* may differ from family tradition and that there is some confusion and concern about what will happen. Unfortunately, the murder of my son left his estate and *The Onion Express* entirely in her hands. However, I will of course be providing her as much guidance as she may need. So, I can see that the steel framing is mostly installed and I understand that the concrete will arrive in a few days. What will be the next phases of construction?"

It was clear now that Pua, Kainoa's widow, would have control of the project and that she would be signing the checks. Too, the reference to Kainoa's death as being murder was the first time I heard it from anyone other than the police.

I went on to describe some of the next phases of construction. "The concrete pour enables us to progress in several ways," I started. "While the foundations and slabs cure, and we will give that a full week, there is still work to be done tying in the utilities to the city systems. In addition, we will begin defining and excavating the perimeters of the driveways and parking lots. While that is going on, the steel workers will be pre-fabricating structural pieces and cross members to support and tie-in the four floors of the hotel so that we can complete all of the steel framing as soon as possible. Once the main support system is in place, it should begin to look like a hotel and restaurant again," I explained.

With Tommy following, we left the office and continued our conversation as I toured Mr. Kapuulaa through the construction site, which he seemed to enjoy immensely. Several times during the tour we were interrupted by members of the construction crews who were cousins, or just well-wishers wanting to provide sympathy for the loss of Kainoa.

Finally, through with explaining and touring the construction, Mr. Kapuulaa hesitated before returning to the car with Tommy, and requested with a stern look, "You will keep me aware of any changes won't you Jack?"

Fielding the question was like being thrown a hot potato that could not be dropped. "You are sir, as far as I'm concerned, always welcome to come by to see our progress and ask any questions you wish."

With that Mr. Kapuulaa gave an understanding nod and then disappeared inside the car door being held by Tommy who, after closing the car door, gave me a wink of approval.

As the car drove off, I felt a renewed anger toward whomever it was that was responsible for Kai's death, and the resulting turmoil that his family now faced. I was looking forward to my scheduled visit with the police investigators later in the day.

Suddenly, I had a longing for home. I felt a strong desire to see the familiar and friendly faces that populate Boulder Creek. I thought of my poker buddies and how I was going to miss the next few games. And too, I thought of sitting outside Doc Paklan's office and even of chatting with Michelle while receiving my haircut that she performs so knowingly.

Then I thought about Pazzi's, the gathering spot and favorite watering hole for many Boulder Creek locals, and how I would feel if someone were to burn it down or kill my friends who own and manage the friendly and welcoming place. If something like that were to happen, I knew I would be pissed off to no end, as would most everyone else in town.

Luanne came into my office where I had been working on keeping up with the project files and said that Tommy had called and that I should leave now to meet Pua at her chosen restaurant.

With the top down on the red Mustang, I made my way through the tourist-laden streets to the meeting place. The restaurant, formerly The Chart House, was under new and local management. It sits by itself on a small bluff over looking portions of the harbor and across at the island of Molokai.

Pua was already seated at a window table for two when I arrived to join her. "Hello Mrs. Kapuulaa," I said shaking hands with only the finger portion of her extended hand.

So here I was with my new boss and I was feeling a bit awkward. It was clear now that she was at the helm of the operation now, and this was the person who would be signing my checks.

CHAPTER 11.........
A NEW CHALLENGE

"Please have a seat Mr. Bryce," she said while gesturing with her hand.

"Thank you." While seating myself I could not help notice the pungent aroma of her Gardenia fragrance, and how attractive she was. Her face was structured with high cheekbones and her eyes, with lightly highlighted make-up, were a beautiful blue-green. Her body shape appeared to be trim and tone. Pua was smartly dressed in business attire that consisted of a navy blue skirt, matching lightweight coat and a white V-necked blouse open to just above her breasts. Her legs were crossed above her knees and she was sitting almost sidesaddle from the table, showing her high heels that matched the ensemble she was wearing. Pua Kapuulaa was a stunningly attractive woman who was showing no sign of being in mourning.

"Please accept my sincerest regrets for the loss of your husband, Mrs. Kapuulaa. He was a fine man and everyone at the construction site misses him."

"Thank you Jack. Is it alright that I call you Jack?"

"Absolutely. I prefer not to be very formal. How can I help you Mrs. Kapuulaa?"

"I just wanted to meet with you Jack and to give you encouragement to continue on with the re-construction of *The Onion Express*. Kainoa would want things to continue, and for now I want to support that. My husband and I knew that it would make my in-laws happy to rebuild it as it was. So for at least the basic structure, I see no need to make any changes, even though I personally dislike the thatched onion look of the roof."

"I have never seen anything quite like it either," I chimed in with a smile.

"I don't expect there to be any further trouble or delays with the construction, so I am hopeful that you can have the buildings up and functional in the allotted time."

"That might be a little difficult with the two weeks worth of delays we have already incurred." My mind was wandering back to her comment about 'continue for now' and I was wondering how to interpret that. Was there something about the structure she wanted to change? Perhaps it was the thatched onion top roof, or was there something else on her mind?

"You're a bright guy Jack and I'm sure you'll find a way to get done on the original schedule."

Hmm, no pressure there I thought to myself.

I decided to take a direct approach in response. "How do you know there won't be anymore delays?" I asked her in a matter of fact of tone.

"Let's just say that with my husband's death, I don't think there will be any more trouble."

"Why is that?" I continued to press.

"Are you and I going to have troubles Jack?"

61

"No Ma'am," I stated. "I just want to get the job done as promised and I was curious how you could be so certain there would be no more delays. I'll just take your word for it for now, and see what I can do about making up the lost time. It would help though if you would authorize some weekend work to help me get it back on schedule."

"Weekend work is extra money for the overtime right? Why don't you see what you can come up with without the added overtime? If push comes to shove, a little farther down the road we can talk about the overtime if needed."

For sure this lady was hard-core and it would seem she had no intention of easing up on me. "I'll do my best Mrs. Kapuulaa."

"How about we order some lunch? Would you care to have a drink with me first?"

Not wanting to fall into any kind of trap, I said sure and asked for iced tea as opposed to anything with alcohol. "I'm not that bad Jack! You can order alcohol if you like. After all, we are adults."

"Thanks for the offer, but I have to meet with the police this afternoon regarding Kai's murder, and I'd rather not."

"I've noticed you said murder twice so far. What makes you think it was murder?"

"Well, for one thing, his helicopter blew up in mid-air while he was opening some kind of a box that wasn't supposed to be there. Plus, there have been all of the political delays to the construction, like the union and the cement plant not delivering as promised. It seems to me, as it did to Kainoa when we talked about it, that someone around here was trying to keep *The Onion Express* from being rebuilt. Furthermore, the fire that burned down the hotel and restaurant is still listed as suspicious."

"Jack you have a wild imagination. I'm sure the fire was an accident. And as for my husband, we should let the police decide whether or not it was murder. Did they tell you that the pilot, Bob, was a heavy gambler who was having marital problems? It very well could have been a suicide, or maybe even that the box you said they were opening did not cause the explosion. Maybe the helicopter blew because of a mechanical failure. Anyhow, let's order some food and you can bring me up to date on how the construction is going."

I ordered a light meal, which consisted of my iced tea, and a BLT sandwich that came with a side of coleslaw. We spent another hour talking about the project and we both carefully avoided any more talk about Kainoa's death, or the suspect fire that burned down the restaurant. I pretty much repeated everything I had gone over with Kai's father earlier in the day. Based on the questions she was asking, I was surprised at Pua's knowledge of construction, so I asked her where she had obtained her construction knowledge.

Thank you for the compliment Jack. Actually, I'm an alumnus from Purdue where I received a Bachelor of Arts degree in Interior Design. Along with design principles, they also teach a little bit about basic construction as background. Plus, being married to Kainoa, I picked up a lot from business dinner conversations that I attended with him. Finally, my father, who passed away a few years ago, was a General Contractor and I learned a lot of the construction language from being around him. My father was performing a job for Kainoa during my senior year. I was at home tagging along with him during Spring Break when Kainoa and I met. Sparks flew between us from the moment we first met and the next thing I knew I had a boyfriend who was flying out to see me for dates while I was still attending college at Purdue."

We finished lunch and she asked me for a ride to the construction site where she had arranged to meet Tommy. Tommy would take her back to the heliport where she would fly back to Molokai.

I felt strange driving this beautiful, well-dressed woman around town in my rented red convertible Mustang, which had the top down, for everyone to see. I mean the woman had buried her husband just yesterday, but to look at her, or even talk with her, you would never know of her recent loss. I had a feeling that Veronica would not think too highly of the lady sitting beside me right now, and I would have to agree.

My working relationship with Pua Kapuulaa promised to be, to say the least, a challenging task.

CHAPTER 12........HAI?

Arriving at the Lahaina police station, I signed in for my appointment and then waited for Lieutenant Ho to appear. I was already thinking about what he was going to ask about my relationship with Kainoa, and what I might offer that he didn't already know. I thought about my exchange with Pua Kapuulaa and her comment to me regarding my imagination, and whether or not there were any murders. I was deep in thought when, from within two feet in front of me, a slightly balding man, not more than five feet three inches in height, was studying me intensely and interrupted my thoughts by asking if I might be Mr. Bryce.

"Yes. Jack Bryce. You must be Lieutenant Ho? I cross-examined while rising to shake hands with the person I had surmised from his appearance to be a homicide investigator.

"Please follow me Mr. Bryce," he said as we marched through a swinging wooden gate and passed through a brightly lit, open office area filled with maybe ten low-walled cubicles, all filled to the brim with seemingly busy people. As I followed behind, he made a right turn into a narrow hallway, and then into the third door on the right. "You are going to interrogate me?" I asked. The room had a single table with three chairs, no windows and an obvious two-way mirror on the wall.

"It's not an interrogation Mr. Bryce, but as with most public agencies we operate on a tight budget, and these rooms fulfill many different purposes. But you are right that this is one of our interrogation rooms. Please have a seat Mr. Bryce. There will be a scribe with a recorder joining us shortly. May I get you a cup of coffee, or a soda?"

"Thanks, no coffee or soda but some water would be great if you don't mind?" I asked.

"Sure, no problem Jack. Is it alright if I call you Jack?"

"No problem," I replied and the Lieutenant left me alone, presumably going in search of my water. I found it curious that three times today, people had asked permission to call me Jack. Yet, in each case, requestors failed to establish the same kind of informality for themselves. The elderly Mr. Kapuulaa remained a Mister; his daughter-in-law Pua remained, to me, a Missus; and Lieutenant Ho remained Lieutenant.

Within a few moments, or so it seemed, Lieutenant Ho returned with my water and a young uniformed officer named, Officer Li, who carried a recorder and notebook.

I figured why stop with the informalities now, so I introduced myself to her as Jack and for some unknown reason she seemed to blush with shyness. "Officer Li will be recording our conversation, but I want you to feel that this is an open exchange of information."

After the lady officer was all set with her equipment and notepad, the Lieutenant opened with getting my name and address information for the record. As is usually the case, it took about five minutes to explain that Boulder Creek is not in Colorado.

We started by going over all of the information I had given in my initial interview, just after the aircraft explosion. Then the homicide investigator started getting down to the reason I was there. "Jack you alluded to things that you think might make this a murder case, and I'd like you to explain that to me in more detail."

I went over the things that Kainoa and I had discussed such as there are people out there that would rather not see *The Onion Express* rebuilt for reason of competition and or labor and hiring practices. We also went over all of the construction delays and the comments made by each company or person involved in the delay, such as the loadmaster at the harbor, and people from the cement plant who conveniently changed our concrete order from one hundred and forty yards to fourteen yards. We even went over the part where the cement was to be delivered instead of at our job site, and Kainoa's interest in who that might be.

"So all of this leads you to believe that Kainoa Kapuulaa and his pilot Bob were victims of a murder?"

"Yes, I do. And I also believe that the two people who died in the fire at the burned-down restaurant and hotel might also be victims."

"Who do you think then is behind these murders?" asked the Lieutenant.

"Who killed Kainoa and the others? I would think that is your job Lieutenant. Am I the only one around here who thinks there is a murder here? Don't you think exploding helicopters and burning down businesses, all impacting the same family, is just a little suspicious?"

Before answering me, the Lieutenant asked the lady officer doing the recording to go ahead and close up her machine and leave. Then the Lieutenant did something I hadn't expected. He grabbed me by the elbow while escorting me out of the tiny interrogation room and asked, "Do you drink Jack? If you do, I'd like to get out of here and buy you a cold one at the bar around the corner. What do you say?"

"Sounds good to me Lieutenant Ho! You buy the first and I'll get the second."

"Deal," replied the homicide investigator. "Only now that I'm off duty you don't need to call me Lieutenant anymore. My name is Hai."

We were outside the building now, and I stopped our progression toward the bar. "Wait a minute. Did you just tell me your name is…"

"That's right, but I'm only going to explain this one time, okay? Yes, my name is Hai Ho, and I've had to live with that for forty-three years. It is a Japanese name that was given to me by my father who was a real jokester. When I asked him why he gave me that name, he said, 'It was either going to be Hai Ho or Heidi Ho,' because they, my parents, thought the names to be…cute! Now, how about that beer?"

CHAPTER 13......MO BETTAH?

The inside of the bar was done in Asian with bamboo framed glass tables and bamboo framed chairs with dark red cushions, lots of Asian art and dangling strings of glass beads used as separators between groups of tables. The atmosphere was cool and dark, which was a welcome change from the over-lit police station, and we were the only customers in the place.

My new friend, or so it seemed anyhow, picked the table farthest away, evidently to not be heard. "Listen Jack, I know I put you through a lot of crap in there, but it was my job. You asked a question in there that I did not want to answer, because nothing is sacred in that place and the walls have ears. Therefore, to give a straight answer and not a lot of bullshit...yes, I think this is definitely a homicide. In fact I think it is four homicides all tied into one case, but as yet the only thing I've got to tie it all together is the family. There is no provable evidence linking anyone or any group to what is happening. At least not yet there isn't, but I'm working on getting the proof. In fact I think you might be my key."

"Great, here I go again!" I said aloud but aimed at no one.

"What do you mean Jack?"

At that point I was committed to informing him of my involvement in the murder and robbery at PharmaLabs and then at the amusement park. By the time I was through explaining all of that, Hai gave a little whistle and said, "That's juicy stuff Jack. I know some homicide detectives who have full careers with less action than that."

"Gee, thanks Hai, that makes me feel a lot better…not!" I said, downing what was left of my first beer and signaling the bartender for two more.

"Suppose you tell me something I don't know about this case," Hai prodded me.

"What makes you think I have anything else?"

"It's my job to read people, and right now I'm reading you as holding back."

"Hmm, what else could I tell you? The family is full of mistrust and suspicion and for what will happen with *The Onion Express.*"

"Nice try Jack but the whole island knows that. What else are you thinking?"

"One faction of the family thinks Kainoa was murdered and the other doesn't, or at least doesn't want to admit to the possibility it was a murder."

"That's interesting. Tell me who said what?"

"Okay, but I'm going to need to switch to iced tea or I won't be able to drive home."

Hai and I ordered some finger food and kept after the beers, and since I was *batching it,* and since Hai was single, it made for an ample evening meal. We talked about the meetings I had had earlier with Kainoa's father and Pua where I tried to recall the details of each conversation for my new friend Lieutenant Ho. By the end of the evening I had Hai talking to himself with confusion, which I thought was only fair because I was already confused enough for two people regarding the things and happenstances surrounding *The Onion Express* and its owners.

When Tuesday morning arrived, I woke up a little late and had to ask Luanne if she could get Tommy to pick me up because I had had enough to drink the night before that it warranted Hai to call a cab for the both of us.

When Tommy picked me up, he could tell I was feeling the negative effects from the night before. So, he took me right back to the same bar, next to the police station, where my car was parked. Once there, he literally dragged me back, while ignoring my feeble protests, into the bar where he ordered the bartender to make something I had never heard of before, it was in Hawaiian, and then he stood next to me until I finished swallowing the last drop of the vile concoction that didn't seem fit for human consumption.

"What that hell was that Tommy? It tasted like shit!"

"Yeah, brudah," he replied. "But it is going to make you mo bettah. Now we go to your work where you can be da big kahuna and I bring you back for your car dissafternoon. We go now okay?" He told me more than asked. Before I could argue, even if I wanted to, which I didn't, we were back in the car and on our way to the office trailer.

Although I am not quite sure, exactly what it is was that I drank, sure enough as Tommy said, by the time we reached the trailer I was feeling "much mo bettah."

CHAPTER 14.........
ANOTHER LONG DAY

It was still early in the week, only Tuesday, and even though I felt better from the concoction at the bar, my feeling was this was going to be one of those extra long workweeks.

I didn't hear from any of the family members. However, I did receive direction from the architects that I should, per instructions given by Pua Kapuulaa, attend a meeting on Friday afternoon to review and discuss the details of the interior design, with the intent of making changes. My response was supportive to both the architect and to the new boss lady that would be signing my checks, "Well, better to hear it and plan for it now. I'll be there on time," I said closing the conversation.

With the long awaited concrete pour all set, and everyone performing the final acts of positioning steel framing supports and checking casings for the drilled piers Tuesday was, in it, an important day needing scrutinizing of the structural details. For management, engineering and even the city inspector, it was a long day that went well into the evening. We reached sign-off that we were, in fact and as specified, totally ready for the big one hundred-and-forty yard concrete pour scheduled for the next morning.

Luanne, to her credit, stayed the course as well, helping to document the completed specifications and collecting sign-offs from the appropriate engineers, contractors and myself.

Finally, it was just after 10:00 PM when I got back to the condo where I picked up a recorded voice message from Jim Alverez, "Vickie and I will be landing at 6:08 PM on Flight 1388 which leaves from SFO, so I guess we'll see you then and thanks for putting us up Jack. You are a true friend to do this for us."

There was a second message from Veronica, who wanted to talk to me about some good news, so I called home, "That's great Babe! Acing both tests is a fantastic accomplishment! Wow! Way to go honey!" I said in support to my excited wife on her significant achievement needed to step up to a new and higher position in the school district where she works.

Veronica, for all her inherent intelligence and quick wit, sometimes lacks the confidence to deal with the business community. I attribute her feelings, which I think are similar for many stay-at-home moms, is that they feel they have missed out on that part of life and that makes them somehow inadequate. Even though Veronica was a straight A student through school and has pretty much mastered the modern world with its computer technology, I have always had a hard time convincing her of her worth in the business arena. Anyhow, today, she was ecstatic over her accomplishment (rightly so) and I was really proud of her...as I have been each and everyday that we have been married. That is not to say that everyday of our marriage is blissful, but regardless of any angry or frustrating moments, which happen to us all, I always have been and always will be proud to be with her.

I related my Monday happenings with the exception of having had too much to drink. It wasn't that I wanted to hide anything from her, but rather I didn't want her sitting more than 2,000 miles away worrying about me. Anyhow, I figured I wouldn't be drinking too much again any time soon.

After hanging up with Veronica, I hit the sack, figuring another long day had ended and that I'd better get some sleep as I needed to be at the office early the next morning.

CHAPTER 15......
A BAD DAY GONE GOOD!

I arrived at the small trailer at 5:00 AM sharp, and well ahead of first daylight. For the first time ever, I seemed to have managed to beat everyone else to work. In fact, I was the only person at the site, meaning the evening security sentry was nowhere to be found.

Lacking the guard who was supposed to be on duty, and being concerned about his absence, I took a stroll along the perimeter of the site guided only by the remaining moonlight and nearby city street lamps.

It was while passing one of the construction trailers that I heard, too late, "Now!" and then felt myself in the grasps of someone's arms and being driven to the ground hard as if I were a tackling dummy on a football training field.

Once down, and with the person who had tackled me releasing me, I saw the outline of a second person swinging a long thick object, maybe three to four feet in length, toward my head. Luckily, I had enough time to roll toward the assailant, causing the brunt of the blow to hit the ground behind me. As I started to get up, the person who had tackled and then released me, now drove his knee into my mid-section bowling me over and leaving me gasping to regain the wind that been knocked out of my lungs.

"What should we do with him?" the younger of the two asked the other.

"Let's just leave him and get the hell out of here. The guy at the cockfights said if we were to run into anybody we should just leave!"

Luckily for me, the two decided it was time to leave, and they departed hurriedly before I could regain my composure enough to even think about chasing after them.

From a distance, I heard the closing of two car doors and the sound of a car's engine starting, and then the vehicle sped away into the pre-dawn darkness and the still quiet streets of Lahaina.

I was pissed at myself for not having been more cautious, and not having been able to get my hands on either of the intruders. I got up, dusted myself off, verified that the right side of my ribs were sore to the touch, and made my way back to the trailer where I put in a call to Lieutenant Ho, where I left a voice message referencing my bruised dignity and the possible new development.

I brewed a pot of coffee and made a note that at first light there would need to be a verification that the pre-pour prep work was still good and that we were ready to go forward the day for which we had waited so long. Then, I put in a call to the security company where an answering machine directed me to an emergency pager. I called that number, left my call back number, and then waited about five minutes for a return call. The responding person was the graveyard supervisor who had no clue as to where his assigned guard was. He promised to get someone over there right away and to get back to me with why there was no sentry at our site.

The security call now completed, I poured a cup of the fresh brew, and sweetened it with a sugar substitute I have grown to like. Luanne, who uses it due to her Type II Diabetes, introduced it to me.

Next, I called the cement plant to confirm delivery. I was pleased to hear that the first few trucks had already lined up for filling and would soon be on their way.

I was on hand to greet the first workers, the steelworkers, who were followed by framing carpenters and concrete finishers. Together we toured the site and found that my two assailants had managed to destroy several of the forms that had been built to support the foundation pours of the restaurant. We made an urgent call for more framing material, and four more carpenters to arrive immediately. The thought was that we would pour several of the drilled piers first, thus giving the framers a chance to rebuild their forms ahead of the impending arrival of concrete trucks to be used for the foundation.

There was no way I wanted to reschedule any part of the concrete delivery. We had waited too long already, and my construction schedule had already been shortened to the point where the project was going to be a couple of weeks late. Furthermore, the added forming material and extra carpenters were going to add to the cost, which I also didn't need.

It was at about the same time when the first cement trucks and the two special concrete pump trucks arrived that I heard from Lieutenant Ho. "So Jack, how did you like our native cure for the common hang-over?"

"Hi Hai!" I guffawed, while stumbling to get out the two same sounding words. "That is nasty shit and I don't even want to know what it was that I drank. But, I got to admit, it seemed to bring me back to life. So, you got my message about the greeting I got at work this morning?"

"Yeah brother. Sounds like you are okay though, right? Two against one aren't the best of odds," he conjectured for me.

"Well, I should have been smarter than that. I should have expected the unexpected," I grumbled. "Anyhow, apparently they were on a mission to disrupt construction, because the only damage was to our pour forms which had to be purposely knocked down. There was no sign of trying to break into any of the gang boxes that house tools and there was no evidence of trying to get into the trailers for computers or printers, or the other type of office equipment in them. This was strictly an attempt to mess up or delay the Kapuulaa family from reopening *The Onion Express*," I reported.

"Want to come down and spend some time in the Mug Books?"

"Nope. It was too dark…I could barely identify myself," I clamored loudly as the noise from the heavy equipment was penetrating the walls of my office.

"So what do you want me to do Jack?" The Lieutenant asked.

"Not much you can do Hai. I just thought you should know that whatever is going on here didn't stop with Kainoa's death. This thing that is happening here, whatever it is, it isn't over."

"Well, one thing I can do is to increase extra surveillance around the construction site. And in the meantime…I'll focus my ears on the street to see what's humming out there in the way of rumors and scuttlebutt."

The Lieutenant ended the conversation by imposing a lunch date on me for the following week, followed by a "I want to hear anything and everything if you think it is the least bit odd."

I agreed to all of the above and went back to watching the crews pump, pour and apply finishes where needed on the new concrete.

As the day went along, the schedule was tight and we had as many as three trucks pouring at the same time. I had Luanne documenting, the progress with pictures of the action for each concrete pour. The picture portion is something I always do as verification of the process not only for the owners, but also for any inspection agency wanting records. In this case, we also documented the vandalism, or more likely sabotage, for insurance purposes, hoping that I could get them to cover part of the loss to avoid project over costs.

All in all, and considering getting the crap kicked out of me so early in the morning, the day turned out to be successful. The saboteurs, probably because I had arrived so early, failed to cause any delays to the new construction schedule.

In the end, even though the day had started so badly, it had been a good day...or as I put it...it was a bad day gone good!

CHAPTER 16.........
A FRIENDLY VISIT

Wednesday night I slept soundly. A couple glasses of David Bruce's finest, followed by three Advil to cover the pain from my bruised ribs, did the job nicely. The next morning I woke up feeling refreshed, except for a little bit of residual pain from the rib cage, which was to be expected.

Thursday went without a hitch, as much of the day was spent watching the concrete dry...not really. Although the concrete did need time to cure, there was plenty to do for the various subs as well as for me. In particular, with the concrete now poured, I was able to work on the schedule, where I focused on trying to make up for the lost time. I was targeting opportunities to reduce duplicated efforts, or otherwise make use of similar circumstances that would allow separate trades to work in the same area at the same time. One way I achieved a little time saving was due to being able to stagger work times. For example, by staggering the start times of the plumbers, the electricians and the mechanical contractors, they were able to work in the same areas without getting in each other's way. What surprised me most was that when I met with the leads of each group, there was absolutely no resistance or worries about who started early and who started later. Pretty much the only comment I got back was, "Okay brudah, you da Kahuna. What you say...is what we do!" At home, that could never happen.

After everyone was gone, I stayed a little longer to ensure that our new security sentry was on site, and to take opportunity to review the interior design in preparation for the Friday meeting with the architects and Pua Kapuulaa.

Finally, at about 9:00 PM, I arrived at the door of my tenth floor condominium to hear music coming from inside. I got really excited thinking that Veronica was inside waiting for me in a surprise visit, she had kept a key for when she would return, and I fumbled in the breezeway getting the door open as quickly as I could.

Finally, I opened the door slowly to find the place dimly lit with gardenia-scented candles burning on the breakfast bar, the coffee table and the dining table as well. I put my stuff down on a chair, and taking the hint I stripped to my boxers and followed a trail of flickering light illuminating the short hallway and emanating from the master bedroom. Being a guy who's been without the favors of his wife for quite a while now, I was very excited and ready for some spontaneous lovemaking. You might even say I was enthusiastic with anticipation as I rounded the corner of the bedroom and dove straight onto the four-poster gliding just above the foot of the bed.

It was in mid air that I discovered the person in my bed was not my wife. Panic took over in mid flight, and when I landed I was grasping for the pillows to cover my engorged enthusiasm, which was now dying rapidly.

"Pua? Mrs. Kapuulaa? What are you doing here?" I gibbered nervously.

"You look surprised Jack. Surely you knew my interest in you from our lunch meeting the other day. Didn't you?"

"Uh..," I stammered. Pua was wearing a form fitting silk, lavender colored nightgown that hugged every curve of her body. I was surprised to the point of being speechless, and as I fumbled for words I edged myself off of the bed maintaining the pillow in its covering position.

Finally I got the words out, "I guess I missed that memo!"

"You're being silly Jack. What are you hiding behind that pillow?" she said teasing me into further embarrassment.

"Uh…" I stammered again. "How did you get in here?" I asked, stalling her to regain my composure. In addition, I had a hard time averting my eyes from her, as she looked beautiful and very sexy. The lady definitely knew how to get to a guy.

"You are being silly again Jack! This is my place. Remember? Of course, I have a key to my own place. Now come back over here and sit down on the bed. Let's talk this over," she said while patting a place on the mattress next to her and smiling at me lustily.

"Pua, I'm married. Remember?" I retorted to her while still backing away toward the door to the hallway.

"I can see you are uncomfortable Jack, and I don't want to force you. Let's be adults here. My husband is deceased and we really hadn't been together for a long time before he died. And as for you, well, the little woman is more than two thousand miles away so what's the harm? Why can't we, as adults, mix a little business with pleasure?" she said while lightly rubbing her hand over her right breast. "I don't want a lasting relationship here Jack. I just want to have some fun because I'm attracted to you, and I wanted a chance to talk a little business before we meet with the architects tomorrow. Now come back over and have some wine with me," she said while indicating the full decanter on the bedside table next to the Tiffany lamp. "I promise not to bite…at least for a little while," she said while patting the mattress beside her again and pouting toward me with extended ruby red lips.

I regained my composure now and I didn't even have to think about my next response. I stepped toward the edge of the bed, ensuring good eye contact and then I said, "I'm happy to talk business with you any time you wish Pua, but not in my bed…"

Before I could finish Pua said, "Well, great. Then just get in here and we'll talk business while being comfortable."

"Uh…no, you don't understand. I can't be with you that way, Pua. My wife and I have a special relationship and we've been together for more than twenty-five years. I have never cheated on her and I never will."

"Never Jack? That's admirable and I like loyalty, but maybe it's time you did. What makes you so sure she's not cheating on you back in Boulder Creek?"

I couldn't believe she would remember where I was from. "I don't believe, not even for one minute, that my wife would cheat on me," I snapped in response to her suggestion. "My wife and I are best friends and I feel bad for you that you don't know what is to have trust and faith in someone else. For me, I would never risk hurting or losing her," I persisted. However, realizing my situation, I felt a little stupid giving a sermon on the sanctity of marriage while standing in my bedroom wearing only my boxers and addressing a scantily clad beauty that was lying on my bed offering what every man wants. Then, to remove myself from the situation, I tossed the pillow back on the bed and turned to walk out the bedroom door and to the chair in the living room where I had placed my clothes.

Pua followed me out of the master bedroom and, leaning against the wall with her wine in one hand, watched me quietly as I put my pants on one leg at a time and then writhed them up my torso finally buttoning them around my waist and closed the zipper. "If you want to talk business Pua you are going to have to change into something more suitable. I'll be out on the deck."

I moved toward the darkened veranda, leaving her leaning against the dining room wall, watching my backside as I stepped out the sliding door. A few minutes later Pua joined me, though this time she was wearing blue jeans and a pink, cotton, button down long sleeved shirt. "So what about those Giants?" I asked to open a new conversation.

Pua smiled, handed me a glass of wine she had carried out for me and said, "You win for now Mr. Jack Bryce. But I don't give up all that easily. Anyhow, let's talk about some of the changes I have in mind for the hotel and restaurant."

"Yes Ma'am, you're the boss!" And then I added, "When we are talking about the restaurant and hotel."

She smiled without comment and the suspicious side of me wondered what else might be the reasoning for this *friendly visit.*

CHAPTER 17........GRANDEUR

Friday's meeting with the architects went pretty well. They listened intently to the ideas handed out by the new boss, and everyone was aiming to please her. For the hotel side, the end result was fewer rooms for rent. Instead, each room was the equivalent of a suite designed to bring in a higher paying clientele. Besides the sleeping area, each room color coordinated to include a three person cushioned couch, a large coffee table and two over stuffed armchairs. Each room, because she wanted to attract business travelers as well, included four phones (two near the beds, one at the desk and another on the wall in the bathroom), high-speed Internet connection at a solid wood desk with an adjustable office chair for ergonomics. Entertainment was to include satellite reception of over one hundred free television channels, music stations and ceiling mounted speakers for sound distribution.

The lobby was being upgraded too, to include a larger foyer, which would be decorated with Pacific Island artwork, rare Hawaiian artifacts, and modern hand-blown glass chandeliers. There would be all leather furnishings surrounding a brass railed horseshoe and hand hewn teak bar equipped with sports televisions from every angle.

There would also be a small wooden dance floor constructed with white oak planks to replicate a ship's deck and an area for the small bands and or piano entertainment. Surrounding the bar area there was going to be several groups of separated and intimate seating areas, consisting of two opposing two-person couches, a square teak coffee table and two armchairs. Each of these areas would be equipped with phones and Internet connections, too.

In addition, there would be a fine restaurant, with capacity to seat one hundred and fifty guests, catering to the tastes of the rich and the richer.

The result was a reduction, about one third, of originally planned available rooms for rent, but the trade off was higher priced clientele paying three to five hundred dollars per night instead of the one hundred to two hundred dollar a night original concept. The hotel section, it seemed, would not be meant as a hangout or gathering place for middle class locals.

For the attached restaurant, Pua decided that instead of an all open-air dining and bar area, half of it would be converted to enclosed, air conditioned, upscale, banquet rooms with the latest in audiovisual technology, including large screen videoconferencing capabilities.

All of these changes were fine as far as I was concerned. Pua had renegotiated my contract very favorably, on the balcony of my condominium the night before. My charge for the new design was an incremental increase, commensurate with whatever the new added costs would equal plus, a larger bonus if I kept the original construction period. If not, the extra time to complete the work would not be compensated. It was a risk I was willing to take.

The architects saw the opportunity for added business and they eagerly, as did I, accepted the new challenge.

The added grandeur was accepted by everyone, as was the authority now being provided by Pua. How these changes would be accepted by the Kapuulaa family was not a mystery to any of us involved in the change order. However, the issue of the added grandeur was a family matter. Our mission was to build as directed, and to do it as efficiently as possible.

Chapter 18.........
From Tears to Cheers

"She has put the entire family at risk with her delusional building designs," reported the senior Kapuulaa family member over the phone. "My worst fears are realized, and my hands are tied!" he exclaimed angrily with a great deal of emotion in his voice.

I explained that the matter was out of my hands and the hands of anyone else involved in the project. "I understand how you feel sir, but this is a family matter and the project crews are not involved."

"Not involved? How can you say that? My son hired you and many of the construction people are part of our extended family," he agonized.

"Mr. Kapuulaa this crew will build whatever it is told to build. If you convince Pua to go back to the original design then that is what we will do," I explained.

"I know," he replied. "I know this is not your fault but I beg of you to work with me in the name of my son who hired you," he groaned sadly to me.

Each time Palakapola Kapuulaa mentioned his deceased son, I felt a sear of pain and the weight on my shoulders increased. Mentally I kept rationalizing that this was not my fight, but my heart was having trouble accepting that.

The conversation ended with me confirming that I would do my best to keep an eye on things and to keep him advised of the construction process. I kept the seduction attempt to myself, not wanting to add to the old man's existing frustration and sorrow. I truly felt bad for the older gentleman and in truth, his plea regarding Kainoa hit home, causing me confusion and guilt at my having agreed to manage Pua's changes.

Luanne snapped me out of my deep thoughts by reminding me that I need to get to the airport to pick up my friends.

The drive was slow and congested, just as I expected for a Friday evening, and I used the time to review my thoughts and feelings.

- The Kapuulaa family had suffered more than their share of tragedies with the loss of Kainoa and *The Onion Express.*

- Outside influences had caused construction delays and apparently the sabotage efforts were still going on with Wednesday morning's attempt to disrupt the concrete pour.

- Local police concur that something is going on but as yet have no idea as to who or why.

- Pua Kapuulaa, Kainoa's widow, was beautiful, intelligent and someone not to turn your back on.

- Finally, home was more than two thousand miles away and the anticipation of the family joining me after school let out for a fun summer in Hawaii was waning. The dim circumstances and the cautious surroundings in which I found myself caused me concern for the safety of my family.

The exit for the Kahului Airport leaped unexpectedly into my view, causing me to snap out of my thoughts and turning my concentration back to the task, which was to pick up my friend Jim Alverez, a homicide investigator from the Bay Area, and his girlfriend Vickie.

My timing was good. Just as I walked into the baggage claim area, I spotted Vickie and Jim emerging from a crowd surrounding a baggage carousel loaded with newly arrived luggage.

"It's so great to see you and to be here!" Vickie exclaimed, while practically leaping into my arms and crushing my neck in her arms. I might have complained except…I like hugs.

"Hey buddy!" said Jim Alverez, with a big smile and giving me a hug around the shoulders.

"It's great to see both of you, and on behalf of the Island of Maui, Aloha," I said presenting them with the fresh orchid leis that Luanne had purchased for me to present to my friends.

Suddenly, all of the things that had laid so heavily on my mind were now forgotten. I was back to my old self, enjoying my time with friends that I had not seen for the past few months. It seemed I had gone from tears to cheers in a few short nanoseconds.

CHAPTER 19......
HAPPY TOGETHER

Jim and I followed Vickie as she masterfully maneuvered the shopping cart around people, other carts and special displays in the huge, card-member only, grocery outlet. The stop for supplies, which was only a few blocks from the airport, was my idea, and was because I had just been too busy to get it done before my guests arrived.

I was brought back to the workweek when Jim, after I had commented about what a great-looking gal Vickie was, gave me an elbow to my still sore ribs, from where I had been kneed by one of the job site vandals on Wednesday morning.

Noticing my wince from his playful elbow jab, Alverez lowered his sunglasses and raised one inquisitive eyebrow while giving me a discerning look. However, before any verbiage could break out, Jim's questioning look was interrupted by Vickie who was asking me questions about any other needed supplies for the condo. "Do we need anything like toilet paper or paper towels?" I assured her that Veronica had left me well supplied and that the condo's shortcoming, as related to supplies, was pretty much just related to food and beverage.

When we left the huge chain store, we were loaded with enough basic supplies to last us the seven days that Jim and Vickie would be spending with me on the island.

The ride from Kahului to Kahana was for me, long as usual. But for the two newcomers it was a new adventure. I was playing chauffeur and guide, as Jim and Vickie sat together in the tiny cramped back seat of the red convertible as I drove us across the island and then up the coast toward the condominium.

It was kind of cute to see the two adults, via my rearview mirror, acting as giddy as a couple of high school kids on a date. Finally, arriving at the beachside tenth floor condo, Vickie and Jim were just as ecstatic with the accommodations as were Veronica and I when we first arrived. As I watched them, I smiled to myself. Jim got hung up on the view and the binoculars, just as I had, while Vickie was not only into the gorgeous views but the condo's furnishings and décor, too. During the morning, before work, I had managed to move my stuff out of the master bedroom and put clean sheets on the bed for my guests. Again they were as excited as kids in a candy store and wouldn't you know it, Vickie also made a big deal over the tiffany lamps as had Veronica.

I recalled it had only been last night when I found Pua Kapuulaa waiting for me, seductively, in the very same bed I was now giving to my friends. For the time being, I had no desires to neither relate that incident to anyone nor explain that she had stayed in the guest room that night after previewing her construction changes and renegotiating my contract. I was only glad that she had removed her stuff, made up the bed and left the place looking like she had never been there...or so I thought.

Vickie, at first, protested my giving them the master bedroom, but it didn't take too much convincing for them to accept the bedroom with its private veranda and panoramic views of the ocean and Molokai.

Jim and I left Vickie in the kitchen to rustle together some eats while we braved the windy breezeway and elevator to retrieve what was left of their luggage and groceries.

"So who was she and why are your ribs so sore?" Jim asked once we were out of Vickie's hearing range.

"My ribs are sore from a little thing that happened at work the other day and what do you mean she?" I contended.

"The woman who left the strong scent of gardenias in your condo, and all of those recently burned candles everywhere," he persisted.

"Thought you were on vacation," I retorted.

"Can't help myself. I am what I am," he chortled in response. "So?" he resumed the questioning.

"This is the boss lady's condo. She was here last night to get my buy-in on some construction changes she is initiating as well as to renegotiate my contract," I defended.

"I see. So the two of you, she heavily scented with some kind of gardenia-scented perfume, reviewed construction drawings by candlelight while drinking wine. Interesting boss lady you have there Jack. By the way, isn't she recently widowed?"

"Damn. Not much gets by you!" I exclaimed with a shake of my head.

I knew Jim was not going to let go, and since we are friends, I let loose with what was going on with the Kapuulaa family, the job site and everything else.

"How do you do that?" Jim inquired.

"Do what?"

"How do you mange to get yourself involved in other people's dilemmas?

"It's a personal fault I guess, or maybe I'm just lucky."

"I got news for you Jack. The predicaments you get yourself into aren't what I'd call luck! I do it because it is my job. You do it because you are who you are. You're a good guy who's always trying to do the right thing for the people around you."

"Well, being the only child in my family, I got pretty used to taking the trash out. What's your excuse again?"

"Are the locals involved?" my inquiring homicide detective friend queried me some more.

"Yeah, as a matter of fact. I seem to attract you homicide types. His name is Hai Ho and he is the only homicide detective in Lahaina."

"Did you say his name is Hi Ho?"

"No," I said. His name is Hai Ho."

"Oh. Huh?"

"Never mind, he reminds me a lot of you, only he's a shorter version."

We finished unloading the Mustang using one of the luggage carts provided by the condominium management group, and then made our way back upstairs via the elevator.

"I see why they call this a breezeway," Jim stated as we fought the winds after getting off the elevator. "Is it always this windy up here?"

"Nope. In the late afternoon, when the trade winds hit, it's much worse," I quipped. "However, if you find the temperature to be too hot or humid…this is where you want to go to cool off in a hurry."

"I thought you boys had got lost or something because you've been gone so long," Vickie said as we brought the rest of goods and luggage through the now propped-open screen and front doors.

"Sorry," I replied. "We're just getting caught up on what has been happening for the past few months. Wow, that smells and looks great Vickie."

Vickie, in the short time we had been gone, had managed to get some fresh veggies and pork chops cooking on the stovetop. Smelling the food and seeing my friends, made me both grateful for the company, and homesick for Veronica and the family that kept life so full and active back in the Santa Cruz Mountains.

By the time we finished eating, it was getting pretty near 10:00 PM. Since Vickie had done all of the cooking, I pushed the two lovebirds out the door for a private walk along the beach while I took on the task of cleaning up the kitchen.

Later, with Jim and Vickie still out on their moonlit beach stroll and the dishes all washed and put away, I called home to talk to my honey, whom I was missing a lot right now. I avoided the stuff about my getting beat up and as for the episode with Pua, I told Veronica about her having spent the night in the guest room. Veronica's reaction, just as I had expected, was better than if she had told me some guy had spent the night in our guest room while I was away. I imagined that Veronica might not have been pleased with the overnight situation, but I also knew she wouldn't show concern. First, Veronica has too much pride to show that kind of emotion, and second, our marriage has trust.

The next morning the three of us took off to play tourist on Maui by taking a trip along the infamous "Road To Hana," which is pretty much an all-day event. We retraced our drive from Kahana back towards the airport and across the island picking up Highway 360, which would take us to Hana via a narrow and twisty drive filled with many of the scenic wonders of the paradise island.

The trip and the company made for a great day. We picked up a Hana Cassette Guide, which brought us great amusement in itself, and then we followed the cassette voice stopping at all of the points of interest along the way. We also stopped here and there to sample local food and fruit being sold along the narrow road at various family run road stands. In particular, we were all quite pleased with some smoked Marlin on a stick, which we agreed was extremely tasty.

Finally, nearly five hours later, we reached Hana and its famous Seven Pools. Since I already knew about this place, we had the foresight to wear swim gear so that we could take a dip in the famous, ancient pools. Choosing the fourth pool because it was less crowded, I was the first in our little group to climb onto the rocks and dive into the beautiful, clear, deep pool. Not to be out done, and more likely to show off a little for Vickie, Jim climbed to the next higher level and performed a dive that would have warranted a good score from the judges had there been any. Seeing the one-up-man-ship, I felt I had to respond. So, for my next dive, I climbed to the highest diving point possible for this upper pool. I estimated that dive to the pool below would be from a height that was more than forty feet. Having been a swimmer and a diver in high school, I intended to give a little show of my own. Bending my knees and springing up and out from the rocks, I first tucked my knees doing a 360 degree forward roll, opening to a fully stretched out position with intent to then turn downward and to enter the water headfirst, arms extended straight ahead with as little splash as possible. Unfortunately, I hadn't taken into account that just like for Captain Hook, in Peter Pan, the ticking clock of time had finally caught up with me too. Time, it would seem, had run out on my mid-air aerobics, and the water came up too fast. My angle didn't get steep enough fast enough, and the ensuing belly flop brought immediate pain to my not so flat any more stomach, my still hurting ribs and the sensitive parts of the male body. Furthermore, I tallied yet another bruise to my battered ego.

When I surfaced, there was a multitude of open mouthed and startled looking people staring at me with cringes on their faces. Vickie broke the silence from across the pond by yelling out loudly to overcome the sound of the waterfall. "Jack. Are you alright Jack?" she asked with genuine concern and adding to my embarrassment.

I could only nod to her as I made way to a small ledge in the cliff from which I dove. Once I got there, it took everything I had to muster a smile at my companions who were on the beach side of the pool.

I clung one handed to the rock ledge, and with my back turned to the crowd on the rocky beach, I took inventory of all my critical body parts and a little time to recoup from the self-imposed trauma.

Finally, Jim swam up behind me. "Are you okay buddy?"

"Think I'm gonna live," I gurgled with my lips just above the water. "Your turn," I goaded.

"Not likely pal! I saw what happened to you, and being on my honeymoon, I need the use of all my equipment!"

"Honeymoon?"

"Yeah. We were going to tell you tonight at dinner," Jim continued. "We got married in the courthouse Thursday afternoon with just her parents and mine attending. The ceremony was performed by Judge Black."

"Well, hot damn, Jim. Congratulations my friend!"

Jim replied, "Thanks. We are both pretty excited. Did you want to try another dive, or should we get back on the road?" he expostulated to make me re-think.

Together we decided that leaving before we hurt ourselves anymore was the wiser move.

Advice from road signs at the end of Highway 360, the car rental company, and from the end of the Road To Hana guided tape, said that we were supposed to turn around and return the way we came.

Not us. Driving the red Mustang with the top still down we ventured forward along the coast over an unpaved and loose gravel covered road. As it turned out, the road wasn't that bad, albeit the landscape was barren on the inland side of the road which looked up toward Haleakala, while the coastal side was spectacular with waves crashing over the lava covered beaches. It is on the slopes of Haleakala, Maui's world-famous dormant volcano, that Maui's famous sweet onions, the namesake for *The Onion Express*, are grown. Maui Onions are considered to be among the best and most flavorful onions in the entire world, and they only grow in the deep red, volcanic earth found on the upper slopes of Haleakala.

Later we reached the small town of Ulupalakua and visited the Tedeschi Winery. There, I bought a couple bottles of the local wine, some breadsticks, pepper jack cheese and three sweet mangos, which we took to the nearest beach where we toasted the new marriage and picnicked in the setting sun.

From there, the happy-looking couple, cuddled in the back seat while I drove the final leg back to the condominium.

CHAPTER 20.......
ON HIS BUTT AGAIN

On Sunday, I drove the honeymoon couple to Veronica's and my favorite snorkel spot, Honolua Bay.

We arrived at about 9:00AM and the place was already crowded, however, we found a spot for the Mustang along the road, and then made the trek down to the rocky beach and the small bay. It was the same place where Veronica and I had encountered the big Tiger shark and the dolphins that came to our rescue when I had first come out to start the job.

This time, having learned from my earlier experience, I had a little less difficulty putting on my flippers. I also found it somewhat amusing that after having had so much trouble before, that I was now helping Vickie and Jim to get their gear on.

The ocean water around the reef was clear and the fish were brightly colored, beautiful to see in their habitat and plentiful. When we eventually ventured out to the edge of the reef and the deep water below, Vickie signaled she wanted no part of it. "I'm not going to go swimming out there in that deep water you guys," she said when we gathered at the surface.

"No problem honey," Jim told his bride. "Let's see what's out there by the point," he said pointing toward the rocky end of the shoreline.

We continued to snorkel even after it began to rain and many of the Honolua Bay visitors had left. Finally, having had enough, and because the water was beginning to get murky from the muddy runoff, we decided it was time to go.

By now, our towels and gear were soaking wet, so we just grabbed our stuff and headed up the trail towards the giant Banyan tree and the parked Mustang. Just as we approached the Banyan, we noticed that the trail we came down on now had about a fifteen to twenty foot wide stream cutting into it, hence the cause of the water in the small bay becoming too murky to see fish. I went first across the little river of rainwater. The plan was once I made it across, Vickie would be next, with Jim bringing up the rear.

I successfully probed my way through and across the stream, finding that at the deepest spot, the water was just above my knees. However, the water seemed to be increasing in speed and depth at a rapid rate, probably because the stream was being fed by other gullies from the small mountains above the road. Vickie came next. I grabbed her hand when she neared my side of the stream helping her to step out of the flowing runoff rainwater. Jim came just behind her, but he lost his footing and went splat. He landed on his behind in the water, with shoes and towels floating away. For me this was a familiar sight. It reminded me of an earlier fishing excursion in the San Lorenzo River during steelhead season, where Jim had also lost his footing and wound up sitting in the river looking ridiculous.

Anyhow, I got Vickie out of the water and made a grab for the swept away shoes and towels, but I came up empty handed. I turned back to Jim who was still sitting in the water making a funny expression about having fallen, when I saw something alarming. I yelled, "Look out Jim!" I then stepped back into the water toward my friend, reaching out with my arm. With less than a second to spare Jim grabbed my extended hand, pulled himself to his feet and narrowly missed being hit by a small log rocketing down the runoff trough.

"Thanks, Jack. That could have put a damper on the honeymoon."

"No problem buddy. Let's get out of here," I said. "Anyone remember if I put the top up on the car?" I kidded.

"By the way Jim, I want you to know how good it made me feel to see your ego bruised a little. Especially after my diving fiasco at the Seven Pools yesterday in Hana."

Covered with mud and yuck from the trail, we finally emerged from the jungle-like setting, making it back out to the road and the awaiting Mustang. As I looked around, I realized we were the last car in the area. Of the three of us, Vickie seemed to be the cleanest so we elected her to drive us back to the condominium.

CHAPTER 21......
DON'T COUNT ON ME!

I left the honeymooning couple alone on Monday morning and hitched a ride with Tommy to work. I figured now that Vickie and Jim had seen a lot of the island that I should get out of the way of their honeymoon. In fact, I was thinking about getting a room someplace so that they could be alone.

"How was your weekend Tommy?" I asked as I climbed into the front seat next to him in the limo.

"It's not good for da Big Kahuna to sit in da front seat with me," Tommy complained.

"I don't feel much like The Big Kahuna my brother," I responded. "I'm more of a team player. I like it best when everyone takes responsibility for his or her part of the job and we all work together. Besides, the only Big Kahuna on this project is Mrs. Kapuulaa now."

"Ain't dat da trut brudah," Tommy chided. "Now Pua, she da one who got control. Hey, I hear she go to your place last week. Every ting okay der?" Tommy quizzed.

I wasn't surprised that Tommy would know Pua had been to the condominium, and I wondered who all knew that she had spent the night. After I arrived on the island, it didn't take long for me to figure out that the locals had a pretty tight network, and that there weren't very many successful secrets.

"Yes, it was fine Tommy. Mrs. Kapuulaa came for a business meeting regarding *The Onion Express.* In fact she spent the night in the spare bedroom." I said not wanting to hide anything. I also assumed, sometimes a dangerous thing to do, that Pua realized others knew she had been there, too.

"Dis was okay wit yer missus?" he asked out of curiosity I figured.

"Yes it was okay with my wife. I told her all about it," I said, realizing that I hadn't been completely honest with Tommy. Nor did I intend to reveal everything else that happened that night.

The job site made it through the weekend without any vandalism, and most of the subcontractors were already at work and performing according to the schedule.

With the concrete foundation now poured and set, the construction would now take off rather quickly. A new shipment of pre-fabricated steel frames was in the process of being unloaded as I walked into the office trailer. For the first time since the project began, things were going without a hitch...I wondered why.

I continued working on tightening the schedule and I was totally amazed that each time I adjusted the schedule these friendly Hawaiian contractors and workers went along with the changes offering no complaints. Back in the Bay Area, I often felt the need to bring out cheese to go with the whines of a project change.

At lunchtime, Lieutenant Ho dropped in without any notice that he was coming. In front of Luanne I maintained professional formalities with the Lahaina Police Detective. "How can I help you Lieutenant?" I asked extending an arm to shake hands.

"Hello, Mr. Bryce. I came by to talk to you concerning the vandals that assaulted you last week. May we step outside?"

"Sure, Lieutenant. How about we walk over to Bubba Gump's and get a bucket of shrimp or something?"

"Hi Hai," I said with a smile after we got away form the trailer and out on the sidewalk. "Did you find something out?"

"Rumor is Pua Kapuulaa has a high-powered boyfriend. In fact, the rumor is that she and this guy have been seeing each other for quite awhile."

"That can't be good. Does the family know?"

"They know where she spent Thursday night," he said catching me off guard. "Would you care to tell me what she was doing at your place all night?"

"The family knows, huh?"

"Yep. What was she doing there Jack?"

"You say that like I'm a suspect," I replied.

"At this point you are a suspect, as are most of the people on the island."

Now at the restaurant, the server took our orders and I resumed the conversation by letting Hai know everything that happened in the condominium on that Thursday night.

"I believe your story Jack, but I'm not sure anyone else will. What do you think she was really after?"

"What? You don't think she wanted me for my body?" I laughed.

"What do you think Jack?"

"No. I don't think she just wanted to use me for sex. However, I think she was selling me sex to get me under her control. I didn't buy!"

"You know that, and she knows that, but I don't think anyone that knows you were together is going to believe that. Including Papa Kapuulaa."

"Hey, you ought to come by the condo in Kahana and meet my friend Jim. You two have a lot in common. He also likes to paint dim pictures of me in no win type situations. So I was honest with you. Do you want to tell me about this supposed boyfriend?"

"Well, he is like you."

"What do you mean he's like me?"

"Let me finish will you? His name is Jude Makala and he's a builder/developer type. He's running a new housing project on the east side of the Island, and he's connected."

"Connected? How is he connected Hai? I don't think you are trying to tell me he's put together with nuts and bolts," I scoffed at the Lieutenant.

"Believe it or not our little island paradise has its own crime syndicate. Everything from cock fighting and prostitution, to drugs, gambling, legit hotels, resorts, and housing developments."

"Sounds pretty big Hai. Do you think Pua Kapuulaa is in with them?"

"I'm not sure about that part. But if she isn't in with them, then she is probably being used by them. That's where you come in Jack."

"Whoa there Hai! You're moving a bit too fast for this mainland country boy. Just exactly where is it that I come in?"

"You're in a great spot to bust this open. If they think you are playing ball with them, we might find out who killed Kainoa and who burned down *The Onion Express* with part of its staff in it. Think about it Jack."

"Uh okay. I'm done now. There is no way in hell I'm going undercover for the Lahaina police department. See? That was easy!" I boasted.

"Come on Jack. Don't you want to get these guys? They've already killed four good, innocent people. And you may have an opportunity to help us put them away."

"Do you like fishing Lieutenant?"

"I'm Asian Jack. I live on fish heads and rice for Christ's sake. Of course I go fishing. What's that got to do with it?"

"Well, I like to go fishing, too. But I'm the kind of fisherman who trolls with lures from a long distance, meaning I'm not much for fishing with live bait. And by that I mean I'm not willing to be your live bait Hai. I'm getting ready to enter the golden years of my life where I get to spend my time spoiling my grandkids and chasing my wife around the bedroom any time I want. I can't do that if I'm permanently attached to the bottom of the Pacific Ocean!"

"Just think it over Jack. We'll protect you every step of the way."

"I like you Hai. I really do. But don't count on me!"

CHAPTER 22......
WHO'S USING WHO?

"Hey, we'd like to pick you up from work and buy you dinner," Jim Alverez offered over the phone.

"Sounds fine to me buddy. Do you know how to get here?" I gave Jim directions and we agreed that he would pick me up at the job site just after five. We were going to stop for a beer someplace and then go back to get Vickie herself and have dinner at the Outback in Kahana.

Apparently the architects had put in some time over the weekend and they wanted to meet in the small conference room of the office trailer with Pua and me to review what they had done. Basically they wanted a *gut check* to make sure that what they were doing was on target.

From my office, I heard Pua dismissing Tommy, and come into the office trailer telling Luanne that she would be in my office and that we weren't to be disturbed.

"Good morning Mrs. Kapuulaa," I said rising from my desk and offering a handshake.

Instead of taking my hand she came around the desk grasped me in both arms for a hug and kissed me on the neck, just below my left ear. I gave her a quick hug back, taking my arms away after a brief moment, but Pua held on. "It's so good to see you, Jack!" she gushed while studying my face for reaction with her head still on my chest.

"Yes, Ma'am," I replied. "You are a little early for the meeting. It's not for another hour," I said as she finally withdrew from the embrace.

"I wanted to come so I could spend some time with you and see more of the construction site Jack. By the way, I love the name Jack. It is very masculine and its fits you. How is the schedule going Jack?"

"Quite well actually. With the concrete done, almost all of the trades are here now starting to put the shell together. I think that within two weeks you should have a pretty good outline of the shape of the buildings."

"That's fine Jack," she said not really showing interest. "Tell me about your friends that you have been showing around."

"Well, actually they surprised me with news that they got married just before coming over here."

"Good for them! So that's why you gave up the master bedroom."

"Saturday we did the trip to Kahana and Sunday we snorkeled and picnicked over in Honolua Bay," I related to her while wondering how on earth she would know that I gave up the master bedroom to Jim and Vickie.

"So it sounds like you are being a good host Jack. How about you? Is there anything you want from me?" she asked leaning over my desk and showing a lot of cleavage.

Damn it! I thought to myself as she caught me looking, and then smiled at my reaction. I averted my eyes away from her bosom, which was still being offered for viewing.

"I hope you don't mind that I'm sharing the condo with them?" I asked her, changing the subject back to Jim and Vickie.

"Not at all Jack. It is your place to use as you like for as long as you are here. So, is there anything else I can do for you?" she said with a wink, obviously enjoying my discomfort.

"Nope, things are going well here. Would you care to don a hard hat and take a walk around the site with me?"

"Sure Jack; let's do that before the architects arrive."

Heading to the door, I grabbed two named hardhats. My own of course, and the one I had had tagged for Kainoa for when he visited the job site.

When I handed Kainoa's hardhat to Pua, she looked up at me with a different look than I had seen before. There was actually some sadness in her eyes and for a moment I felt sorry for her. "Could you adjust this for me Jack? Kainoa's head is a bit larger than mine," she said softly.

In front of Luanne, Tommy and the construction crew, Pua maintained a *business* distance from me. She was keeping her hands clasped behind her back, and asking lots of questions. I give Pua credit for being a sharp and intelligent woman and I flashed to Lieutenant Hai Ho stating that a crime syndicate might be using her...but I was thinking that maybe it is she who is using Jude Makala and the crime syndicate to get control of what she wants.

CHAPTER 23........
WHAT TO DO?

I was still in my office when Jim arrived alone to pick me up. "This place is just like the one that burned down at the amusement park isn't it? And, by the way, I almost forgot, Karen and Maggie McCarthy send you their best wishes. Anyhow, how can you work in a place like this again when the last trailer you worked in was set on fire with you it?"

"Karen and Maggie? Really? You saw them? How are they doing?" In my last construction project, I had made a connection with Karen and Maggie McCarthy. The place I was re-constructing had been severely damaged by a roller coaster that had crashed into it and Karen's husband Ian, and their son Josh, were passengers of that ill-fated roller coaster which had been rigged to intentionally crash.

"They are doing fine Jack. Karen just wanted me to tell you again how thankful they are to you. Identifying the killers allowed their family to get on with the rest of their lives. You really helped them a lot Jack, and you should be proud of that."

"I just did what I had to do. Anyone would have done the same thing."

"Not true Jack. Trust me. I see many people who are affected by killings and most of the time, other people don't want to get involved. Believe me buddy. So let's blow this joint. I'm thirsty for one of those famous Hawaiian drinks."

"I got just the spot then. Let's go!"

"The Lahaina Police Station is not what I had in mind Jack," he said as I pulled into their parking lot.

"Trust me here buddy," I stated as I led him around the corner and into the quiet and darkened bar where I had met with Lieutenant Hai Ho.

As arranged without Jim's knowledge, Hai was waiting for us in the same booth as before.

"Hi Hai!"

"Hi Jack," the Lieutenant said shaking hands.

"Hai this is my friend Jim Alverez who is currently staying at the condo with me. He and his bride, Vickie, were just married a few days ago."

"Hi Hai," Jim said.

"Hi Jim, it's a pleasure to meet you. Welcome to Hawaii!"

"All of these Hai's are making thirsty," I said. "How about a Mai Tai for my friend here. And two Buds for the Lone Ranger and myself," I said, not sure if I was endearing our new friend or not, but the waiter got it and gave me a quick wink.

The two detectives hit it off immediately, and although I tried to follow their conversation, the two seemed to have started talking in some sort of Homicide-eeze. I've learned over the years that each profession, whether it be mailroom worker, mechanic, engineer or lawyer, all seem to have their own language. After about twenty minutes I interjected with "How about them Giants! Do you think they can get into the pennant races this year?"

The two stopped their conversation, looked at me as though I needed to be reprimanded for the intrusion, and then started right back into their talk where they had left off. It rather reminded of being at dinner with Veronica and just the girls. On those occasions, when Warren and Patrick weren't around, my role was pretty much to order, eat and then pay the fare while the ladies reviewed the day's happening to the finest details.

I let them go on a few minutes longer. I understood their commonality. Finally, thinking of Vickie who was back at the condominium waiting for us, I interjected again. "Sorry to interrupt you again, but there is a beautiful young lady waiting in my condo, and I need to go reassure her that marriage to my friend is still a good thing and that she really hasn't been abandoned by her new husband of five days."

"That's right!" Alverez suddenly realized. "We've got to go!"

"Finally!" I reiterated, drawing scornful looks from both detectives.

"Before you dash out of here for Jim's little woman, and congratulations on the marriage, Jim, I want to know if anything happened today when you met with Pua Kapuulaa, and if you've thought anymore about our conversation?" Hai Ho said shifting the burden to me.

"Hmm," I mumbled. "I got an extra long hug, a kiss on the neck, a view I'm trying to forget, no new information and yes...you've managed to make me feel really guilty about Kainoa."

"Really?" Hai breathed. "I really got you thinking?"

"I'm just thinking Hai, no commitments to put my ass on the line," I scowled back at him.

112

"Then I did my job and it's been a good day after all!" the Hawaiian Lieutenant proclaimed with a broad grin.

My friend Alverez looked at me with a raised eyebrow and an observing expression on his face, which I interpreted to mean we would be talking more about this a little later.

We said our goodbyes and good lucks and left the coolness of the darkened, cool bar, venturing out to where we had parked the car. A young traffic officer was writing me a ticket because we were parked in an area apparently reserved for police officers. Without saying a word, Jim Alverez flashed the young officer his badge, and just like that the ticket disappeared.

We hadn't even left the parking lot when Jim asked, "What is it they want you to do?"

"They want me to help catch Kainoa's killers."

"I know that Jack. How do they want you to help them?" Jim pressed.

"They don't want much," I snickered. "They just want me to play around with the local syndicate."

"Jesus, Jack. Are you going to do it?" he pursued.

"Think I have to," I replied honestly. "I tried to say no, but my conscious isn't having it. I know what I have to do."

CHAPTER 24......HOMESICK!

For their last night on the island Vickie, Jim, and I went to a Luau where, as is the custom for these shows, all the newlyweds were brought on stage. I was quick to volunteer Vickie and Jim for the event, and they good heartedly joined several other newlyweds. The task on stage was for the brides to pair off with the native male dancers and for grooms to pair off with female native dancers. The audience was left to laugh hysterically as the native dancers tried to instruct all of the newlyweds how to perform the native Hawaiian wedding dance.

"How'd I do?" Jim said laughingly when the couple returned to our long banquet table.

"The truth?" I asked.

"Yeah, but keep it clean."

"Well, it looked like Vickie had all the right moves. You were looking pretty sexy up there Vickie. You and your teacher made for a good looking couple!" I teased.

"It was really fun. My partner was a really good dancer. But he wasn't nearly as good looking as my Jim!" she smiled.

"Well, beauty is in the eye of the beholder," I replied. "Jim, I had no idea you were so talented. Where'd you learn to imitate a drunken ostrich like that? You were an act all of your own!" I raved loudly so that all of the people at our table could hear.

Anyhow, we spent nearly three-and-a-half hours at the very entertaining luau complete with an in-the-ground roasted pig dinner and a terrific show involving a world famous fire dancer. Later, we shopped the souvenir booths where Jim and I each bought our ladies really nice puka shell necklaces.

That evening the couple strolled the beach one last time while I retired to my bedroom to read James Patterson's latest and greatest whodunit.

The next morning, while Vickie showered and began packing her suitcase for the trip home, Jim sat outside on the lanai with me, drinking some great Kona coffee I had freshly brewed.

"How much longer will the project last?"

"If all goes per schedule, my part of the job should be complete by October. The restaurant should open by then and the hotel should open about thirty days later. The idea is to have the place ready for a grand opening in November so as to be ready for the Christmas holidays, which is the busiest time of year here."

Back inside for a refill on the coffee, Jim asked, "Are you going to work with Hai to help solve the case?"

"Don't think I should work against him."

"You know what I mean Jack."

"Yes, I know what you mean. I'm thinking about just getting this place built as planned, and then getting myself on home to Boulder Creek. I haven't had a good haircut since Michele last made jokes at me in the mirror of her little shop. I also miss sitting in the window of the B.C. Café eating breakfast. And then there is nothing like a great Long Island Iced Tea and Pepper Steak at Pazzi's. But most of all, I miss sitting at the little glass table on our deck at home and having intimate talks with my wife while overlooking the Santa Cruz Mountains with a glass of Bonny Doon's finest wine."

"Well, that sounds like a good plan Jack. Keep your nose clean. Enjoy your family when they come out next month and then get yourself home. Maui is a warm and beautiful place to live but your home is the Santa Cruz area. We want you back home in one piece okay?"

CHAPTER 25......JUDE MAKALA

Jude Makala, Pua's *connected* friend, was waiting for me. He was in my office trailer when I arrived at work after dropping Vickie and Jim off at the airport for their flight home. It had been a great week with them and I knew that I would miss them when I returned to the empty condominium later that night.

"What can I do for you, Mr. Makala?" I asked while shaking hands with him.

"Mr. Bryce, I represent an association of businessmen who are interested in this hotel and restaurant that you are building."

"I'm just managing the construction project. I don't own the place," I informed the well-dressed man sitting across my desk.

Jude Makala, I observed, was wearing crisply pressed Armani slacks, a blue silk Hawaiian shirt with white coral designs and fine hand made Italian shoes. He was also wearing a solid gold Rolex, and there were at least three fingers adorned with men's diamond and jade rings.

"My associates understand that Mr. Bryce, and we wish to not interfere with your construction project. We only wish for you to continue building as directed by Kainoa Kapuulaa's poor widow, Pua. We think it is important for you to keep your nose clean by staying out of the family's personal problems so as to get yourself home to Boulder Creek safely and on schedule."

My hackles went up immediately, as I recognized the very words that Jim Alverez had said to me earlier in the morning inside the condominium. I tied that info together with Pua's off-handed remark about my giving up the master bedroom for my newlywed friends and immediately surmised that the place where I was living was bugged. "Shit!" I said to myself under my breath and then I began to wonder what else they might have heard. They must know, too, that I have been meeting with Hai Ho. Now I knew the reason for the visit from Jude Makala…I was being warned.

I couldn't help myself from being brash, "So you're telling me that if I stick to doing my job and stay out of the family affairs that you'll let me finish this job without any further delays?" I said clarifying the conversation.

Jude studied me intensely for nearly a full minute before responding. "I'm not sure what you are implying Mr. Bryce. My associates and I are merely supporting Mrs. Kapuulaa's desire to build a place intended to attract the affluent and higher-class business professionals. We wish merely to see her succeed in her endeavor."

"Meaning that the kind of place she wants to build won't compete with your businesses which are designed to attract the middle class tourists and vacationers."

"I see you are an astute businessman Mr. Bryce. Building *The Onion Express* to attract high-end clientele is a 'Win-Win Situation' for everyone in Lahaina. Helping us to that end ensures your project will be completed on time…maybe even sooner so that you can achieve your negotiated early completion bonus."

"And what happens to the rest of the Kapuulaa family and their holdings?" I retorted.

"Our concern is only for what is best for Lahaina. The Kapuulaa family, I assure you, will remain a well known icon within the islands."

"So then Papa Kapuulaa gets to keep the onion fields, cattle ranches and other businesses?" I pushed.

"Let's not go there," Jude Makala hastened. "We need only concern ourselves with this project."

"Right!" I responded. "I just need to finish my project and get myself on home to good old' Boulder Creek."

Rising from the chair on the other side of my desk, Jude extended his hand and grasping it for the goodbye shake. "I'm glad we see things clearly," he said laying a business card on my desk. "Please don't hesitate to call if my associates or I can be of assistance in helping you to complete your task," he smiled and left the trailer with a cordial goodbye to Luanne.

"So that's Jude Makala," I heard Luanne soliloquize from the other room.

"Know him?" I asked exiting my office and moving toward her.

"No. I've never met him before. However, I know who he is. Now I know that he is as good looking as people say. All I know about him is that he is a very important man in these Islands and he is not someone you want as an enemy. What did he want with us?" Luanne prodded.

"He said he wanted to help us be successful in rebuilding this place," I declared without wanting to further the conversation. "Want to get some lunch with me? I'm buying!"

As we headed downtown and toward the docks to find some fish and chips, I tried not to think about what had just transpired, favoring food over worry time. I'd think some more about Mr. Jude Makala later.

CHAPTER 26........MARIE

I made a stop at MacDonald's drive-thru where I picked up a Big Mac, fries, vanilla shake and an apple turnover to go.

Once inside I set the food on the dining room table and put on an Eagles CD, playing it louder than usual. With *Hotel California* playing, I took a bite of the burger, a swallow of the milkshake, grabbed a couple of fries in a napkin and then started looking for bugs.

I began with the master bedroom and was surprised to find one so quickly. It was right next to the bed attached to the back of one of the Tiffany lamps. I left it there, untouched, and headed back to the dining room table for another bite of burger and swallow of the vanilla milkshake.

Satisfied with food for the moment and moving happily with the rhythm of music, I moved about the dining and kitchen area looking under, around and inside of things decorating the area. Again, I found a bug without too much effort. It was attached to the refrigerator in the form of a magnet that looked like a ladybug. What made it so easy to find was, there were no magnets on the refrigerator when Veronica and I first moved in. Although the design of the bug was cute, it hardly seemed original. So far, whoever had planted the bugs appeared to not be a professional.

Since they were so easy to find, it made me even more suspicious. So, I continued my search. I checked the air registers, supply and return, in the walls and ceilings. I checked the phones and I checked the light fixtures, finding nothing. On a hunch I fired up a cigar, yes I smoke one occasionally like when I play poker with the guys, and went from smoke detector to smoke detector setting them off with the smoke from the cigar and then resetting them quickly so as not to alarm any neighbors. When the one in the living room failed to go off from the cigar smoke, I put out the cigar and washed out the taste from the cigar with some more of the vanilla shake, burger and fries.

I returned to the failed smoke detector and pried it open as quietly as possible. Sure enough, where the nine-volt battery should have been, there was instead a listening bug. This time, with *In The City* now loudly playing in the background, I removed the bug and re-fastened the smoke detector. I thought about re-installing the bug inside the toilet tank so as to give the listeners a rush every time the toilet flushed, but decided against that tactic. Instead I destroyed the bug, hoping that the listeners who planted it would just figure it failed and that instead of three bugs they had two. It was my intent not to let on to the listeners that I had discovered any of their devices.

Since it was Jude Makala, paraphrasing my morning comments with Jim Alverez, it was clear that Syndicate was responsible for installing and listening to the bugs. My concern was that the listener's or the recording device had to be nearby. It seemed I was going to have to be watchful of my condominium surroundings. However, for now, I had the upper hand as to what would be heard.

I changed out of my work clothes and into a pair of walking shorts, and, an "Old Guys Rule" black t-shirt. Then I gingerly made my way to the beach below where I strode through the sand barefoot to do some thinking about what to do next.

I had left the two poorly placed bugs in place thinking they might be useful. I was also guessing that Pua and Jude had probably combined efforts to plant the bugs as a means of monitoring me. Did they know about my meetings with Lieutenant Ho? Were they concerned that I would be working with Kainoa's father and against them? If I were working with Palakapola Kapuulaa, what do they think I could do? Pua has legal control of *The Onion Express*. How could I build anything but what she wants? The payoff question I really need to answer is …what is it about me that have Pua or the Syndicate worried?

I looked up to the sky noting a gorgeous, full moon and I wondered if Veronica might be looking at it too. Having reached as far as I could go along the beach, I turned around and headed back. Interestingly just as I turned around, I got a glimpse of someone seating themselves at the top of the sandy beach, and the hairs on the back of my neck began to rise, signaling my usual internal warning that something was not quite right. Had I been followed?

I pulled out my cell phone and put it in camera mode, and when I got near enough to what I could see was a *not dressed for the beach* man, I stopped in front of him, said "hello" and snapped a picture. The man flinched at the flash of the camera phone.

"Sorry! Just taking a picture of my condo from the beach side for the folks back home," I said as I forwarded the picture to Marie's identical cell phone for safekeeping.

The man grumbled something non-intelligible, and turned his face away form me.

"Sorry again," I said to the seated man, still not sure if he was following me or not, and then I continued my trek along the beach and back toward the condominium. I was sure that even if he was following me before it would be unlikely that he would continue after my having taken his picture.

About fifty yards further down the sand, the beach curved and put me out of view of the man on the beach. So, I took opportunity to turn the table on him. Instead of continuing down the beach I headed inland over a recently mowed lawn of a neighboring condo complex. I was noticing how good the cool grass felt on my bare feet as I moved in and behind the position of the man seated on the beach. As I was looking for the guy, a voice from right behind me said, "Hey!" As I turned, startled, a huge right fist landed on the side of my jaw, and I crumbled onto the cool grass. Still dazed from the punch, the man was easily able to pluck the cell phone from my hand, and then he darted off into the darkness while I struggled to regain my balance to follow.

"Crap! Nice move Bryce!" I cursed to myself. Now the person who had been tailing me had my phone and all of the numbers I had stored in it. He would even be able to see the last call I made which was when I forwarded the picture to Marie a few minutes ago.

I quickly made my way to a nearby phone booth, and called Jim Alverez asking him to contact Marie and to download the picture.

"Of course I will Jack, but damn Buddy, I only left you a few hours ago and you're already in trouble!"

"You know me," I responded. "There is never a dull moment. Anyhow, please get the picture off Marie's phone and get it to Lieutenant Ho would you? Meanwhile I'll get a hold of Veronica and let her know you need the phone and let her know what is going on, which may be the toughest thing I have had to do in a while. I'm guessing it is not going to be received real well."

"You think?"

"Apparently I don't think enough or I wouldn't have let myself be caught off guard like that. At the very least I should have put my phone back in my pocket so it couldn't have been grabbed so easily," I said reprimanding myself.

"Take it easy Jack. If you are dealing with a crime syndicate they already know everything about you and your family anyhow. They probably didn't get any new information from your phone. However, you've likely embarrassed them by making the tail and then getting his picture. Keep your eyes open though, just in case."

I had called Jim from a phone booth at an ABC Convenience Store not too far from the condominium complex. I then called Veronica to alert her as well.

"Let me get this straight," she complained. "You're twenty-five hundred miles away from home. You have gotten yourself involved in another murder case, and you're telling me the bad guys know our children's phone numbers and where we live in Boulder Creek?"

"Geez, you're good at this detective stuff Honey! Have I said how much I love and miss you? What are you wearing?"

"A concerned face!"

"Yeah, I figured. But I'll bet it's a beautiful concerned face," I cajoled. "I need your help here." I went on to explain about the bugs in the condo and to arrange to call her back from there in few minutes, which is just what I did next.

"Hey sweetheart, how are you and the kids doing?" I said when she picked up the phone. We went on to express some I love you(s) and I miss you(s) and what was going on with the kids, and then I related how my cell phone had been stolen when I was returning from a walk on the beach and how I had just sent a picture of the condo to Marie's cell phone. Then I went on to talk about a new opportunity I had been given by some local businessmen that might help me get the job done earlier and thus earning a bigger bonus.

The idea was to lay it on convincingly, but not too thick. I was hoping to create the impression that I was going to play ball, so to speak, and that there was no need for anyone to worry about me. My biggest concern was, of course, for my family and in this case in particular I was worried for Marie. I didn't want someone grabbing Marie to confiscate her cell phone and the picture I had sent her.

CHAPTER 27......KAPPY

At work the next morning, before Luanne arrived, I searched the trailer for bugs and I found two. One was in my office at the back of the center drawer, and the other was in the supply air vent serving the small conference room. I left them intact.

My paranoia was now consuming my thoughts. "Who else might be involved?" I questioned to myself. The answer I returned was alarming…just about everyone! Although I had no reason to suspect anyone in particular, I decided it was in my best interest to rule out no one. A syndicate can be a powerful entity with the ability to corrupt or apply pressure to anyone. "Could I really trust Luanne? How about Tommy?" I thought to myself. "How about the contractors? Most of them are related to the Kapuulaa family but can they all be trusted?" All of the unanswered questions I had been asking myself were beginning to take a toll on my psyche.

"Okay Jack," I said to myself as I continued to work things out. "Who on this island can you trust? Papa Kapuulaa? Hai Ho?" The for sure answer was obviously the senior Kapuulaa. Furthermore, I felt it highly unlikely that Lieutenant Ho could be involved with the syndicate but I really couldn't say with 100% conviction that he was or wasn't, and I needed to find out that answer. I decided I needed to talk to the one person I could trust.

At lunchtime, I walked to the mall by myself, checking frequently to see if I was being tailed and it appeared that I wasn't.

In the mall, I purchased a new cell phone, with a camera and text messaging options. For the moment, I planned to give the number to only a few trusted people, which were of course Veronica, my friend Lieutenant Jim Alverez and Palakapola Kapuulaa, who was my first call.

"Mr. Kapuulaa this is Jack Bryce. How are you sir?"

"I'm fine Jack but I wasn't expecting to hear from you. I thought you had decided to support my daughter-in-law?" he posed questioningly.

"Well sir, she certainly is in control of *The Onion Express* and in that role I certainly have an obligation to build what she instructs." Just in case the Kapuulaa's phone was bugged I needed to structure my conversation. "Anyhow sir, Kainoa had told me that you are an expert at fishing for the big billfish in these waters and I was wondering if we might go out together?" The truth was that Kainoa had told me that the only kind of fishing his father did was with a net along the reefs and that try as he might, he could never get his father to join him for any kind of deepwater fishing.

"Kainoa told you that huh?" He asked checking the question.

"Yes sir. Kainoa told me how much you loved deepwater fishing, and I thought that maybe you would like to go with me? With my family back on the mainland, I seem to have plenty of free time when I'm not at the construction site. I've heard the big fish are running good right now and I was hoping we could go out soon."

"I see," he answered and then hesitated, obviously considering what was going on here before giving me a direct answer.

"I was actually hoping we might go out tomorrow," I pressed trying to signal that I wanted to talk with him sooner than later.

Finally I got the answer I was looking for, "How about you meet me on Dock H in the morning? 5:30 AM okay?" he asked.

"I'll be there Mr. Kapuulaa! I'm looking forward to it."

"Jack. My friends call me Kappy."

"Thank you Kappy. I'll see you in the morning."

CHAPTER 28......
YOU KNOW WHY I'M HERE

I intentionally left the condominium early thinking there would be fewer cars on the road and that I could watch for any headlights that may be following me. To be on the safe side, I took the Lower Honoapiilani Highway, which winds its way along the coastal homes, condos, beaches and shops, toward Kaanapali, stopping several times to see if I were being followed. I wasn't.

When I arrived at the designated spot, Dock H, I was surprised to see the senior Mr. Kapuulaa already waiting for me. "Good morning Mr. Kapuulaa," I said extending my hand for a greeting.

"Good Morning Jack, and please just call me Kappy. Okay?"

"Yes sir. Wow, what a great boat Kappy," I said while admiring the nearly twenty-eight foot Bayliner "289 Classic" that was moored just behind him. The name on the side of the boat read Kainoa I and I thought to myself that it was appropriate considering the conversation I was about to have with Kainoa's father.

"Yes, she's all set up for trolling to catch the big ones. Kainoa loved this boat and sometimes he'd take it between the islands. That is, when the weather was right," Kappy replied.

It was just the two of us and I watched the shoreline for any unwanted observers as I untied the boat from the moorings and we cast off heading out of the harbor area. Inside the harbor, the maximum speed was posted at five knots. "There's coffee and some cups in the galley Jack. How about you getting us each a cup while I take us through the harbor?"

"Great Kappy! Do you want anything in yours?"

"Just black Jack." He smiled at the rhyme. I remembered my smiling at Hai Ho and figured that turn-about is fair play. "There is some sugar and powdered cream packets in the drawer below the coffee pot if you want."

Going down the ladder to below the main deck I entered the galley, which looked to be very organized, well stocked and it was neat and clean with everything obviously secured in its assigned place. Ahead I could see the sleeping quarters, which looked to contain a queen-sized bed across the bow and in front of that were two built-in singles on either side of the same cabin. Behind me was the head.

I returned to the bridge with two commuter type mugs that Kappy had left out for us near the fresh-brewed pot.

"Thanks for meeting with me, Kappy. There are some things going on with *The Onion Express* I wanted to talk to you about. So I'm really glad you accepted the fishing idea."

Kappy was dressed in old blue jeans, a pullover long-sleeved red shirt and sneakers, which reminded me of Gilligan from the TV series only without the hat. He studied me with one eye slightly squinted. "So I gathered from your phone call Jack, but why talk to me now? I approached you before and you ignored me."

"Well one reason," I explained, "Is that your daughter-in-law signs the checks."

The older man scoffed at me with an unintelligible grunt while raising his hand in the air as though to brush off the comment, but saying nothing.

I went on. "Don't forget that I'm the middleman between a father who lost his son and a wife who just lost her husband. I'm also, now involved in what I think was the murder of your son, his pilot and the two restaurant workers who died in the fire. Under the circumstances, I'm hoping you'll understand that I needed a little time to see things for myself."

Kappy looked at me again briefly, but returned his attention to maneuvering the craft towards the open sea buoy marker now just a few hundred yards ahead. "Well son, err ah Jack, now that's the first thing you've said that makes sense. So what is it you've figured out, and what is it that brings you to me?"

"Well sir........."

"Kappy!" he snapped.

I was beginning to see the senior Mr. Kapuulaa in a new light. What I was seeing, for the first time, was a well-seasoned and tougher old bird than I had realized before. Moreover, I was beginning to appreciate his frank candor and the make up of his character. I recognized too, that much of what I had appreciated about Kainoa was present in his father as well. Kainoa was a chip off the old block I thought to myself.

"Well Kappy, here's what I have figured out so far. Your daughter-in-law wants to build an upscale resort designed to attract a more affluent clientele and businesses wanting a classy place to hold meetings and seminars. And you, sir, you want to return the place to being a favorite of the locals and also for it to be attractive to tourists wanting a more authentic atmosphere while vacationing in the islands. The problem being, of course, that Pua has control of the hotel and the restaurant and how they are being built and furnished."

"It's taken you all these weeks to finally figure that out?" he said sarcastically while pushing the throttle forward for more speed as we now passed the open sea marker, which released us from the slower speed control.

I ignored the comment and went on, carefully choosing my words, as the boat sped toward the open ocean with Molokai on one side and Maui on the other. While he listened intently, I explained about my meetings with Lieutenant Ho, Pua and recently, Jude Makala, which caused eyebrows to rise. I held back the part about Pua visiting me in the condo, figuring there was no need to add further grief for the old man.

"You met with Jude Makala? You're telling me that Jude Makala visited the construction site offering his help to you to avoid any more construction delays?" Kappy slowed the boat and shifted it into neutral focusing his full attention on me. "I've spent a lifetime building and maintaining a good reputation for my family. We run businesses where people are treated honestly and fairly throughout these islands, and we've done that with our own sweat and blood. Now you are telling me, with my son out of the way, the syndicate is trying to move in on us?"

"That's about it," I replied, being a bit frank.

"And the relationship between my daughter-in-law and Jude Makala?" the senior Kapuulaa asked staring at me. "Is there a relationship?" he pressed.

I didn't answer.

"My God!" Kappy shouted out loud. "My son's wife and the mother of my grandchildren, is involved with the mob. Things are much worse than I thought!"

"That is part of why I'm here Kappy. The other part is that, except for you, I don't know whom I can trust. It seems Jude Makala is pretty well connected, and I'm not even sure I can trust the local police. My condominium is bugged, the office is bugged, the police want my help, the syndicate wants my cooperation and your daughter-in-law wants me to build something that you don't want."

"Why are you even here Jack? Why not just fold up your tent and go home? None of this is your affair so why are you still here?"

"That's a good question, but I think you know why I'm here," I stated with coolness in my voice.

"My son?"

"Yes. Yourself and the people I'm working with as well. I'm not the kind of person who can just walk away when things get a little sour," I replied in earnest.

Kappy seemed to ponder that for a minute and then replied, "Well, let's get on out to the deep water and see if we can't catch you a trophy." He returned the engines to drive and pushed the throttle about three fourths of the way forward.

Chapter 29.......Baby Blue

The weather and the ocean scenery combined for a spectacular environment as we distanced ourselves from the islands, which eventually became nothing but vague silhouettes in a background that seemed so very far away.

"Kainoa told me you didn't like the deep water and billfish type fishing," I said as I followed his lead in rigging the poles and putting out the lines on the stingers.

Kappy obviously knew what he was doing. He had used the boat's electronics to guide us to the desired fishing waters and then, just as if he did it everyday of his life, he rigged three poles with marlin lures. One pole was rigged with a large, chrome jet-head, another with a smaller jet-head, neither of which I had never seen before, and the third was rigged with a simple blue skirt and hook. "You never know from one day to the next what kind of lure they will hit, or even what color. We'll just drag these around for a while, and if we don't get any strikes we'll change 'em up. The big marlins, the blues, are over by the Kona Coast. We get some big ones here, too, but the best blue marlin fishing is over there by Kona."

"Kappy, you're pretty good for a guy who doesn't like doing this," I said looking at him quizzically.

"Kainoa was right; this is not my favorite form of fishing. I prefer the native way of fishing, which is less like fishing and more like food gathering. In the traditional way of fishing, we use skiffs and nets to work and gather the fish. However, don't let fishing with nets fool you into thinking it's easy. The traditional way the natives fish is far more dangerous than this sissy stuff!" he declared, and then laughed aloud at his own humor. "Anyhow, just because I prefer the traditional ways doesn't mean I don't know how to do this."

That outburst of laughter seemed to ease us from the tensions of our earlier conversation. We made several runs through the area with various lures before we got our first action. It finally came on a smaller, green and yellow skirt lure attached to the middle and longest stinger, which was running out from directly above the bridge. We had three poles in the water when we got the strike. Kappy took the fish first and ensuring we had a good hit, and that the fish was truly on. Then he handed it off to me. "Small one," he said almost nonchalantly. "Probably 125 to 150 pounds."

Considering the biggest fish I had ever caught was a thirty-five pound king salmon in the Monterey Bay, I thought Kappy was crazy. Hell! That big salmon had taken the better part of thirty minutes to get on board, and my arms had ached for two days afterwards!

Nonetheless, this was my chance of a lifetime, or so I thought, as I began the struggle against the blue marlin on the other end of the line.

"Pull up and reel down!" Kappy barked as he cleared away the other rigs and headed up to the bridge.

About fifteen minutes into the fight, the blue broke water and I got my first glimpse of what I considered to be a beautiful monster.

"Just a baby," Kappy yelled out from the bridge as he positioned the boat to ease my fight.

"Right!" I managed to mumble between breaths, wondering if my arms were going to fall off my shoulders. The fish cleared water twice more before sounding again.

Finally, after what seemed like forever, he came back to the surface rocketing his full body out of the water getting good air. It was beautiful, exciting, and exhausting all at the same time. I kept wondering if Kappy was going to come grab the rod from me, but he stayed on the bridge barking out things like "Don't let him tangle you in the prop!" and "Keep that tip up!"

Finally, more than forty minutes later, the blue and I were both tuckered out, but I had won the battle. I managed to tire him enough to get him along side the boat, where Kappy took a picture, with a waterproof disposal camera, that seemed to come out of nowhere, and then he released the blue, which swam slowly away from the boat, looking nearly as spent as I felt.

"First marlin hey? Well, that was very well done there Jack. How ya feeling now brudah?"

"Going to live I think," was the weak reply that emanated from a shaky and breathless voice box, which I tried but couldn't hide.

Surprised again, seemingly from nowhere, a bottle of traditional Mexican Mescal, complete with worm, was dangling in front of my face. "This will revive those tired muscles. Take a few swigs brudah, and then let's get those lines out again."

Somewhere during the day, Kappy became familiar enough with me to call me "brudah," just as Tommy often does and I took it as an honor. "Thanks, Kappy. Thanks for bringing me out here and thanks for listening." I said still trying to get the jelly feeling out of my arms.

"Well, we will talk some more about this situation we are both in, but we can do that on the way back. Let's have a little more of this fine Mexican booze and catch ourselves another fish!" Even though I was still pretty much exhausted from the fight with the fish we had just released, I didn't argue.

And we did just that. Within twenty minutes, the old man was battling his own blue, bigger than mine, while barking out orders for me to clear the gear and maneuver the boat. That day with Kappy Kapuulaa, was one of the greatest fishing days of my life. And I'll never forget the *baby blue* I had fought with, or the time spent with Kappy.

CHAPTER 30.......
FINDING A VICE

"So we both know what Jude is, and who he represents," I said as I sat next to Kappy for the ride back home. "But what about the police? Can I trust Lieutenant Ho?"

"Hai? Absolutely. He is a good man, who comes from a good family. My family has known his family for all of our lives. What does he want you to do?"

"He wants me to get to know Jude and his friends. He thinks maybe they had something to do with the helicopter explosion and burning down *The Onion Express.*" I saw Kappy wince when I referred to the helicopter incident, and I felt bad for him.

"Are you going to do it?"

"I'm leaning that way."

"I can help!" the tough old man stated. "The fact that there is a syndicate of organized crime in the islands is not news around here. Everyone knows it. It's been going on here since well before the big war. It's pretty much just like back on the mainland. There is prostitution, drugs, politics, and cockfighting. Cockfighting is big in these islands, and it's hard to control. It's a very big business. If those bastards are responsible for my son's death, then I'm in! I'll get you anything you need."

"I appreciate your offer on that, but what are you going to do about Pua?"

"What can I do? She is my only son's widow, and as such she has inherited his holdings, which are several of the family businesses I had turned over to him. Now I am in a hard place, because if I drive her away, I may never see my grandchildren again."

"What about Tommy? Where does Tommy's loyalty lie? With you, or with Pua?"

"Tommy? He is just like part of our family. He and Kainoa grew up together. I'm sure Tommy can be trusted to help, too."

"You don't think the Syndicate has any holds on him or anything? Do you?"

"No way. If Tommy were in trouble he would come to me for help!"

"Has he been in trouble before?"

"Yes, but it was a long time ago. Tommy ran up some gambling debts and Kainoa and I helped him out. He has never been in trouble again that I know of."

"Gambling debts?" I questioned.

"Cockfighting. Tommy got into gambling on the fights, and when he got in over his head in debt, we helped him out."

"Could Tommy tell me where to go if I wanted to attend a cockfight?"

"I guess so, but why would you want to go to a cockfight?"

"If I'm going to get in with the Syndicate, they might as well think I've got a few vices." I smiled and winked at Kappy.

CHAPTER 31......
"CHICKEN JACK"

For the rest of the trip back to Maui, and the harbor from which we had left, I spent the time asking questions about the family and its businesses. I also thought about Kappy and his family predicament, where nearly everything the family had built over its history now resided with his son's widow. What about Pua? Was she truly involved with the Syndicate? Why? Had something gone wrong in their marriage? Had she just married into the family for its wealth? Had she orchestrated Kainoa's murder to gain control of the family fortune? Was she even capable of doing that?

Turning my thoughts to cockfighting, I imagined myself in a barn, somewhere in the Maui countryside, dressed in khaki shorts, rubber sandals, wearing a wild colored Hawaiian shirt, sporting a white Panama fedora styled hat, and smoking a premium Cuban cigar. I laughed quietly to myself as I thought about what my poker buddies might think of that sight. "They'd laugh, too," I answered to myself.

Of course the reality of that picture was not really so different from playing poker at someone's house on a hot summer night, in the Santa Cruz Mountains. We would be wearing shorts, sandals and maybe our club t-shirts, that Pablo had made for us. The fronts are titled, "B.C. Poker - The Best Hands." On the back of the shirts, there is a picture of a Royal Flush. Maybe the Santa Cruz Mountains and the islands of Hawaii are not so different, I thought to myself.

After being dropped off at the dock, I did a quick check at the construction site. There, I found that Pua had left messages for me to contact her immediately.

"This is Jack, Mrs. Kapuulaa, how can I help you?"

"I can think of lots of ways you could help me Jack, but for now I'd just like to know what you were doing with my father-in-law this morning? Do I need to worry about you, Jack?" she said with coyness in her tone.

"I'm not hiding anything. We went fishing. And now I've just gotten back to find your messages."

"Just fishing Jack?" Really? You are too cute! How about dinner tonight? We can talk business."

"It's a tempting offer Mrs. Kapuulaa…err uh Pua," I said lying through my teeth. "Afraid I've already got a date tonight with my wife."

"Oh. I didn't know the little woman was here. When did she arrive?"

"She's not here, she's still in California. We have a date to meet on-line. In fact, the whole family is meeting on-line."

"Well, if you ever decide you need more than a computer relationship, give me a call. Meanwhile, I've decided we need to change some of the sub-contractors."

"You've decided that, huh?" I stated. "Why so?"

"Because Jack, the teamsters and the other unions are well integrated, and if we want a professional job without further delays we need to get them on board."

"Do you mind if I ask you who told you that?"

"I'm a big girl. I don't need people to tell me what to do. Considering the delays you've already encountered, it makes sense to join with the union," she said.

"You are aware that many of our subs are relatives and close friends of your family?"

"What family is that Jack?" she asked being coy again.

"The Kapuulaa family," I quipped.

"Oh, well they are just going to have to understand the needed change," she responded as though it was no big deal to summarily dismiss them without cause.

"I see," I replied without emotion. "There is another thing you are not considering. Per the contract, I personally approve all of the contractors."

"Are you going to give me hard a time on this issue Jack?"

"No Ma'am, there is no hard time from me. I'm just not making any changes. Is there anything else I can help you with?"

"Yes, there is Jack, but your wife would probably object," she toyed with me changing the subject to amuse herself. Finally she said, "I'll be in on Monday at noon, please be available to meet with me," she hung up the phone before I could respond.

"Everything okay with Pua?" Luanne asked when I walked into that part of the trailer.

"Everything is fine. Could you get a hold of Tommy for me and ask if him he could meet with me please?"

"Today?" Luanne asked for clarification.

"Yes, please."

About thirty minutes later Tommy showed up at my desk. "The big Kahuna need some ting from me?" he asked with a smile.

"Yeah, Tommy. Do you have a few minutes to come with me?"

"Sure brudah, I can go witchu."

Tommy followed me out to where I had parked the mustang. At first he balked about me driving him around, but with some convincing I got him to get in and we drove off. I drove along the coast for about two miles and then parked amongst some trees near a beach that ran parallel to Highway 30.

"You unhappy wit me or sumpin brudah?" he asked as we got out of the car.

"It's nothing like that Tommy. What I want is your help." I said looking into his concerned eyes. "I want you to take me to a cock-fight tomorrow night."

"No can do brudah. I don't do cock fights no more. Not for a long time now."

"I know Tommy. Kappy told me what happened in the past. But I need to be introduced to a fight where I can make some bets, and meet the people who run the fights."

"Dat bad business Mr. Bryce. First, it's a bad group of folk at doze places, and second dey don't like no howlies at doze places. You want to gamble den I find you a good poker game some place. Okay brudah?"

I sat down on the white sandy beach and got Tommy to sit next to me while I explained what I was doing, and why. "What you going to do is crazy brudah. You could get yo'self killed if you don't be careful!"

"Dying isn't part of my plan Tommy. However, finding out who is out to destroy the Kapuulaa family is what I am after. Are you with me?" I asked giving the big man a pat on the back.

"You don't tell my missus and den I try to help you. If my missus find out I go to a cockfight, den she going to kill me before anyone else can do it!" Then the big man laughed.

"I just need you to introduce me the first time." I explained to Tommy whose posture seemed a bit awkward sitting in the sand. "After that I'm on my own,"

"No brudah. I no let you do dat. I tink we both gonna do this togetta. Kainoa, he was my best friend in di whole world. We go to school here in da islands when we just kids, and I been wit him ever since. No, Mr. Bryce, you wanna find out who got it in for da Kapuulaa family den I'm wit you all da way. No way you can say no to me brudah."

"Alright Tommy, what time should you pick me up tomorrow night?"

"Okay brudah, I gonna pick you up at 10:00 PM. But first I got to find out where dey have da fights nowadays."

I dropped Tommy off at the limo where he had left it, and headed back to the condominium planning to grab a short nap before dinner and meeting the family online for the pre-scheduled Texas Hold 'Em game.

On the drive back to Kahana, I remembered *Chicken George,* from the TV series *Roots,* but when I tried *Chicken Jack* it just didn't seem to work as well. Oh well.......

CHAPTER 32...
"A STICK TO BEAT THE LOVELY LADY WITH?"

I stopped along the way and bought marinated flank steak and a bundle of fresh asparagus for dinner that night, along with some lunchmeats and beer, because the fridge was running low on supplies.

Finally arriving at the condominium, I changed into khaki shorts, my *Salty Dog* T-shirt (a gift from my in-laws), and flip flops I had bought at the local market for a buck ninety-nine. Next, I put on a Beatles CD, which started with a twelve-minute version of *Hey Jude,* which is a favorite. Then, before leaving to barbecue the steak down by the pool, I grabbed a Primo beer and turned on my computer so that it could start warming itself up. I wanted to be on the Internet where I could join Veronica and the kids for Texas Hold 'Em.

I found I was in luck when I finally got down to the swimming pool area and the barbecues, which are located on the inland side of the complex. My luck was that there was still an open barbecue for me to use. Even at 9:30 at night, there is usually a wait to get a turn on one of the three provided propane units. I fired up the open grill and then stretched out the long thin strips of teriyaki-marinated skirt steak evenly over the medium low flames.

Next, I took up a position on a patio chair, leaned back, and took a swig of my still frosty cold beer, and reflected on my long day. Talking frankly with Kappy, catching my first ever, blue marlin, disagreeing over sub contractors with Pua Kapuulaa who was still offering sexual invitations, and making plans with Tommy to attend the local cockfights. "Pretty productive day," I thought to myself.

Suddenly, a large Hawaiian woman, dressed in a native muumuu, offered me a piece of smoked Ahi. "Thank you!" I said taking a piece of the offered fish. "Wow, that's really good!" I said tasting the savory piece of fish.

"You're welcome," she smiled back at me. "If you want more I have plenty to share."

"No thank you," I replied while turning over the long strips of steak and explaining that I needed to save room for my dinner.

"Are you sure? I have too much for just myself."

It seemed like I needed to take another piece of fish, so I did. I thanked her profusely as I ate it gratefully. Then I washed it down with the last of my beer. The lady continued talking to me while my steak finished cooking, I came to know her as Mary, and she lived in number 810, two floors directly beneath my own unit. It seemed she was the proprietor of a local fish store located two blocks south on the Lower Honoapiilani Highway.

After removing the steak and balsamic vinaigrette braised asparagus from the barbecue grill, I cleaned the grill with a provided wire brush while assuring Mary that she had just made a new customer.

After eating and putting the dishes in the dishwasher, the family began showing up on-line one-by-one. Ashley and Rusty were there from Davis, Marie and Jeff from Jeff's parent's house in Boulder Creek, Veronica from our house, Patrick and Ally from their dorm, and Warren & Kathy from her parent's house in Ben Lomond. I thought it amazing that Veronica could get this whole thing coordinated, but there we were, the ten of us, all seated on an on-line Texas Hold 'Em table provided by Yahoo. But then, Veronica has always been an amazing woman, which is one of the things that attracted me to her. We began with chatting over the screen...

Myself: Hey everyone...sure miss you guys!

ASHLEY: Hey dad,...we miss you, too. How's Maui?

MARIE: Don't forget about me...I miss you too!

Myself: I could never forget you baby girl! Maui's great! I responded to Ashley.

ASHLEY: We all miss you too mom.

VERONICA: I was wondering if I'd get a turn?

PATRICK: Okay...we all miss each other.

WARREN: I second that. Hey dad let's play some cards...I'm feeling really lucky!

We chatted together for nearly two hours, while gambling with pretend money and at the end of our play yours truly had kicked butt on the whole crew, with Patrick coming in a distant second in the money count. My poker buddies would have been proud! Afterward I called Veronica. "That was fun Babe, thanks for getting it all set up. It made me feel like I was close to everyone... even if it was just for a little while."

"I've been thinking, Jack. Maybe taking this job was a mistake. With Patrick and Ashley living away from home, Warren and Marie dating Jeff and Kathy nearly every evening, and you being a few thousand miles away, our family seems almost broken or at least a little fragmented. I wish you were here. It's definitely not the same when you are gone, and at night I don't sleep as well without you next to me."

"I'm sorry Honey, it must be tough on you being there alone. I hope the dogs give you some level of comfort at night though," I said trying to make her feel a little better.

"Ralph and Pogo do help a little, but honestly Jack, when you're not here I don't sleep well because I feel like I'm on guard duty all night long."

"You know what? I agree with you. Nevertheless, when we accepted this job we knew it would be tough. And we also knew we needed the extra cash for the college tuitions."

"I know. You are right of course. I guess I'm just a little low tonight. I know we will get through this and that everything will be all right. So how is it going over there? Is that woman still hitting on you? Do I need to be worried about that too?"

Her even asking about Pua told me that it was on her mind. "It's only you, Babe. It's been only you for the past twenty-five years and I'm good to go with just you for another two or three more months at least," I joked with her.

"Whew! For a minute I was worried there, Jack. By the way, do you remember that lady in the news who cut off her husband's penis?"

We both laughed aloud at that and then, after about another twenty minutes of talking about what is new around the Santa Cruz Mountains, we said our goodbyes. It was sad, but unfortunately necessary, as it had been a really long day and I was fading fast.

After hanging up, I flipped through the channels on the bedroom TV finally landing on the old classic, *The Quiet Man,* with John

Wayne and Maureen O'Hara. The last scene I remember, before falling into a deep and long overdue sleep, was John Wayne angrily walking Maureen O' Hara back to her brother's house to collect a dowry. A crowd of cheering townspeople was following the duo and an elderly woman ran to catch up with John Wayne offering, *"A stick to beat the lovely lady with?"*

CHAPTER 33...
SATURDAY AT THE BEACH

I woke up on Saturday morning to the sound of an excited ESPN broadcaster announcing time trial laps of Formula I cars at Indianapolis. Still feeling a little groggy, I wondered what had happened to John Wayne and Maureen O'Hara?

After a cup of fresh hot coffee and a slice of cold, left-over steak, I did a minimal clean up (a splash of cold water, teeth and hair) and changed into my swim gear.

Arriving on the beach, with a little Styrofoam boogie board under my arm, I noted several surfers out by the bigger breaks, already enjoying the early morning surf. Thinking why not, I headed their way hoping to catch a few fun rides. As I paddled my way toward them, I stopped to watch for a minute. I was blown away when I saw two surfers riding the same wave side by side, exchanging boards with each other. Their timing had to be perfect in order to switch boards with each other, but they made it look easy. Never sure if the surfers are going to except some klutz on a boogie board, I caught up with the surfboard-swapping duo and was further amazed that one of them was much older than the other. "Good morning!" I offered when I got to within hearing range of the two men. "That board swapping was awesome. I've never seen anyone do that before,"

"Aloha," they chimed in unison. "Thanks. We've been doing that for lots of years."

"My name is Bryce, Jack Bryce, and I'm staying in a condo right over there," I pointed behind me. "Do you mind if I get a few rides too?" I asked trying to be polite.

"No problem brudah. The ocean is a very big place and it's free. My name is Kimo and this is my youngest son, Paolo. Are you visiting our Islands?" the older gentlemen asked with a broad and welcoming smile.

"Sort of," I replied. "I'm working for the Kapuulaa family helping to re-build *The Onion Express.*"

"The Kapuulaa family are good people. It is such a tragedy for what happened to Kainoa. A terrible thing for the whole island really. Many people are very upset by what happened."

Just then, Paolo, who had thus far remained silent, pointed and commented that a good wave was coming, wherein we all began to paddle frantically to catch the wave.

I took the outside lane so as not to get in their way, and three of us took off down the wave's face. There we were, a father son team of expert surfers who had probably been surfing all their lives, and me, a semi-old guy hanging on to his boogie board. I was excited about being on the face of a nice wave, and half scared to death that I'd fall off and have to chase my little Styrofoam board all the way to the shoreline. It turned out to be a good ride where I was able to do a couple of quick 360s, one clockwise and one counterclockwise and then I pulled off the flattening wave at about the same time as Kimo and Paolo.

I stayed out there, chatting and riding with Kimo and Paolo, where we had the good fortune of catching several more waves over the next two hours before I begged off. Before paddling away on my little Styrofoam board, I promised to meet both of them at the same place again on the following weekend, but this time with a surfboard. While I was heading back toward the condominium to make some needed calls, and although it was difficult to tell for sure because of the distance, I thought I glimpsed someone loitering near the side of the condominium towers peering in my direction. The brief sighting of the person looking in my direction was enough to cause the little hairs on the back of my neck to rise, giving me warning that all may not be right.

As I emerged from the water I kept a careful eye on my surroundings, but I saw no one who looked out of place. I moved to the back of the beach to rinse off the salt water using an outdoor shower adjacent to the condominium pathway. After rinsing, I grabbed my towel from the nicely trimmed hedge where I had left it. As I lifted it from the hedge, a note fell out of the towel and to the damp ground near my feet.

The hand-written message on the note was simple and very clear, *"Bryce, go home now!"* I glanced around and again saw nothing out of the ordinary so I made way to the elevator; the tenth floor and then down the breezeway to the condominium, which seemed secure from intrusion. Nonetheless, I searched the place to satisfy my own level of comfort,

It was 10:00 AM now meaning it was 1:00 PM in Boulder Creek and I wondered what Veronica and the kids were doing. Wanting to make phone calls to home, as well as Lieutenant Ho, I poured myself some coffee, grabbed an un-toasted bagel, put on my *Hookers* baseball cap I got from a local fishing store with the same name, grabbed my cell phone, and again made my way downstairs. But this time I went to the lawn area and found a chaise lounge that seemed to have my name on it.

"What's new in the land of the redwoods?" I asked when Veronica picked up on the third ring.

"Same old stuff around here. I have the flower and veggie garden growing nicely now. I really missed you though when I had to fix the drip system on my own,"

"It' great to be missed and to know that I am sometimes useful too!"

"Well, Pogo and Ralph miss you too. In fact without you around to throw the ball for them they are driving me freaking crazy!"

"I never knew I had so much importance! And to think that all this time I thought I was only a sex toy."

"Nice one honey. It's good to see that Hawaii hasn't spoiled your charm." she replied with humorous sarcasm. "Yesterday I had to tell the Boulder Creek Art & Wine volunteer coordinators that it would only be me this year, because you are over there."

"That's right!" I replied. "It's that time of year again. I should have remembered when I woke up to the Indy cars doing time trials this morning. Are you going to go ahead and volunteer?"

"Yes. I have it all worked out with Jenny and her new beau, Henry. You are going to really like him. They seem to be a perfect fit."

"Well, good for Jenny! I'll look forward to meeting Henry when I get back."

I didn't mention anything about my warning letter or the fact that I was going to attend illegal cockfights tonight. Instead, we talked a while longer about the kids, Marie's soccer team, and the upcoming tournament being held in Maui next month.

Next, I called my new friend Lieutenant Hai Ho. "Hello Hai! Jack Bryce here."

"Hey Jack. Is something new happening? Are you all right?"

"Yep. Except for some mind games, all is fine here," I stated a little light heartedly.

"Mind games Jack? What mind games?"

I went on to tell the Lieutenant about the man observing me in the water while I had been out on the waves with Kimo and Paolo, and then about the note I found in my towel.

"Jack! Wait a minute Jack," Hai interrupted. "You were surfing with Kimo and Paolo? Do you know who they are?"

"Couple of guys I met on the water. Father and son I believe."

"Jack, Kimo, in his day, was <u>THE</u> World Champion Surfer, and his son Paolo is the current favorite to take the title next year. And you surfed with them? That's amazing!"

"World Champions huh? I could tell they were very good, but they just seemed like nice people to me. They invited me to meet with them next week. I guess I should be honored huh?"

"You are invited to surf with them again? Did you say yes? That's so cool Jack. You are a lucky guy. Hey, can I come too?"

"First, I wasn't exactly surfing. I just went out to ride some waves on one of the Styrofoam boards from the condominium. But when I meet them next weekend I intend to rent a board. As far as you coming with me…why not? Like I said, they seemed like really nice folk and after all, 'The ocean is a very big place and it's free,'" I stated remembering the words Kimo had said to me earlier in the morning.

Like an excited little kid Hai Ho continued, "I'll be there Jack! And I have extra boards so you don't need to rent one."

"Hai, although I have surfed some, I'm not all that good. Those guys can swap boards back and forth in the middle of a ride, and they can do handstands too. Me. I'm lucky to make it all the way in without falling. Anyhow, I guess what I'm saying is that I need a big board. Nine foot six or better. Do you have anything big?"

"No problem brudah. I got three boards, including an antique *Big Gun*, which is just over twelve feet."

"Great then. Six A.M. at the beach directly behind my condominium here in Kahana. Now can we get back to why I called?"

"Sure, but I can't believe I'm going to surf with Kimo and Paolo. Wait until my wife and friends hear about this. So why did you call again? Oh I remember...the mind games."

"Besides the mind games, Pua called me yesterday wanting me to fire all of the subcontractors in favor of going fully unionized."

"There is nothing wrong with the union Jack," Hai responded defensively.

"I know that Hai. In fact, I find the union people to generally be the most skilled craftsmen. However, *The Onion Express* is already well underway and the team of contractors building it consists of many of the Kapuulaa clan and their friends. I'm not going to change teams at this point. Besides, this team of subcontractors knows each other and everything is working out really well scheduling and the quality of work. Moreover, I sense the request is really coming from someone other than Pua, like probably Jude Makala."

"Does that mean you argued with Pua to keep the existing contractors?"

"By contract I have the right to choose and approve all of the subcontractors. I told Pua no way, which is why I probably got the note this morning suggesting I go home now."

"I see."

"On top of that, I've scheduled myself to attend some cockfights tonight."

"Cockfighting is illegal Jack, and why go there at all. Are you into that sort of thing?"

"No. I'm not into cockfighting. However, I am into helping the Kapuulaa family and finding out who killed Kainoa. I figured seeing the local Syndicate in action might prove useful. To really understand the trash you need to spend sometime in it. Besides, one of the guys who attacked me at the job site referred to someone at the cockfights as having hired them."

"I'm not so sure that is such a good place for a howlie from the mainland," Hai said admonishingly.

"I've been tangling with these guys ever since I got here. I've seen and fought with vandals trying to delay the construction. I have been followed, observed, and even bugged by these people ever since I got here. I even tangled with one of them who ripped my cell phone out of my hand. I've met one of the active leaders of your local crime Syndicate, and I was listening and talking to a good man, a friend, and his pilot who were blown out of the sky. So going to the cockfights to mingle with the trash is a move I want to make for a couple of reasons. One is to see if I can spot any of these assholes that have been harassing the project and me. Another is to lay down a little money to get their attention so they know I'm close."

"How are you going to get into this place? What makes you think you can just walk up and that they will let you in?"

"Tommy is going to try and get us in there tonight. He has had some past experience."

"That might work Jack, but I want to put a bug on you and personally tail you."

"Not this time Hai. I'm thinking they might want to search me going in the first time and if I get caught with a bug on we will all lose… especially me. Besides, Tommy makes for a hell of a bodyguard."

The sun was beating down on me now, and the skin on my back, as well as the back of my legs, was developing long deep groves from the vinyl webbing of the chaise lounge where I was sitting.

"I'm okay with you tailing us from a distance though," I continued. "Having you around in case I get into trouble will give me a little more comfort while I'm inside. Besides, when this investigation is over, you can go back and bust the persons responsible for the inhumane cockfights," I added showing my feelings on the subject. Raising creatures to destroy each other for entertainment is, I truly believe, despicable and the bastards who do it should be put away for a long time. "By the way, what have the police found out regarding Kainoa's murder?"

"With some help from the Navy, we gathered up what was left of the helicopter. The crime boys now know that the explosion occurred from inside the cab of the helicopter, probably from the rear seats, and that it was likely two sticks of dynamite tied to an electronic detonator. We're searching sources of dynamite on the island, but we already know that there are several construction companies out there that use it routinely…including some of Kainoa's own people."

"Any more leads or ideas on who might have done it?" I pressed the Lieutenant.

"Nothing new there. We're thinking the same as you. Either someone wanted to take down Kainoa and the Kapuulaa family to eliminate business competition, or Kainoa's wife wanted him out of the way so that she could have the power. Or, seeing there is some kind of relation between Pua and Jude Makala, it could just be a love triangle where the two of them plotted to get rid of the husband."

"Well, whoever or whatever the motive, the Kapuulaa family deserves better. I can't help but think that the two *Onion Express* employees who died in the fire were also murdered. What do you know about them?"

"They were Mark Malone, who was the General Manager of *The Onion Express*, and John Chu, who was a cook. Malone was a straight up okay person who did a good job of running both the hotel and the restaurant. He was a graduate from the University of California at Berkley with a Master's Degree in Business Economics. He left a wife and two kids behind when he died in the fire. He was a popular guy around here with the locals, and he was very close to the Kapuulaa family. John Chu was one of the top cooks who worked in the restaurant, and known to be a little bit on the wild side. John was very popular with the younger set, who always had good-looking women around him and he was known to party a lot. It is purported that *The Onion Express* was his personal hunting ground for picking up women."

We chatted for a few minutes longer and agreed that I wouldn't tell Tommy about the tail, and that Hai would be waiting nearby when Tommy picked me up at 10:00 PM. The rest of my day was spent broiling myself to get a better tan, and reading a Dick Francis mystery book.

CHAPTER 34...
SATURDAY NIGHT AT THE FIGHTS

I was already waiting in the lobby area of the condominium complex when Tommy picked me up in his personal car.

"Do you still want to go tru wit dis brudah?" Tommy asked after I climbed into the front seat with him.

"No, but let's do it anyhow."

The drive to where the cockfights were being held took us nearly an hour. I tried, without drawing Tommy's attention, to see if I could spot Lieutenant Ho. He was supposed to be following behind us, but I didn't see him, which left me with an uneasy feeling, wondering if he was tailing us or not. When we arrived, I noted that we weren't too far from the Makawao Rodeo Grounds in an area of Maui known as Olinda. The final stretch of the drive was on a short dirt road, which led us around a small jungle-covered hill, and finally into someone's small ranch that included a horse arena, several outbuildings, and a large barn with nearly fifty cars parked around its perimeter.

Before we got out of the car, Tommy said, with a big grin on his face, "Okay. I be da big Kahuna now. You just follow my lead and I tink everyting gonna be okay."

I agreed and when we reached the barn doors a big Hawaiian man, nearly as big as Tommy, greeted us. "How come we never see you anymore Tommy? Dis da guy you called about bringing?"

"Yeah dis da guy. And da reason I don't come no more is cause I lose too much and my missus she say no more!"

"Well you know the routine Tommy. I gonna search for weapons and stuff."

"Okay brudah...it's no botta to us. Just don't take our money befo we get a chance to bet on da fights." Tommy replied with a friendly chuckle.

Tommy was searched first and when he was done, I stepped up for my turn. "Dis man name is Danny and he going to search you now," Tommy said surprising me with the introduction.

"You go to da fights on da Mainland brudah?" Danny said as he patted me down and looked me over,

"Yeah," I replied. "I like the action."

"Where is it dat you go?" Danny asked while bent over patting down my legs.

"Do you know the Santa Cruz area? They have some fights in the mountains and also down by Watsonville."

"I don't ever go der but I have heard dat dey have dem in dat area," he said finishing his search and standing up again to loom down on me. "Okay you give twenty dollars each for da house, and you can go in now. But if you cause any trouble in der den you gunna have to deal wit me," Danny stated matter-of-fact to both Tommy and me.

I paid the twenty for both of us and we made our way through the entrance.

When we entered the barn, I observed that there was a small wooden fenced fighting ring surrounded by three portable bleachers, with standing room next to the fence and a small canopy type tent with tables where the betting took place. I followed Tommy over to the canopy where he introduced me, "Dis Mr. Jack Bryce from da Mainland who be da big Kahuna rebuilding Da Onion Express."

"You know how it works?" asked a short heavyset Caucasian man smoking a long wet sloppy looking cigar.

"No problem here. Where can we look at the birds?"

"They're over there behind the stands," said the short man who was now busily arranging the money he held in both of his hands, nodding in the general direction of the birds without looking at us.

As we made our way amongst the other gamblers and people attending the fights, I looked for the two people who had jumped me at the construction site. I also kept a close vigil for the person I had tangled with at the beach behind my condominium who had gotten away with my cell phone.

Arriving at the bird's staging area where the caged, and some un-caged roosters were being held, I was immediately saddened by the site. Owners and handlers of the birds were agitating them by thrusting them at other birds repeatedly, all the while explaining to the gamblers the wisdom of betting on their particular bird. Tommy had explained to me earlier that each owner got a share of the betting pool with the winner receiving the larger share. Owners with strong winning records usually drew the largest bets.

It was there in the staging area that I spotted one of my two assailants from the construction site. I clearly remembered him as being the younger one who tried to club me after his partner had driven me to the ground.

I pulled Tommy away and pointed out the person I recognized, asking him if he knew who he was. "No. I never see him befo," Tommy replied. "You want me to go get him and bring him outside?"

"Not yet Tommy. I don't think he recognizes me. Let's watch him and see who he hangs out with."

"Okay brudah. You just tell me when you ready and I get him fo you!"

Just before the next fight, I went to the betting area and laid three hundred dollars of the money that Kappy had provided on a brown and red bird not really knowing anything about what I was doing. The short, heavy-set man who took the bet now gave me his attention. "Three hundred dollars?" he asked while looking me over and sizing me up as if I were one of the birds who would be fighting.

To view the fight I chose a place in the bleachers two rows behind the man I had recognized. He was now sitting in a group of other people, one of which was his partner from that morning when they had been paid to sabotage and disrupt the construction site. So far, it would seem, my hunch about going to the cockfight had paid off big time.

The cockfight lasted only about three minutes with my bird on the bottom. The opposing bird, using the small curved sickle shaped blade attached to his leg just above his own natural spurs, crippled the bird I had bet on very quickly and then it was just a matter of time before the fight would be over. The crowd, excited at first, turned quickly to boos and jeers as the fight ended too swiftly for their liking.

For the next fight, I handed the agent five hundred dollars on a brown and white bird named Tornado. "It was a shame your bird got crippled so fast," he said with a big smile, obviously enjoying the fact that I had lost my wager. "I think you have a better chance this time. This bird has already won a few fights and comes from a good trainer."

I returned to the seats where Tommy was waiting without notice by the men we were seated behind. This time the fight lasted much longer, with both birds bloodied by the attached blades. The birds would circle for a moment or two, looking for an advantage, and then, with their tiny wings outstretched, they would fly to engage each other while screeching loudly and spewing blood over the cheering onlookers.

Tornado won the grueling fight, but he looked so battered I doubted he could ever fight again. The owner of the defeated bird picked up the barely moving carcass, and swiftly snapped its neck in front of the crowd while still in the fighting arena.

This time while betting, with the senior of my two assailants' right behind me in the betting line, I placed my bet. "Let it ride on Ball-O-Fire."

"That's going to be nearly a one grand bet! I need to check with someone to see if we can cover that kind of action. Just a moment please," said the short heavy man still gnawing on what seemed to be the original wet sloppy cigar he had when we first arrived. He then moved over to the middle row and end seat of the second set of bleachers, where he conversed with sports jacket and slacks kind of guy. The man he was talking to kept looking over at me. When he returned he asked, "Who are you here with?"

"Tommy." I replied with a nod in Tommy's direction. Then, as an after thought, and just to test the water I said, "My name is Jack Bryce and I'm a friend of Jude Makala."

Makala's name got the raised eyebrow. "Just one more minute please," the man said, and without waiting for a response, he scooted back over to the sport coat to deliver the info. This time the sport

163

coat came over to talk directly to me, while the other man now took the bet of the person who was waiting behind me.

"Hello Mr. Bryce! Folks around here call me Blaze. My associate tells me you know my good friend, Jude Makala."

"And you are?" I pressed with a false indignant attitude of superiority, trying to get a last name from Blaze.

"Just Blaze," he stated, searching me with his eyes and not taking the bait.

Lately, with all of these people sizing me up, I was beginning to understand how an attractive-looking woman might feel when every guy on the street checks her out.

"How do know my friend, Jude?" Blaze queried me as a test.

"He's friends with my employer, Pua Kapuulaa. I'm on assignment to help rebuild *The Onion Express*," I expressed to Blaze with extra authority in my voice. I also noticed that my response quickly got the attention of the man, my senior assailant at the construction site, whom I guessed to be in his early thirties.

"Well, Mr. Bryce, we are very pleased to have you with us tonight, and though your wager is unusually large for us we will, of course, be happy to take the bet."

"Thank you." With that done, I made my way back to Tommy.

"Everyting okay brudah?'

"Everything is fine Tommy. I just let my bet ride and, because it was kind of large, they wanted to know who I was with." Just then, the entire group of five guys seated in front of us, including my two assailants, turned to look at me as they had apparently been informed of who I was. I paid them no attention figuring I'd somehow get to even the score for the roughing up they had given me at another time. Of course, it was a big assumption on my part that I could handle either of them let alone both of them at the same time. Most people, because of the way we have been brought up within our society, have delusions of grandeur when it comes to sex, fighting, and gambling... and I am no different from most guys. And just like most people, there are times when I am aptly able to lose at all three.

As the next match got underway, I was a bit nervous over the money. I was very hopeful that the fight would turn out in my favor, because the money I was betting really belonged to Kappy and I didn't want to have to tell him I had lost it, even though he knew he may never see it again.

With fingers crossed, I watched the cruel fight with disdain and guilt for being involved in any way.

Luck was with me again though, as Ball-O-Fire bit and clawed his way to victory. "Good win brudah," said the short, fat, cigar-smoking bookie.

"Hau'oli," I said blandly.

"Huh?" asked Cigar Face.

"The next bird. Its name is Hau'oli. Let it ride," I commanded. Hau'oli, when translated to English, means happy, Tommy had told me. He selected the bird after reviewing the hand-written program, distributed to the event attendees when entering the barn. I struggled to understand why someone would name a fighting bird, "Happy," but I went with it. The picks I was making were strictly based on input from Tommy, and to his credit, he seemed to know what he was doing. However, Tommy never moved from his bleacher seat and never made a bet of his own. I gave him a lot of credit for restraining himself from what I understood to be a chronic, personal problem.

Cigar Face looked over to Blaze and held up two fingers indicating that I now wanted to bet two large. Blaze gave the okay by replying with a simple nod.

On my way back up the bleachers to sit with Tommy, I stopped directly in front of the group of five men we were seated behind. Looking directly at my two assailants I said, "Jack Bryce, good to see you guys again!"

The younger of my two assailants started to say something, but an elbow to the ribs from his partner, seated right next to him, silenced him. He looked at his partner, and looked back at me and said nothing.

"Don't tell me you boys have forgotten me?" I said questioningly.

"Never heard of you friend. You must be mistaking us for somebody else," said the senior of the two.

"Nope. I'm sure it was you guys. Remember? At T*he Onion Express* construction site? In the early morning hours, a few weeks back. You tackled me, and your friend here tried to bash my brains in!" I said pointing to each of them for the actions they had taken.

"Look Brah. We already said we've never seen you before, so leave us alone."

"Well then that's too bad. I was going to let Blaze and Jude know what a good job you did. But since it's not you then I guess you're just a couple of lowlife punks not worth mentioning." I said walking to the side and then stepping to one row above them.

"I'm gonna fuck you up like…." the younger man started to say. He rose from his seat moving toward me, but before he could reach me my size 11 ½ hard right shoe responded to the threat. I caught him against the left side of his jaw, knocking him backwards and into the lap of one of his friends that I didn't know.

The elder of the two rose quickly as if to challenge me, but stopped cold in his tracks when he saw that Tommy had moved to right beside me. "Good thing you brought your own protection or

I'd be kicking the shit out of you right now," the man said without making any sudden moves to provoke me.

To my chagrin Tommy joined in. "Hey brudah! I only be here so dat you friends stay out of dis. If you want to fight wit da Kahuna den dat okay wit me...you go ahead and we see who do what to whom." Tommy said it almost laughingly, adding to the anguish and frustration of the man facing me.

The younger man was still groggy and not up to helping his friend and the other three acted as if they didn't want to get involved. That left just the other man to face me and he reconsidered. "Like I said I've never seen you before so it ain't worth fighting over." He then promptly turned his back on me while seating himself to face the arena.

Tommy and I took our seats and I looked over toward the other bleacher, where Blaze was seated, and I saw that he was watching with great interest. I gave him a salute and a thumbs-up, which he acknowledged with a return salute and smile, which I took to mean that he knew exactly what had transpired.

The bird owners started the new birds in the middle of the ring, and again, Tommy had picked well as Hau'oli won the fight in dramatic fashion. He had to come back from an early and serious wound to put his opponent down to a point of its only movement being its heaving chest.

Together, Tommy and I collected the winnings, which were about seventeen hundred dollars after commissions, and we made our way out of the barn. Just as we got to Tommy's car a voice from behind stopped us in our tracks. "Mr. Bryce!"

It was the elder and more reasonable of my two assailants, and he appeared to be alone.

"Yes?" I said now facing him.

"You really know Jude?"

"Jude Makala? Yes I do."

"Well, we were just supposed to cause some delays to the project, but you arrived early and surprised us. If I had known you was a friend of Jude's, we'd never have messed with you. I don't want Jude being mad at us, so I'm sorry about the mistake."

Jackpot! I thought to myself. I gathered my wits quickly, figuring how to play the information I just received. "Okay." I said as sincerely as possible. "I got even for the mistake, so let's just call it a draw okay? I won't say anything to Jude," I added. "What's you name?"

"Sounds good to me! People call me Lou," he said accepting the offer with a big sigh of relief.

Before he could turn and walk away I asked, "So Lou, do you do odd jobs for other people…like if I wanted to hire you for something?"

"Well, not really. We only did what we did because we owed some money to Blaze, and Jude said the debt would be square if we could cause the project some delays."

"So if I wanted to have someone messed up a little you aren't the right person?" I asked him point blank.

"No. No I, err, uh, we don't do any heavy stuff. If you want heavy stuff you got to go to Blaze his-self. He's the one who does the heavy stuff."

I figured I had learned all I needed to know for the moment from Lou so I said, "Okay then. Let's you and me forget we ever had this conversation, and we'll all call it even. Deal?"

"Deal!" he said turning around and walking away.

After we turned off of the dirt road and out of the vicinity of where the cockfighting was being held I said to Tommy, "Hey brudah…we make an awesome team! "

Just then a flashing red light and siren behind us got our attention. "Heck, I not speeding or any ting. Why dey pulling me over now?"

"I think it's not you they want Tommy."

"Say what? You got some ting happening here dat you don't tell me about?" Tommy stated with great alarm in his voice.

"Just a little insurance Tommy. The police want to catch Kainoa's killer too. Do you know Lieutenant Ho?"

"I don't tink so," the big man replied looking at me with uncertainty.

"Well, Lieutenant Ho has been escorting us since we left my place in Kahana." I figured I needed to be upfront with Tommy now. Not only because he had stood beside me, but also because he was now involved. Lou and his friends would now associate Tommy with me. And, of course, Cigar Face and Blaze would do the same. And Jude Makala would hear it through his own grapevine.

For sure, the "Saturday Night at the Fights," were rewarding in more ways than one.

Chapter 35...
Hai Ho Rides Again!

Both Tommy and I met Lieutenant Ho between the two vehicles. "Hi Hai. This is my friend Tommy." I said making the introduction.

"Hello Tommy. So this guy is dragging you into this mess huh?"

"It okay. If we gonna git da guys who got Kainoa den I want to be der too!" he said gripping Ho's outstretched hand, which totally disappeared inside the grasp of the big man.

"We got lucky in more ways than one. Not only did we make a few bucks for Kappy, but we got names and faces of people you'll want to know." I explained to Ho.

"Me too," said Hai. "I got the makes and plates of every vehicle on the property!"

"Well then, when you run all the numbers we should be able to match the faces and names."

"So, did you find anybody of particular interest?" asked Ho.

"Lou. No last name. He was one of the two people that tried to sabotage the construction site. We met the other one, too, but I neglected to get his name."

"Yeah," Tommy chimed in. "Da udder guy met with his right foot. It was so quick dat I almost missed it!"

Hai looked at me with raised eyebrows.

"Military training." I replied shrugging my shoulders.

"Military?" Hai pressed obviously wanting to know more about me.

"I spent some time in Thailand during the Vietnam War, and one of the locals, our hooch boy whose name is Boon, gave me lessons in Thai kick-boxing during my spare time.

"Okay. Meet anyone else?"

"Well, there was a guy I called Cigar Face who took all of the bets, and then there was a man named Blaze, who took time to personally introduce himself to me when my wagering got a little heavy. That's about it, other than a few of the bird owners."

"That's it?"

"Did I mention that Lou told Tommy and me that he was hired by Jude?"

"No! Hai replied. "I think you missed that detail."

"Well, Lou told us that he owed some money to Blaze, and that Jude said if he delayed the project at *The Onion Express,* the debt would be squared. Is that right Tommy?" I said looking at him for affirmation.

"Dats right pah! He definitely said Jude."

"Well, I'll be!"

"You'll be what?" I asked the Lieutenant who looked starry eyed.

He responded, "I'm one lucky Hawaiian cop since meeting you! We've solved your assault and vandalism case, which is linked to one of the biggest crooks in the Islands, and I've not only found out where the illegal cockfights are held, but I now know who attends them, who takes the bets during the fights and who actually runs the games! I'd say it was A VERY GOOD DAY!"

CHAPTER 36......
FROM GOOD TO BETTER

We all agreed to meet and talk later. Since it was nearly 3:00 AM, we all decided it was best to head to our homes for a little shut-eye.

"You pretty good wit your feet!" Tommy said after about ten minutes of quiet driving time.

"Just a little something I picked up while stationed at Tahkli Royal Thai Air Force Base in Thailand during the Vietnam War," I replied with a yawn.

"Well it looked pretty quick!"

"Thanks," I replied. "And thanks again for backing me up in there. I might have been able to make a dent in one or two of them, but I couldn't have handled all five."

"A 'ole pilikia, which means you welcome brah!" We both laughed.

After getting back to the condominium, I decided to take a short stroll on the beach before going up to bed. The full moon was shining brightly overhead, and its reflection danced delicately on the gentle rolling waves coming in from the very tranquil late night seas.

The short quiet stroll must have totally relaxed me as I don't even remember my head hitting the pillow when I finally went to bed.

It was 10:00 A.M. when then phone woke me from what seemed to be a very deep sleep. "Hey Jack! This is Kimo. You alive up there and ready to surf?"

Crap…I thought to myself as I raised myself to a sitting position on the edge of the bed. I had forgotten all about meeting Kimo and Paolo today. "No. I'm here but I had a late night last night and I haven't gotten out to rent a board yet."

"No problem Jack. Paolo and I loaded enough boards for the three of us and a few more. Besides, there is a person down here named Hai who is asking to join us. Says he knows you."

"Yeah. I was hoping you wouldn't mind if he surfed with us. Is it okay?'

"Yeah it's cool," Kimo replied. "It's a really big ocean, the surf is up, and besides, were the only ones out here!"

"Are you already here?"

"Yep, and we've been waiting for you, but it is no big deal brudah. You come on down as soon as you can, and we'll leave the big board on the beach for you so you can come out and join us."

I moved to the deck off the bedroom and I could see Hai, Paolo and Kimo standing on the beach below and I gave them a wave."

"Hey, I'm ten floors below you and I can tell you look like shit my friend," Hai said after taking over the phone from Kimo.

"That bad huh?" I said still trying to get the cobwebs out of my brain. "Just give me ten minutes and then I'll join you guys out on the water."

I put a cup of instant coffee on high in the microwave, ran through a cold shower, slipped on a knee-length Hawaiian swimsuit and a tank top. Then I grabbed a towel, my sunglasses, a cup full of very strong, hot coffee and made my down the breezeway to the elevator. Then I went out onto the beach adjacent to the condominium.

"Mahalo nui loa!" I said, finally arriving at the ride area about 300 hundred yards out from the shoreline. The board they had left for me to use was not quite as big as an old *Big Gun* but it was fine for me.

Kimo replied with an "A ole pilikia" while Paolo just said, "You're welcome."

We all had a great time out there, along with a growing crowd of surfers who seemed to migrate to our area. Hai and I tried to mimic the father-son professional duo without much success. I was able to make a few moves up and down my board without falling, but when Hai and I tried to swap boards, do hand stands and some of the other tricks that Kimo and Paolo were doing, all we did was create some great laughs for everyone who was watching.

We surfed for about five hours or till just after 3:00 PM when Hai, Kimo and Paolo said it was time to head home for Sunday dinner with their families.

I had had a great time on the water and not once did I think about work, or the murder mess I was involved in. Hai seemed to be enjoying the same mode, and he too had forgotten about his work and everything that had happened the night before.

When I arrived back upstairs, I was surprised to see some new groceries on the sink, and then I noticed a trail of woman's clothes leading down the hallway towards the bedroom. Damn! I thought to myself. Pua just won't take no for an answer.

"What are you doing here?" I asked rounding the door and heading into the master bedroom.

"Surprising my husband!" was the response I got from Veronica. She was wearing a skimpy bikini, sitting in a chair on the balcony, and holding two glasses of red wine.

Expecting to have been facing Pua Kapuulaa and telling her to leave the condominium, instead I found myself speechless…for all of about three or four seconds. I don't even remember walking past the bedroom furniture, but in those few seconds I crossed the room, removed the wine glasses from her hand and picked up my more beautiful than ever wife, and carried her to the big bed. "When… err…a…how…oh to hell with it!" I finally stammered giving up on conversation and letting my lips fall on hers for one of the longest kisses of our marriage.

"Glad to see me?" Veronica said when our lips finally parted.

"Oh God yes!" I said gently into her right ear and unwilling to let go of her.

"Just wait here for a minute." Then I ran into the shower not caring whether the water was cold or hot. When I returned, we continued to hold each other closely making love for nearly two wonderful hours.

It had started out as a very good day by surfing with my new Hawaiian friends, and then with Veronica's surprise visit the day obviously just kept getting better. After a light homemade supper of pasta, salad, garlic bread and wine on the livingroom balcony, we adjourned to the beach below for a hand-in-hand, slow stroll through the gentle warm waters of the tropical Pacific.

CHAPTER 37.........
A SPECIAL LADY

The second thing I did was to show Veronica where the listening bug was located inside the condominium.

"One of the reasons I'm here Jack is that I'm worried about you. The situations you get yourself involved in never cease to amaze me."

"Me too!"

"Come on Jack. You know what I mean," Veronica said catching my gaze and holding my eyes to hers.

"What do you see in there?" I asked, honestly wanting to know.

"I see you, Jack. I see what's going on inside you when I look deep into your eyes. Your eyes always tell me what's going on."

"What are they saying right now?"

"Right now you've got that little boy look you get when you are excited. You're very happy that I am here, but there is something else you are trying to hide but can't quite pull it off. Am I right?"

"You're always right," I said, stopping our gingerly walk, pulling her toward me, and kissing her amazingly sensuous lips, and each of her inquiring blue-green eyes, closing them and ending her search.

"I love you to death Jack, but I also worry about you all the time. I don't ever want to lose you, and I know that you feel the same about me. So I don't understand how it is that you get involved in all of these dangerous situations."

"I think you do understand, and that you have always known who I am. These situations seem to find me honey. I don't ask for them...they just seem to arrive on my doorstep. And when they do, there are usually people, really nice people, who need help and I can't let them down. I'm not made so that I can turn my back, or just look the other way. You should know that about me by now. I am who I am, and I don't think I'm going to change. Can you honestly say you want me to change who and what I am?"

"No, of course not. I know you have to do what you can to help people, and I admire that. I think you are wonderful. It's just that I don't want to lose what we have. We have a great marriage, great kids and a terrific life. You and the kids are my whole world."

"And you are ours. I know we have a good thing, and the kids do too. I will be as careful as I can, and I won't take unnecessary risks. But I won't run and hide, and I won't turn away when I can help someone who needs me."

We were walking again, with Veronica holding my left arm in both of hers. We walked all the way to where we ran out of beach, and then we turned to walk home, re-tracing some of our earlier steps that the gentle waves had not yet washed away.

We made love again before falling asleep in each other's arms, and in the morning, I took Veronica back to the airport where she boarded a plane. Once back in San Francisco she would then drive herself home to Boulder Creek where Warren, Marie, Pogo and Ralph waited for her return.

During the ride back from the airport, I reminded myself of what a special lady I had, and that I had better not screw it up by doing something stupid.

CHAPTER 38.........
STRIKING A NERVE

"Have a good weekend, Luanne?" I asked while pouring myself a cup of fresh coffee.

"I had a great weekend. Thanks for asking."

"Me too! Veronica came in for a surprise visit," I told her without going into details.

"That's wonderful, Jack. I'll bet it was very special."

"It was. What about you Luanne? What made your weekend so good?" I asked wanting to know more about Luanne and the things she likes.

Luanne told me about going to a wedding held at the Pukalani Golf Course, and then having gone to a house warming for some friends who had just moved into a new tract home. The new tract home got my attention when I learned it was the same one being built by Jude Makala and his cohorts.

Construction at the site was moving fast now. All of the steel framing had been secured, the sub-flooring was in, many of the exterior walls on the hotel side were up, and utility connections were jutting from floors and walls everywhere. In addition, both the onion shaped roof of the restaurant and the roof over the hotel had taken shape and been covered, but not yet with the finished roofing materials.

"I heard the little lady paid you a surprise visit yesterday, huh Jack?" Pua said as she unexpectedly entered my office. I was reviewing the mechanical portion of the design drawings to maintain my familiarity as preparation for a walk-thru scheduled with the sub-contractor after lunch. "I'll bet the two of you had a...," she hesitated deliberately pausing for a few seconds while looking me up and down in a way that made me feel embarrassed, "very *special* time together."

"How can I help you, Pua?" I addressed her with an obvious hint of sarcasm in my tone.

"I think I've been pretty clear about that Jack," she said laughing at her own wit. "I'm really here because my friend, Jude, says you've been using his name in places where it is not appreciated."

The statement surprised me, and it must have shown on my expression.

"Come now Jack, surely you are not surprised that word would get around that fast. This is, after all, just a tiny island. Obviously, you used his name for a reason. What is it you were trying to accomplish?"

"Trying to accomplish? I wasn't trying to accomplish anything. Is Jude upset about something?"

"Upset is not the right word Jack. I think it is more a case of curiosity. He is wondering just what it is you are up to."

"Well, please tell Jude that I didn't mean to upset him or cause him any problems," I said with false sincerity. However, the truth was that I didn't really care if he was upset or not. I was finding it very interesting that Jude was speaking to me about this through Pua.

180

I would have expected him to contact me directly. In fact, I was kind of hoping he would contact me personally.

"Maybe I should call Jude and apologize?" I suggested to Pua.

"I'm sure that it isn't necessary. If he wanted to contact you he knows where you are."

Considering the bugs in my office and at the condominium, I had no doubt that Jude knew how to reach me.

"Well please convey my apologies to Mr. Makala," I asked her. "Is there something else that brings you to the construction site? Would you like a tour of how the construction of your hotel and restaurant is going?"

"And what Jack? Have all of those Kapuulaa cousins and their friends leering at me as we walk by? No, no thank you. I asked you to change those people, but you refused, and I'm very uncomfortable around them."

"That's a shame," I replied without really caring about what she might be feeling. "They are really nice folks, and they are very good at what they do."

"I'll be on my way now Jack, but I expect you to keep me posted of the progress, or lack of progress." She turned her back on me as if I were summarily dismissed, and walked quickly away, leaving me no room to respond to her orders.

"How was the Island Queen?" Luanne asked entering the office.

"She was her usual self," I responded with some amusement.

"I honestly don't understand what Kainoa ever saw in that woman!" Luanne exclaimed with some exasperation in her tone.

I had the same thought.

As if it had been deemed Kapuulaa Family Day, Kappy walked in less than five minutes after Pua had left. Luanne said her hellos and departed my office rather quickly.

181

"Hi Kappy. Are you here to collect the winnings?" I said smiling and honestly happy to see the elderly man. "You just missed your daughter-in-law!"

"I know," he replied. "I saw her arrive so I waited around the corner. I don't like seeing her if I don't have to, especially outside of the family compound and away from the kids. No, I'm not here for any money Jack. I'm here to thank you and Tommy for what you are doing. On behalf of everyone in the family, except maybe for my daughter-in-law, we are very grateful for your help."

"It's no problem Kappy. Tommy and I both want to get the bastards who got your son."

"Tommy told me about your run-in at the cockfights, and what you found out while you were there. It sounds like it was a pretty successful weekend."

Thinking about that and Veronica, who must be halfway to the mainland by now, I had to agree. The weekend had turned out to be pretty successful. "Yes, it was a very good weekend, sir."

We chatted some more about what had happened at the cockfights and about the message from Jude Makala, which just been delivered by Pua. We all agreed that Makala's nervousness probably meant that we were on the right track, and we discussed what our next steps might be which included a return trip to the fights for Tommy and myself.

We also decided, since we may have struck a nerve with the Syndicate that we were all gong to have to take extra caution and care in our daily lives.

CHAPTER 39........
ONIONS TO UNIONS

"So why is it that the construction cousins and friends of the Kapuulaa family aren't members of the local unions? Is it the cost or the politics?"

Kappy looked away before providing an answer to my question, which I took to mean as my having posed a more difficult question than intended. "It's definitely the politics Jack. We don't have anything against the union or the people who belong per say, however, there is and has been a problem with the people who control it. Hell, I used to work for the union myself back in the fifties and sixties."

"Let me guess. The Syndicate has their hands on the wheel?"

"You got it Jack. The union came under control of the local crime Syndicate back in the early seventies. The problem was the returning Vietnam War Veterans, and there were thousands and thousands of them after Nixon started reducing the military presence over there, rushed the job market. There were not enough jobs for everyone. The first thing that happened was that the union leader for the Laborers Local #56208 died when his car went off the road and over a cliff. It was a mysterious crash because the car had to travel over one hundred feet and hit the spot just right to go over the cliff. It was more than a nine hundred foot straight drop. Anyhow, the labor union held a special election, and since there were so many workers and so few jobs, the Syndicate promised the men everything. They bought what was being sold to them, and they elected the Syndicate cronies as officers of the union.

I listened intently as Kappy continued his *History of Unions in Hawaii 101* class. "Once they got control of the Laborer's Union it was easy for them to get a hold on all of the other unions, too. Nobody wanted to stand up against them, and those that tried either lost their lives or were squashed into non-existence. Now, the workers are stuck with exorbitant dues and they really have no say in the direction of the unions at all. Moreover, developers are at risk too when they don't employ the union forces. Our family and some of the other established families are trying to fight back, but it's been a tough road and the cost has been…too high," Kappy hesitatingly murmured turning his head and eyes downward. I took it to mean he was thinking about the loss of his only son, Kainoa.

CHAPTER 40............
LOST THE BET!

After Tommy and Kappy departed, a new picture started emerging from within my not so wild imagination. Kappy and Kainoa must have known what was at stake when they decided to rebuild *The Onion Express* using their family members and other non-union contractors. I began to realize that right from the start everyone, even the contractors I chose, knew the risk before even being allowed to choose their own participation. Then, I remembered when Kainoa asked me if I still wanted in, knowing that two persons had already lost their lives, and that he and his family had their share of enemies.

He had laid it all out for me that first day. And I, always eager for a challenge, stood across from him, eye-to-eye, and said it wasn't a problem and that I still wanted the job. What I was also realizing though, is that everyone involved in *The Onion Express* project must have known from the beginning, that there would likely be trouble. Even when they chose me to be the helu ʻekahi (number one), or in this case, the Project Manager, they likely knew the challenges that lay ahead.

Next, I did an internal soul search of what this new revelation meant to me, and I decided rather quickly it didn't mean much at this point. For sure, I was now involved in the struggle along with Kappy, the contractors, and others who objected to the Syndicate involvement within the unions. If anything, I declared to myself silently, the team I was on was bigger than I had realized. That made feel a little better about my situation.

"Hey buddy this is Jack," I stated to my on-duty Lieutenant friend, Jim Alverez, when he answered.

"Jack! How's the Big Kahuna?"

"Things are going as can be expected over here. How's married life? Or has Vickie dumped you already?"

"Thanks for the kind thought pal! Anyhow, married life couldn't be better."

"She's a great gal Jim. I'm not sure what she sees in a cop who works all hours of the day and night…frankly she deserves better!" I teased my friend.

"Yeah, yeah. So, did you call just to bust my chops, or is it because you just can't stand to be away from me for so long?"

"Are you keeping an eye on my family?"

"I encouraged her to make that surprise visit. How's that for keeping an eye out and being a pal?"

"You could be my new best friend ever!"

"Could be Jack? You gotta do better than that!"

"Okay, Veronica's visit was way cool. So how about helping out a buddy here?"

"What can I do for you?"

Since it was business now, I switched from "Jim" to "Lieutenant."
"I was wondering, Lieutenant, if it would be worth-while for you, and by chance for me, to check out some individuals over here who may

have ties to persons over there? Especially if any of them have ties to any persons actively engaged in union activities, or even perhaps to your local underworld."

"What about your friend Lieutenant Ho in the Lahaina Homicide Department?"

"He's doing the same thing from over here. I'm asking you to check it out on your end for the safety sake of my family. If there are any known cronies in your area, then the game changes…at least for me."

"Consider it done Jack."

"Thank you sir. "Now Jim (I switched back to the familiar mode), in a few weeks, Veronica and Marie will be joining me over here because Marie's team has been invited to play in the Maui Championship Soccer Tournament. Warren has a gig house sitting out in the foothills of Aptos at the same time. You wouldn't know of any newlywed apartment dwellers that might want ten days of country loving…err uh I mean….country living with gorgeous sunrises, a secluded hot tub, guest passes to the local country club and of course, the quiet of the mountains that can only be provided by a mostly undisturbed Mother Nature?"

"Hell yes we'd like to…oops…forgot I was married for a minute. What I meant to say was …sounds great! Let me check to make sure my wife doesn't have other plans."

"Damn it!" I almost shouted.

"Damn what?" Jim Alverez asked.

"I just lost a bet to Veronica."

"What bet?"

"I bet Veronica that you couldn't be house broke in less than a year…I just lost!"

CHAPTER 41............
STIRRING THE POT

"Hello Hai! You getting anything besides a headache from this case?" I responded when I picked up the blinking line two that Luanne had put on hold for me. I had been talking with a supplier on line one.

"I'm going nowhere fast with this case Jack. So far, all we have is a link to some ruffians and their brass for vandalism and assault at your construction site. I've got nothing that ties them to burning the place down or to Kainoa's death."

"Well then how about we take another approach Lieutenant? Maybe you can lean on a man named Richard Hatcher. Or was it Thatcher? No, I'm sure its Hatcher." I went on to explain Hatcher's involvement. "Mr. Hatcher sets the schedules and priorities for the stevedores on the docks over on Oahu. He's an Australian who still utilizes words like bloke and chap. Anyhow, Richard Hatcher may have a direct line to the higher ups." I went on to explain to the Lieutenant about Kainoa's and my run in with Mr. Hatcher when the delivery of our steel load was unreasonably delayed. Remembering the incident caused me to laugh aloud. I explained to Hai how Kainoa had the barge that could not be towed and unloaded by the union, towed to Maui by one of his own boats, and unloaded by his own crew. "Richard was protesting to Kainoa that one of their tugs was down for repairs, and that no amount of money or anything else could influence the schedule. However, even as he was speaking, he learned that Kainoa had already begun towing the barge to Maui with one of his own boats. Hatcher was flabbergasted by the news and he turned red with anger. Then Kainoa handed Hatcher a check for having rented the steel laden barge, which was already on its way to Maui."

"So you think this Hatcher person has links to the union's undesirables?" Lieutenant Ho asked.

"It's possible. Of course it's your call, but I'm guessing Hatcher, if he thought you were trying to implicate him in a murder, might be willing to talk if he knows anything."

"You make it sound like the police can just go around harrying the citizens any time they want."

"Well…yeah!"

"We'll see. Anything else you think I should check into?"

"You might try the cement plant. I don't have a name, but they were delaying a delivery to the site too."

"I've already talked to them Jack. It was on the top of my list after Kainoa's chopper was blown out of the sky. I got nowhere except that they claimed the delay was due to a simple transposition error in the amount of concrete being ordered. Even with your document showing the correct number, which I got from your secretary, I couldn't prove malicious intent."

"Did you try it from the union perspective? The cement company's drivers are part of the teamster's union and they are out of the same hall as the stevedores. Maybe there is a connection to Jude or Blaze, or someone close to them. Remember my friend, Lieutenant Alverez? I've asked him to see if he can find any union connections to Blaze or Jude in California."

"You sure you aren't some kind of cop? Maybe you're working for some government agency?"

"Not hardly Hai. I just want to help get the son-of-a-bitches who got Kainoa, and I want to bring them down quick! I declared with an emotional tone of commitment in my voice. "Mr. Kapuulaa, his family, and their friends, are risking a lot and we need to help them if we can."

"Okay Jack. I'll see if I can't apply some heat to the cement plant, as well as to your Mr. Hatcher. Who knows what we'll find. Maybe they'll turn on each other or maybe they'll run for cover, who knows. They might even just be legit business people who know nothing. Anyhow, I'll stir 'em up and we'll see what happens. Okay brudah? I'll get back to you soon."

"Thanks Lieutenant," I said and hung up the phone.

CHAPTER 42........
A SWEET DEAL!

After talking with Hai, a new thought popped into my head, so I called back home to ask one of my long-time poker buddies a few questions.

"This is Pablo. How may I help you?"

"Hey brother, this is Jack. How's everything going in Boulder Creek?"

"Good to hear from you . You back home and ready to play some cards?"

"Still toughing it out in Maui I'm afraid, but yeah, I'm ready for some cards. Who was the big winner at last month's game?"

"Sly Guy and Big Dave pocketed the loot. I lost my ass! We had fun, but it would have been better if you and Cowboy had been there. The table was a little short."

"Where's Cowboy?"

"He's home now, but he missed last game because he was in Italy on business."

"Italy?" Normally, when Cowboy travels for his company, he's somewhere along the Pacific Rim.

"Yeah, he's handling Europe now too. There was some kind of business crisis over there and they sent him in to schmooze the clients and smooth the ruffled feathers."

"That's our Cowboy. He's great at smoothing ruffled feathers. How are Mat-Man and Streaks?"

"Mat-Man is still fighting a slow economy, and Streaks got himself a new lady. She's terrific and he seems really serious about her!"

That's great for Streaks. And Mat-Man has gone through these slow-downs before. He's a survivor. The reason I called was to ask you a couple of real estate questions."

"Shoot brother."

"I thought I read somewhere about how unions sometimes invest in real estate. Is that true?"

"Absolutely. Many of the bigger unions own some of the best commercial properties in Silicon Valley. Its a pretty common practice."

"Where do they get the money to invest?"

"Pensions. Many of them have diverse pension fund investments which include commercial real estate."

"I noticed you said commercial real estate. How about residential?" I asked.

"Residential? Hmm. I don't think that is the normal practice, but I guess they could. It probably depends on how the trusts are set up. Why the sudden interest in unions?"

"Do you know of any circumstances where unions get involved in new housing developments?"

"I don't know of anything like that personally. What's up?"

"Some friends over here have run into a little trouble and I'm just trying to help them out."

"Right Jack. So have you been shot at or has anyone tried to burn you up in your office yet?"

"Nothing like that Pablo, but I did go to the local cockfights, and with my friend's input we nearly tripled our money!" I said feeling proud for having won at something for a change.

"Are cockfights legal in Hawaii? Isn't that just a little in-humane on the birds?"

"It was just something I needed to do. You're right though, it was pretty bloody and disgusting. I have a feeling that this particular event is going to get closed down pretty soon."

"Let me guess…you have something to do with closing down the illegal cockfighting? How in the hell do you get yourself involved in these things?"

"Just lucky I guess. Hey thanks for the info bro. You've been a big help…like always." I said, sincerely thanking him for the information provided.

"You going to make the next game?"

"Not sure yet. I still need to finish this project and then Marie is coming over for a soccer tournament in a couple of weeks. I guess I'd better say no, I won't make the next game, but I know it's my turn to host the one after that. I'm pretty sure I'll be home by then."

We said our "goodbyes", and then I sat back to think about the information I had just gained. I was wondering who was in control of the local Hawaiian union's pension plan. The thought that kept coming to me was, wouldn't it be sweet for Jude and his friends if they had control of the pension fund and directed the investments. How great of a deal would it be to use pension plan money as backing for housing developments? You don't have to put any of your own money at risk. You pay the pension plan fair interest on the exposed capital, you use union labor to keep the member work force happy, you reap the profits from sales of the new homes, and if you are financing any of the purchases, you make money there too.

As I continued to think about that scenario, I envisioned all other sorts of ways they might benefit. There would likely be kickbacks from suppliers, and the contractors who supply the labor trades. If for some reason the homes didn't sell right away, like the bottom falling out of the market, such as it did when the Japanese economy took a dump, pension plan losses would just be written off and explained as a downtrend for the current year. Jude and friends are non-the-worse because they had no personal risk. "What a sweet deal!" I thought to myself.

CHAPTER 43.........SHEE _ IT!

The rest of the week at work went well with only a few minor interruptions, which is expected on just about every larger construction project. In fact, things had gone so well for so long, that we had actually made ground on the schedule. However, it meant I had to beg, borrow, and negotiate like crazy to accelerate our material delivery schedule in order to keep pace with the work being performed.

In preparation for Veronica and Marie's arrival, I hired one of the women who cleans and services the rental units in the giant complex to do the same for me.

For once, everything seemed to be going as planned, which was why I figured I had better not relax. When all the stars and whatever are in place, and all the cylinders are firing on time that is exactly the time something goes unexpectedly wrong.

Tommy and I made our plans to hit the cockfighting circuit again on Saturday night. This time Lieutenant Ho and I agreed there was no need for him to follow us. However, he did inform me that Tommy and I should make this our last visit as there was a bust being set-up for the following Saturday. Since I already had a dislike for the happenings at cockfights, it was fine with me that this would be the last time I would attend such an event. Besides, Veronica and Marie would be here the following Saturday. The plan was for them to be here for a few days prior to the rest of the team's arrival.

Veronica and I had it scheduled, with lots of Luanne's help that we would be at the Kahana condominium for three days, and then stay in Kihei with the soccer team for seven full days and nights before returning to Kahana and meeting up with the rest of the family. Being with the team during the tournament was always fun for the players and the parents too. Even though this was a team of seventeen-year-old girls, who pretty much did their own thing, the parents had also established camaraderie and we truly had a great time together. In fact, there were times when the two coaches, Art and Chris, had to get the parents in line so that the girls could get a good night's sleep before a game.

When Saturday night rolled around, I was already waiting in the parking lot when Tommy drove up. "You're sure your family is okay with this Tommy? I feel bad that I am dragging you out and away from them two Saturdays in a row."

"It okay brudah. My wife...she a good woman. We get along pretty good and besides, she knows dat I am out wit da Big Kahuna and she happy I am getting paid. Or at least dats what she tinks."

The cockfights were being held in the same location as before, which caused me to consider that the organizers might have become too relaxed. Their operation showed no concern for the police showing up for a raid, or bust, or whatever it is the police call that sort of thing. The bouncer at the door was the same man as before, and he remembered both Tommy and I as we parked and walked up to the door. However, he searched us nonetheless. Inside the barn, the setup also remained the same. The place was set up with the same bleachers, the same staging area, and the same fighting ring and then Cigar Face was there too. As we walked through the staging area, supposedly looking at the birds, my eyes searched everyone in the room trying to find Blaze, Lou or the younger man who may still have a bruised ego. None of them seemed to be there and I was disappointed.

The first part of the evening was uneventful. The handlers teased the birds to a frenzied state, turned them loose, and then they fluttered, and flailed at each other spewing blood around the ring and splattering some of the closer on-lookers. I kept my bets small and actually lost each time. It was right after the third fight that Blaze came through the door with Lou and his friends right behind him. Just like the time before, Blaze took up a position at the end of the bleacher closest to Cigar Face. Lou and company sat as a group in the bleachers across from where Tommy and I were seated.

To ensure that Blaze was aware that I was there, I bet one thousand dollars. The bet was on an all black bird that looked mean as hell, and whom Tommy thought had a good chance to win at high odds. As soon as I handed over the money to Cigar Face, and he did have a raunchy sloppy wet stub of a cigar sticking out of his mouth, he looked around me toward Blaze, raising one finger as an indication of the size of my bet. I looked back at Blaze, too, and gave him a nod and slight grin acknowledging his presence.

As it turned out the little black cock fought his heart out, but in the end, he was so badly damaged that his heart stopped beating and his abandoned carcass was removed with a shovel.

"Too bad your bird lost," said Blaze as he sat down next to me.

"Win some lose some," I quipped with a wise guy attitude. "That's why they call it gambling."

"I was watching you during that fight and you know what I think?" Blaze asked holding his eyes steady on mine.

"I think you are going to tell me what you think whether I want to hear it or not," I responded maintaining my smart-ass grin and attitude.

Blaze looked at me as if he were deciding to continue the conversation or not. Then he said, "You're right, I am going to tell you. I was watching you and I saw how you reacted to the birds fighting. You don't like it! You're not into this at all and you know what?"

"What?"

"I talked with Jude after you were here last week and he thinks you are pretending to be someone you're not. What do you think about that?"

"To tell the truth, not much. However, it is time for another bet and this time Cigar Face over there is going to hold up five fingers. Can you handle it?" Then I got up leaving Blaze on the bleachers seated next to Tommy and I made my way to where the bets were being taken.

Sure enough, Cigar Face held up five fingers for my five thousand dollar bet, but this time I didn't look back at Blaze to see if he was giving the approval...I knew he had to.

I returned to my seat to find Tommy was still there but Blaze had moved on. He probably realized all he was going to get from me were smart-ass answers.

I searched the crowd and found that Blaze had moved over to where Lou and his friends were sitting, and that Lou seemed to be protesting in vain, to whatever he was being told by Blaze. When their one-sided conversation ended, Blaze headed out the barn door alone.

This time my bird came through. It was a Rhode Island Red, Tommy had explained, and it was a two to one underdog against a larger and more stoic looking bird that looked tougher than it was. I collected my winnings; less the juice, which is the ten percent the house takes. Overall, Tommy and I walked out about seven grand ahead. Again giving Kappy a good return on his investment. As we were leaving, I noticed that Lou and his younger cohort had left their group and I didn't see them anywhere.

As we drove away Tommy declared, "Dat a very good night. You only win da one bet, but it was da big one!"

"It was thanks to you, Tommy. I sure as heck didn't know what I was dong in there."

"Shee-it"

"Shee it? What does shee…." But I never got to finish the comment as Tommy's car was rammed hard from the rear.

"Dat's what Shee-it means. And here dey comes again!" He said while maintaining the steering wheel with both hands.

The hit jolted us and it was hard enough to slam us in our seat belts and give us a little whiplash too.

"Hold on!" Tommy stated rather calmly as he began to take evasive moves.

"You're pretty good!" I stuttered as we endured the bumpy road and Tommy's swerves to avoid being hit again.

"I've had some practice at this," Tommy replied, but without an accent.

Just then, the sedan that had been chasing and ramming us moved along side of us near our trunk, and the passenger let loose with a barrage of bullets. Tommy avoided the bullets by slamming on the breaks, putting the car into a hard right turn and a slide that took us to just off the side of the road and onto its dirt shoulder. Having slid in the dirt, we created a huge cloud of dust, which was eerily highlighted by the headlights of Tommy's car. Tommy quickly turned off the lights and we both got behind my side of the car.

"Get down and stay down!" Tommy commanded as he pulled a revolver out from under his shirt, quickly firing two shots at the other car. The other car had stopped in the road with its two occupants taking up positions behind it for their protection. Then he looked at me, smiled and yelled out to our two assailants, "FBI! Throw down your weapons and come out with your hands behind your head." Then he said to me, "I should have said that first," and he gave me another big smile and a wink.

I would have been floored by the news if I weren't hugging the ground behind the car.

The response to Tommy's two shots was another short barrage of about six or eight shots, all of which hit Tommy's car and all of which were too close for me.

"Got another gun?" I asked.

"No and stay down!" Tommy replied. Again, I noted there was no accent.

Just then, Tommy left the protection of the car moving to his wide left, and all the time he was moving he was firing. Apparently his move worked. I heard one of the men scream loudly, yelling to his partner that he had been hit. I watched, as Tommy remained erect with his gun held in both hands, pointed at the other car and its occupants.

"FBI!" Tommy boomed again.

A shadowy figure rose from behind an open car door of the other vehicle. The rising figure was wildly firing shot after shot and marching directly toward Tommy, who stood his ground stoically and unmoving. Tommy, taking careful aim, dropped the wildly firing figure with two quick shots that seemed to collapse the man's chest. The wounded man went limp. His hand opened, letting the gun fall free, and then the man dropped to the hard asphalt without any further movement.

I moved cautiously, along with Tommy, toward the downed men ignoring his commands to remain where I was. When we arrived at the other vehicle, an older beat-up green Ford, the one man lay face down in the street, still not moving, while the other sat leaning against the car with his legs straight out and gargling blood, which trickled slowly from his half open mouth. He looked at both of us, and was obviously in shock and unable to get up. Tommy, with his gun still trained on the wounded man, tossed me his cell phone directing me to call nine-one-one while he moved our attacker's guns away from their reach.

I got the police on the line giving them our location and telling them of the shooting, plus needing and ambulance. Then Tommy asked for the phone, which I handed back to him. "Who am I speaking with?" Tommy asked. "Well, deputy, this is FBI Agent Thomas Johnson and I'm reporting shots fired, two persons down and I am requesting assistance. I'd also like you to get a hold of your Homicide Lieutenant Hai Ho and let him know that he needs to respond. Got it?"

"FBI?" I asked still exhibiting signs of disbelief.

"You can still call me Tommy if you want, but my name really is Theodore Thomas Johnson. And yes, I'm a real FBI agent."

My head was swimming now with thoughts of what I had assumed was a gentle giant having a heavy Hawaiian accent, who was now speaking very proper English and telling me he was an FBI agent.

"I was recruited after graduating from Harvard Law School," he said still smiling and almost laughing at me. "The accent is easy for me because I was born and raised here in the islands, which is one of the reasons I got the assignment."

"Assignment?" I queried his comment as distant sirens came into the background.

"It's a long story and I'll be happy to clue you in when we get this cleaned up. By the way, you sure seem to have a knack for getting yourself into trouble."

"You got dat shee-it right, brudah" I mimicked. We both laughed a little.

Chapter 44………
The Real Tommy

Kneeling near the wounded man I said, "Thought you didn't do any of this 'heavy stuff'?"

At first Lou just looked at me with an expression of pure hatred mixed with the pain, but he managed to eek out, "The Kid?"

"The kid didn't make it," I said feeling a bit remorseful over the loss of life. "Who put you up to this?"

"Fuck off and leave me alone," Lou responded with a sigh of despair.

"Was it Blaze or Jude?" I asked. Tommy was crouching next to me as the first police unit arrived.

"Eat shit and die ass-hole! Just leave me alone," Lou groaned holding his stomach with both hands.

"Did you kill Kainoa Kapuulaa?" Tommy asked.

Lou forced a grin and then managed a weak "Fuck off!"

"Your buddy is already dead, and you are gut shot, which means the chances of your surviving aren't too good. If you do want to live, and I'm guessing you do, we'll make sure the doctors work hard at keeping you alive…that is if you help us. If not, well, we won't really care whether you live or die. Matter of fact, the tax payers will save a lot of money if you just die now."

"You're bluffing. The doctors have to fix me."

The first paramedics had arrived now, and they were getting their medical equipment out of their truck. Their emergency lights, along with a nearby sheriff's cruiser, were flashing multiple colored lights into the jungle-like countryside.

"Think so? Watch this." Then Tommy turned and said to the approaching paramedics while holding up his badge, "FBI. This one is gut shot, you had better see to the other one first. He's a key federal witness." With that the paramedics headed straight to the corpse laying face down in the street.

"That's not fair man," Lou said while trying to straighten his sitting position, and grimacing from the pain caused by the movement.

Tommy took another turn at him, "Did you want to say something?"

"You guys don't know what you're dealing with."

"Why don't you tell us?" I chimed in.

"They'd kill me."

The paramedics came over to the three of us, as did the police officers, who had already secured the scene and put out roadside flares.

"Give me just one minute guys," Tommy asked. They all backed away.

"Who put you up to this?"

"They own me man. I'm so far in debt to them that they own me. I had to do what they said."

"Who are *they*?" I asked.

"Blaze and his bosses. They put the hit on you. It's nothing personal man."

"Okay guys, see if you can help this man," Tommy directed to the paramedics.

We moved away to let the paramedics do their job. "I'm guessing that Blaze's bosses include Jude."

"Me too. But I'm concerned about the part where he said 'They put the hit on you.'"

"Yeah. I caught that too. Listen, a lot has happened here. Being shot at was one thing, but finding out that the big, friendly, heavily accented family chauffer is a highly educated FBI agent is another. Want to explain? And what about Johnson? You don't look like a Johnson."

"Most of what we told you was true. Kainoa and I were best friends growing up, so the Kapuulaa family really is like a second family to me. As for the Johnson family name, my mother is pure Hawaiian and my father is a mainlander from California. He met my mother while he was on R&R here during the early years of the Vietnam War. Anyhow, Kainoa, Kappy, other family members, many of the local contractors, and several long-time union members asked for help from the FBI because the corrupt union officials have been squeezing them for a long time now. I came in, undercover, to work with Kainoa and start building an anti-trust case, but when *The Onion Express* burned down and the two workers died, it all changed."

CHAPTER 45............MY GIRL

"What about you, Tommy? Isn't your cover blown now?"

"That's probably true. It's pretty tough to keep the lid on something like this. Look over there," Tommy pointed to some arriving media. "Their scanners perked their ears with the first police car dispatched to the scene, but it's okay now. We already have enough evidence for several indictments including anti-trust, vandalism, assaulting you, and now attempted murder on you and me. Lou, Blaze, and Jude are probably looking at anywhere from twenty years to life in a federal penitentiary."

"I also think we have enough evidence to file some anti-trust violations and drive the mob out of the all of the unions in Hawaii," Tommy added.

"Tell me about the anti-trust."

"Well…you actually gave us our first break there. When you got suspicious about the housing development deferring your cement delivery, and connected it to Jude, we just followed the money. In the real world what they did was fraud and even embezzlement but since they did it with union pension funds they broke several anti-trust laws."

"Just following the money, huh? That was going to be my advice to Hai next time we meet, which looks like in about thirty seconds."

"You guys okay?" Hai asked with genuine concern.

"We're fine Lieutenant. These guys tailed us when we left the cockfights and then they opened up on us on the road. It seems they were ordered to *hit* our friend, Jack, here."

"Tommy? What the hell happened to your accent?" Hai asked looking dumbfounded.

Tommy pulled out his badge and said, "Agent Johnson at your service."

"I'll be damned!" was all the homicide detective could muster in response.

Lou was loaded up in an ambulance, and the paramedic's prognosis was that he was in critical condition. The dead man's body had being outlined with chalk, and was being photographed from every angle. The scene had transformed itself from the two autos originally involved into a vast and wide verity of emergency and law enforcement vehicles. I left Tommy and Hai to discuss happenings and theories excusing myself to make a late night call home.

"Uh huh?" the groggy answerer responded.

""I love you."

"Jack?"

"No, it's the boyfriend."

"How are you? Why are you calling so late?"

"Sorry about that...I guess I didn't realize how late it is."

"It's almost five in the morning here. What are you doing up so late? Are you okay? Did something happen?"

"I'm sorry pumpkin. I was out with Tommy and our new friend, Hai, and I just lost track of the time. You go back to sleep and I'll call you later."

"That's okay honey. You can call me anytime and besides…I miss you. Where are you right now?"

"I'm actually enjoying a little bit of the countryside. " I held back about what had happened. "Can't wait for you and Marie to get here next week."

"Me too. I miss you so much. Plus the whole soccer team and all the parents are really pumped for this tournament. I know it is going to be a lot of fun."

"Sounds great baby. I love you tons. I miss you buckets, and my thoughts are starting to get sexual so I'd better go."

"Well, keep those thoughts and save your energy for next weekend. With what I'm thinking, you're going to need it!"

For a few moments, it seemed like all that was around me had disappeared and that there was only Veronica and me in our own safe little world, which was exactly what I wanted out of my late night call. She had put a smile on my face and reminded me of who and what I was.

After our goodbyes, I wandered back to where Tommy and Hai were still talking.

"The last time I saw that kind of a grin on your face was when you wife showed up for a surprise visit. You must have been talking to her just now." Tommy said while studying my face.

I responded, "You are very good at this detective stuff…yep, I was just on the phone with *my girl*."

CHAPTER 46........
ANOTHER LONG DAY

"If you guys are going to get done in time for lunch, we'd better get you back to the precinct and get your statements," Hai said.

"That's a good idea Lieutenant," Tommy stated formally. "Just as long as we all realize this is a Federal case, my case, and you are welcome to play along as long as we are playing by Federal rules." Tommy made the statement without any extra force or assertiveness in his voice. Instead, the clarifying comment was toned to be friendly, and it was said with a broad grin and a slap on the back. Hai didn't seem to have a problem or any argument about the jurisdiction.

As it turned out Hai was not too far off the mark as to when we would get out of the police station. It was nearly 11:00 AM when I exited the elevator on the tenth floor of the condominium, The wind funneling through the breezeway was refreshing, and it felt good after the stale air in the small offices at the police station. On the way home I decided I would just push myself a little to last through the afternoon and then maybe go to bed early for a long night's sleep.

I made myself some strong, vanilla-flavored coffee. The store had been out of hazelnut. I grabbed a few of what Veronica would classify as "must-goes" (must-goes are more commonly known as leftovers) and settled myself in a high back wicker chair on the lanai overlooking the ocean. Molokai looked a million miles away...at least in my mind. Using the binoculars on the nearby table, I decided to check out the wave action, and see if maybe Kimo, Paolo, or both of them might be on the water. It didn't take long before I spotted Paolo in a group of about five other young surfers, who all seemed to be lounging about on their boards waiting for a good set of waves. I decided that I too wanted to be out on the water. Not necessarily with Paolo and his friends, but to quietly challenge a few waves on my own and to let the warmth of the sun melt away the tensions and happenings of last night.

I changed into my swim gear and grabbed the borrowed surfboard I was now stowing on the lanai near the master bedroom. Next, I fought the breezeway winds that were making life difficult as I made my way toward the elevator, where it was a struggle to cram both the board and myself inside the tiny compartment. By the time I got to the ground floor I felt about eighty years old, out of gas, and too pooped to pop, so to speak. So, I found myself a place on the beach, next to the condominium hedges that separates the lawn and the sea. There, I sat down leaning against the surfboard where I promptly fell asleep in the warmth of the sun.

"Where'd you come from?" I groggily asked Pua whom I discovered was lying on a towel next to me.

"Oh, you're awake. You must have had a big night Jack. You've been asleep for nearly two hours."

"I have?" I said trying to shake myself free of the fog clouding my head.

"I found you here and covered you up so you wouldn't get burned."

"Thank you very much. I stopped to take a break before heading out to the waves and I must have fallen asleep. Thanks for covering me from the sun. That was really nice of you. So, what are you doing here?'

"This is one of my favorite beaches. It's not that it is particularly special or beautiful, but it is peaceful here and rarely crowded. And, you are welcome. I'm not really such an awful person you know."

"Well thanks again. Where are the kids?"

"They're with their grandfather. Every since the two of you went fishing together he spends half of his awake hours on that damn boat. I guess I shouldn't complain though as it does give me time like this. Hey, want to buy a girl a drink after she saved you from getting a horrible sunburn?"

I had to think fast as I was truly grateful; however, there was no way I wanted to bring Pua up to the condominium alone. "Tell you what, if you'll wait right here I'll get rid of this board, grab my wallet, and we'll go across the street for some cold ones at the pizza place."

"I got a better idea. How about we just go up to your place and we have a glass of that cold, wonderful Bonny Doon Big House White that you have up there?"

Thinking fast and still trying to avoid her from gaining entry into the condominium, I said, "Actually, I have an even better idea and I won't take no for an answer. I'm going to get rid of the board, rinse off, change, and then I'm taking you to an early dinner at the *Down Under*." Then, while rising and grabbing the board with both arms I moved away and toward the opening from the beach to the condominium complex saying, "I'll be down in five minutes." Then I hurried on without looking back or giving her time to answer.

Again, the larger than normal and slightly antique surfboard and I fought to squeeze ourselves into the elevator. Then, again, I fought the breezeway against what seemed to be eighty-five mile an hour winds. Finally, I maneuvered the big board through the uncooperative screen door gaining entry to my place where I stowed the board back on the bedroom lanai. Next, I peeled off my suit and ducked into the shower to wash away any residual beach still clinging to me. The shower was so quick that the water didn't even have time to get warm before I had finished. I opened the door to get my towel only to find Pua standing there, holding it for me. She was staring at me and smiling a dangerous smile.

"Pua!"

"Yes?"

"What are you doing here?"

"Handing you your towel obviously," she said playing at being coy again.

"I told you I would be right down," I said taking the towel and starting to dry off while covering myself at the same time.

"Yes, you did Jack, but you left in such a hurry you didn't hear me say I needed to use the potty. Being the gentleman I know you are, I knew you wouldn't mind if I came up to use the toilet."

"Okay. However, would you mind using the other bathroom and leaving this room so that I may get dressed?"

Leaning back, against the bathroom doorframe with her hands behind her back, Pua continued her cat and mouse game, "You have a handsome body, Jack, and there is no need to be shy around me."

By then I had pretty much dried off so I hung the towel across the top of the shower door, strode right past Pua in my birthday suit, and got dressed without bothering to look back.

"Why do all men put their pants on one leg at a time?" Pua asked.

"It's not our style to sit on the edge of the bed and do it all at one once. Putting your pants on one leg at a time is the great male equalizer. No matter what your rank or status we all seem to put our pants on one leg at a time. I'm heading over to the *Down Under*. If you would like to join me for a drink and a bite to eat, that is fine. If not, I'm sure you can find your way out."

"Isn't that being a bit rude Jack?"

"Give the lady a Kewpie Doll! Are you coming with me?"

We did not say much during the five-minute walk to the restaurant.

Although they are a bit sweet, I love drinking an occasional well-blended Pina Colada, and I managed to drink three while listening to Pua. She was telling me how she and Kainoa had grown apart and how much she loathed the confines caused by being part of the Kapuulaa family. I finally said sarcastically, "I see. So, now that Kainoa is dead, you are glad to be free?"

She looked at me for a second with angry eyes before saying, "That's an awful thing to say Jack!"

I looked at her trying to decide if she was really hurt or not, and for the first time ever, it seemed I had struck a nerve with the woman who thus far had seemed so cold and uncaring about the death of her husband.

"I'm truly sorry I said that Pua. You are very right. That was an awful thing for me to say. I was out of line and I apologize."

"Apology accepted. However, you don't understand what it is like for me being part of the Kapuulaa family. I have felt like an ornament every since we got married and I need more. I need to feel more alive and to be a bigger part of the action."

I didn't reply, but my thoughts were not full of sorrow for her life. How many people in the world would like to have what she has? Raising two children, being part of one of the most influential families on the islands, having ranches and farms, restaurants and hotels, a personal helicopter, a yacht, a chauffer, and a husband who cared for her seemed like a good life to me.

From the bar, we moved to a booth where we had our early afternoon dinner. I re-focused our conversation to on *The Onion Express* and Pua's desires to create an environment that would attract business clientele. I had stopped drinking when we left the bar, but Pua continued with glass after glass of red wine, and I noticed her words were becoming thicker. In addition, her eyes had become very glassy.

"Are you going to be able to get home alright?" I interrupted her discussion about having fine Chuihullly made, hand-blown, glass chandeliers throughout the new lobby, the result would be more elegant than that of Las Vegas's most famous hotels.

"I've made arrangements to stay on Maui tonight with a special friend. But I'd rather you were my special friend tonight Jack."

"You never give up Pua. In a way you and I are alike."

"How is it that we are alike Jack? This sounds intriguing. Are there possibilities?" she was beginning to slur her words as she was rolling the wine around in her glass and nearly spilling.

"No Pua. Sorry. There is no possibility for you and me. It's just that you have the same persistence with me as I do with Veronica. For me it will always be Veronica."

"What are you? Are you shum kind of a Boy Scout or sumpin Jack? Here you are, with an attractive and desirable woman, whish you urself have said to me…oops, escuse me Jacque, numeroso times, and who wants to be with you right now, today, with no strings attached. Your little wifey is thousands of miles away from here, and I'm ready please you in whatever way our imaginations and desires choose. And you shit saying no. I'm beginning to think there ish sumping wrong with you, Jack. Most men wouldn't hesitate at a chance like that. So what da ya say? How about we go back to yer place and fuck each other's brains out?" she said getting more and more sloppy with her speech.

I could hardly contain my laughter while listening to her. Finally, I replied to her, "I would say you had better give me the number of your special friend so that I can have you picked up, or maybe I just ought to call Tommy."

"How about if I said either you sleep with me or you're fired?"

"I'd say write me a check," I said crossing my arms over my chest and leaning back in the cushioned booth and laughing aloud.

Pua reached over, putting her hand on my lap, and concentrating on her words, "Don't be silly Jack. I was only teasing. Pleece escuse me while I use the ladies room."

I stood up as she exited the booth and staggered between the other tables on her way to the ladies room. Then I summoned our young server, probably a college student, to bring me the fare.

About ten minutes later, I rose from my seat and watched as Pua made her way back through the dining area. She was still having some difficulty maneuvering around the tables and chairs.

"How about I get a cab for you, Mrs. Kapuulaa?"

"My, but haven't we gotten formal all of a sudden?" she said, lowering herself unsteadily back into her seat.

When she was safely seated, I returned to my seat, too. "I think it is best to keep our relationship formal, but I do want to thank you for keeping me from getting sunburned this afternoon."

"I think that was a mistake." She surprised me with her response.

"Why's that?"

"Maybe if you were all sunburned we'd be in your place applying ointments and that could have been more fun…at least for me!" she smiled. Then she followed with, "Don't shay anything Jack…I already know…you only have eyes for your little wifey. That stuff is cute Jack…but it is also very …B O R I N G! Anyhow, I've called my other friend and he'll be here in about twenty minutes, so what do you say to having one more drink before he arrives?"

"Okay." I said summoning the server again. "I guess we aren't quite done. I'd like another wine for the lady and I'll have a cup of coffee."

"Enough wine already!" she said with a huge sigh. "Bring me a Long Island Iced Tea with a double shot of Myers dark in it would ya honey?"

The server looked at me knowing that Pua had obviously already had too much to drink. I said to the waitress, "It's okay…she has a special friend coming to pick her up." I gave the server another twenty for the drink and coffee adding, "We'll need those pretty quick please."

There was almost no conversation while she guzzled her drink and I sipped at the very hot coffee. When she had finished her drink, I took her to the front of the restaurant where she, although there was a little waver in her body, stood in front of me stating that there was still time for me to change my mind. "You never give up do you?"

"I'm just a girl, standing in front of man, who wants some love."

"I've seen that movie, too. It's not going to work." I replied laughing helplessly.

"There you are again Jack….B O R I N G."

Just then a black convertible Mercedes with the top down pulled up right in front of us.

CHAPTER 47...............DREAMS

"Hello Jude!" I greeted through the open car window, which had just arrived in front of the restaurant. I walked up to the car opening the door for Pua to get in, while in the back of my mind I was thinking that Tommy, obviously, had not yet been successful at obtaining a warrant for his arrest.

"Hello Jack. Get in Pua," he commanded. "If your business here is done, maybe you and I can go have some fun."

I actually felt bad for the man. Having your date so sloppy drunk, before you pick her up, didn't sound like fun to me.

Seated in the car now with the door closed Pua put one hand on the side of her face to hide her lips from Jude and then, talking to me while pointing the index finger of her other hand at Jude quietly said, "Not boring."

Moving my eyes toward Jude, we exchanged a glance, which said a whole lot without using any words. In a brief instant of our eyes meeting and locking on each other, I could see in his eyes that he knew about the shooting the night before, and that his squinted eyes and facial expression were providing me warning. If looks could kill, I would have been dead right then and there.

"Thanks for having dinner with me and sharing your plans Mrs. Kapuulaa," I said, and then patted the top of the door and gestured the way out. Placing one hand on the side of her face toward me and out of view of Jude, Pua gave me the royal finger. It was all I could do not to keep from laughing aloud.

"Until the next time." Jude said and then he peeled out of the restaurant parking lot in his convertible Mercedes like a high school kid showing off his wheels.

I returned to the condominium and called home. "Hey Babe. How's the love of my life?"

"She's busy trying to get ready for spending a month or so on Maui with a good-looking stranger."

"Anyone I know?"

"Umm…I don't think so. But if we run into you over there I'd be happy to introduce him."

"Gee thanks…I can hardly wait. What are our children up to?"

"Your sons and daughters are busily getting ready for the last weeks of school. Marie gets out on Thursday. Warren is the next week and then he is all set-up for a thirty plus hour week with Majid. Ashley has two weeks of finals and then she has a week off before starting summer semester. Warren said he would go up there to help her move to her summer room, which is only going to cost us three hundred and fifty dollars a month. Patrick and Ally, since we won't be home, are going to her folks for a few days and then they are driving down to Cabo San Lucas."

"Excuse me? Did you say Patrick was going to drive down to Cabo? Do her parents know that?"

"Yep. The two of them are staying at a friend's house, which has four bedrooms and a livable trailer parked in the backyard. There are about twelve people going down and Ally's parents, whom I've talked to, are very aware and okay with the whole thing. After all Jack, they are both in their twenties so we really don't get much of a say."

"But how do we feel about this trip?"

"We feel fine about this trip. The kids are paying their own way, they are both in their twenties, they are great, well-adjusted, highly educated kids, and we are happy for them."

"We are?"

"Yes, Jack. Do you remember the first time we went away together? Do you remember how old we were?"

"That was different. Wasn't it?"

"The only difference is that we were even younger and we had to sneak away. At least Patrick and Ally have told us when and where they are going. So yes, we are fine with them going away."

"I'm glad you told me because for a minute there I was having an attack of parental uncertainty. Nevertheless, I think I am going to call Patrick just the same and say the fatherly things I need to say. It's not that he isn't a smart kid, whom we know already has a great deal of common sense, it's more for my own good and my own needs than his."

"That's why you are such a great father, Jack."

We talked for another thirty minutes and during that time everything that had happened over the weekend had slipped to some far away place within my mind and I was feeling fairly normal after a non-normal weekend.

Later, as I lay in bed waiting to be overtaken by some much-needed sleep, my mind replayed the weekend starting at the cockfights, the car chase, the shootout, the figure of the dead man laying facedown in the street, another encounter with the ever persistent Pua Kapuulaa and then the short exchange with Jude Makala. Of all that I was least concerned with Pua; although I'm sure Veronica might have a few thoughts of her own about Pua's persistence to get me into the sack. In addition, I thought about Tommy and Hai Ho, and I wondered whether they had successfully obtained warrants for Blaze and Jude's arrest. Moreover, I imagined Hai and Tommy barging in on Pua and Jude during an intimate moment, flashing their badges and handcuffing a bare ass naked Jude Makala and marching him outside and into the back seat of a waiting squad car, showing the world that he wasn't such a big shot after all.

Trying to get my mind off all of that negative stuff, I forced my thoughts toward Veronica and what she might be doing. When I was finally overtaken by a much-needed sound sleep, my dreams turned to Marie flying down the middle of the soccer field. She was running full bore, with her ponytail dancing and bouncing as if following some imaginary orchestrated movement, all the while dribbling the black and white soccer ball around and through her opponents, to where the difficult shot she had to make was executed perfectly. It was a good dream.

CHAPTER 48...........
THE BASTARD

I arrived at the office trailer feeling well-rested, refreshed from my morning shower, and about two hours late.

"Oversleep?" Luanne asked as I came through the door and headed to the coffee pot.

"Good coffee, but it's a little strong," I said pretending to chew it.

"It wasn't all that strong when I made it two hours ago!" Luanne declared.

I dumped what was left of my coffee in the pot and then made a fresh pot while Luanne told me about her fun-filled weekend.

"How was your weekend?"

"Mine wasn't quite as fun as yours but I did manage to stay busy. What's the status of the kitchen equipment? Is the supplier going to be on time?"

"Everything is looking good Jack, except for the convection oven. It's coming all the way from Baltimore, which means it will be here about two days after the rest of the equipment arrives."

"I can live with that. Good job Luanne. Thank you very much."

We chatted about the status of invoices needing payment, and accounting balances. When the fresh pot of brewing coffee was complete, I took my cup into the office where I fired up my computer while listening to several messages callers left on my business phone.

The first two messages were scheduling questions from sub-contractors, and the third was from Tommy. "Jack, this is Tom. I just wanted to let you know that we have warrants for both Blake and Jude Makala, and that I will be working with Hai and some other locals to pick them up this morning. When we are done, I'll come by the construction site and let you know how it went. By the way, and I am not sure if it's the drugs they are giving him in the hospital or what, but Lou has been telling us everything he knows. If we get any kind of corroboration to what he is telling us, a lot of folks are going to jail. At the very least the crooks that are controlling the unions are history."

The last message was from Kappy. "Jack, Tommy just told me what happened Saturday night and I know that you are physically fine, but I wanted to let you know how grateful my family and I are for all that you have done for us. Cleaning up the union is going to make life better for thousands of people around here who depend on it for a living. You and Tommy have probably saved a lot of pensions. Brudah, when this is over, you and Tommy and your families are going to be the guests of honor fo' the biggest luau these islands have ever seen!" I smiled at Kappy's message knowing that this whole thing had been planned a long time ago. My only regret was that Kainoa, who had a key main role in ridding the union system of its crooks, did not get to see the result.

After listening to the messages the phone rang, "What in the hell did you do Jack?"

"Excuse me Pua, but I don't know what in the hell you are talking about," I said lying through my teeth.

"I was with Jude last night when he got a call from someone who said he was about to be arrested. Jude said you framed him, and then he packed some clothes and left. What is going on Jack?"

"I have no idea what you are talking about Pua," I lied. All I know is that a couple of guys tried to kill Tommy and me around 1:00 AM on Sunday. Thanks to quick action by Tommy, we survived. One of the attackers didn't, and the police have the other."

"And you didn't tell me any of this yesterday?"

"That was why I fell asleep on the beach. I had been up all night giving my statement to the police. That's all I know Pua."

"You're lying to me Jack. You are not telling me something. How are you involved with Jude? Why have you framed him? He was helping me, now what am I to do?"

"Maybe you should ask Kappy for help?" I replied as more of a question.

"The Kapuulaa family? Never Jack! That's who Jude was helping me to get away from."

"Then I can't help you, Pua. I think the Kapuulaa's are fine people, and I think you are wrong for feeling the way you do, but then I'm just an employee."

"I want you off the job today Jack!"

"That's fine Pua. I'll leave as soon as you cash me out of my contract," I said as nonchalantly as I could.

"Fine. You'll have your money today and I want you out of the condominium by the end of the week!"

"No problem Pua. It's your hotel, your restaurant, your condominium and your money. I'm easy…I always have been. I'll look forward to seeing you in a little while then." I said as pleasantly as possible and then I hung up.

"Luanne?"

"Yes sir?"

"This may be my last day on the job. Pua says she is coming over to pay off my contract, and she wants me out of the condominium at the end of the week. Would you mind contacting the place where we are staying with the soccer team and see if it would be possible to check in early?"

"Why would Pua want to do that? She would be crazy to change out the project leader at this point. Besides, if you are on budget and on time why would she fire you?"

"She's the owner Luanne. She gets to do whatever she wants. It has been great working you, Luanne. I would recommend you to anyone. You are very good at your job and I will miss you. I'd really appreciate it if you would call that hotel and see if we can check in a week early."

I left Luanne and the trailer and took a walk through the construction site. I felt good with what we, the whole team, had been able to accomplish despite the delays and problems we had encountered. I walked through the hotel lobby and went up the wide and expansive curving staircase that led to the second floor. From there I made my way up the stairways that led to the roof, where I got a bird's eye view of the rest of the project. It was also a good vantage point for viewing much of the city of Lahaina. I could see the harbor, the little island of Molokini, the island of Lanai on the left and the ocean waters beyond. It is a spectacular view and I was wondering if I would ever get to see it again.

When I got back to the trailer, Luanne had my new reservations all set, and there was another message on my machine. "Jack, it's Tom, and I'm here with Hai. We took Blaze into custody without a struggle, but we missed Jude Makala. We think he has flown the coop so to speak. We believe he flew into Los Angeles earlier this morning and that he is likely heading for Mexico. The Los Angeles branch of the FBI is trying to catch him before he crosses the border. We'll see what information we can get out of Blaze, and, of course, the paperwork we must do for all of this is getting knee deep. I'll call you again later."

There was telltale excitement in Tommy's voice and I was glad for him. His investigation and undercover job had gone well and there was good reason to be proud.

I picked up my ringing phone to hear, "My daughter-in-law is on her way over there to fire you, Jack, and I couldn't stop her." Kappy declared over the phone. His grief was obvious in his tone.

"I know Kappy and it's okay. I would like to have been around and seen the job through all the way to the re-opening ceremony, but apparently that won't be the case."

"I heard they got that guy, Blaze, but that Jude got away. He was the one I wanted them to get to the most. Anyhow, my daughter-in-law is a major disappointment Jack. I am sorry there is nothing I can do to keep her from sacking you. However, you are welcome to come over here and stay with me. You will always be welcome here and if you need any money, cars or anything what is mine is yours. I mean that Jack. You are one of our people now and we take care of each other in Hawaii."

I thanked Kappy for his generosity and explained that Luanne had already made arrangements. I told him where I would be, about Marie's upcoming soccer tournament and that I'd likely be coming back as a witness if there were to be any criminal proceedings related to the shooting.

With Kappy, confirming Pua was on her way; I gathered up my personal belongings and loaded them into the Mustang. I said goodbye to Luanne and then returned to the trailer to wait for Pua's arrival, which did not take long.

When she arrived, I met her outside, and the exchange was short.

"It didn't have to be like this Jack."

"Yes it did."

"We could have had a beautiful relationship on and off the job."

"No we couldn't"

"You're a bastard Jack!"

"Probably." I verified the check was for the right amount and said, "See ya." I made my way to the Mustang, giving her my backside. As I drove away, she just stood in front of the construction trailer watching me leave.

CHAPTER 49........
COLD SHOWER

Driving back to the condominium my thoughts turned to Kainoa and I wondered who was really behind the helicopter blowing up in mid air. Could it have been Jude, or Blaze or even Lou? Did Pua play a part in it? Would it ever be known who had killed Kainoa and his pilot, or who burned down the *Onion Express* killing two of its employees? Maybe it would come out in the arrests.

I picked up my cell and called Tom, "Dis is Jack and I wanted to let you and di utter Lieutenant know dat I am da Big Kahuna no mo', brudah." I was trying to mimic the phony accent he had given me while he had playing chauffer, but it was a little weak in comparison.

"Nice try Jack, but it just doesn't sound the same coming out of a mainlander. So what is this all about?"

I explained to him what had happened with Pua and where I'd be if he needed to get in touch with me.

"Sorry Jack. These islands owe you a great deal, and for the moment, all I can do is say thanks. At least you got fully compensated."

"Hey. I made some new friends, got to snorkel in your beautiful reefs, got closer than I wanted with one of your famous sharks, played with some amazing dolphins, surfed with world champions, and totally enjoyed your wonderful warm beaches. So, it hasn't been all that bad."

"How about you getting shot at and assaulted? Did you enjoy that too?"

"Hey! I'm trying to end on a positive note here."

"I just don't want you to get too relaxed. Jude Makala and several of his cronies are still out there, and they are probably not real happy with either of us. Keep an eye out Jack."

"You're as bad as Pua when it comes to dampening a guy's spirits. Thanks pal!"

"You really do need to keep an eye out Jack. These are dangerous people. Maybe I should get Hai to assign someone to you as long as you are going to be here."

"Well, he'd have to pin his badge on his swimming trunks, and he'd need to carry his gun in a plastic bag because I plan to spend the next several days playing in your ocean waters. So thanks anyhow, but I don't need a sitter. Meanwhile I'll keep both of my eyes wide open."

"Okay. Hai and I will be around to check up on you and to keep you posted on Makala and anything or anyone else you may need to know about. But, again, I can't thank you enough."

"Likewise! If you hadn't been there, I'd likely be lying full of holes along side one of your country roads. You take care to buddy. Your cover is blown, and they now know who and what you are. I'm sure they are equally unhappy with both of us."

Back at the condominium, the first thing I did was remove the remaining bug. The second thing I did was to make a call home.

"We're unemployed again," I said to Veronica when she answered her cell phone. It was 10:00 AM and I had caught her at Nob Hill, where she was stocking up on food supplies for Warren. She wanted to make sure that he would have something to eat while Veronica and Marie were in the islands with me. "Let me guess. Clam chowder (Warren goes nuts over the stuff, often eating it for breakfast...Yuk!), pop-tarts, fish sticks, and flavored almonds?"

"You do know your son. However, I am also getting him some frozen dinners. I feel better with the frozen dinners because if he eats them he will at least get a few veggies and some protein. Kathy's parents are going to have him over for some dinners too."

"I'm sure Warren will be alright. He has a head full of common sense. Can't wait for you to get here babe...I miss you tons."

"Me too and Marie is all packed and ready to go."

"Just knowing that you're coming soon is giving me those warm and fuzzy feelings!" I said laughing.

"Try taking a cold shower Jack," she said laughing.

CHAPTER 50.........ONE LEFT

After changing my clothes, I walked down to Mary's Fish Market. Mary herself pointed me toward some fresh mahi-mahi, which I purchased for my dinner that night. The plan was to barbecue it on one of the grills next to the pool at the condominium. Next, I hit the little farmer's market that utilizes part of a local business's parking lot twice a week, where I bought some locally grown corn on the cob, pineapple, mango, and freshly made whole grain dark bread. One of the vendors was offering free samples of locally made jams, and after trying a few of them I bought two. Finished with my shopping, I started the three-quarter mile trek back to the condominium, laden with the purchased groceries. I enjoyed the walk, but I was definitely ready to shed the load of groceries by the time I got back.

Although I was feeling a bit lonely, the evening was relaxing. I barbecued both the fish and the corn, all the while chatting with a vacationing family from Texas, who had rented one of the two-bedroom condominiums that are available as a vacation rental. Later, I read a new Dick Francis mystery while sitting on the lanai and taking in a gorgeous banded, orange and red sky that made for a spectacular evening sunset. Truthfully, from that vantage point, all of the sunsets are spectacular.

The next morning Luanne called and asked to see me regarding some unfinished business at the construction site. Apparently there was need for some final signatures on things I had ordered. "I'm not sure Pua really wants me at the site, so how about we meet at the Lahaina Market Place on Front Street? I'll buy you some breakfast."

"Thanks. That would be great Jack. See you in one hour?"

"You got it Luanne. Besides, I already miss your smiling face."

I brushed my teeth, showered, and did not bother to shave for a change. I put some coffee in my to-go mug and headed out the door. When I got to the Mustang, the seats were slightly damp from having left the top down. So, using a beach towel I had left in the backseat, I dried off the driver's seat, climbed in, put the key in the ignition, and suddenly stopped before turning the key. My internal warning system, consisting of the hairs rising on the back of my neck, stood straight up, and in addition, I noticed that the hood did not look quite right. Suddenly I was worried that leaving the top down might have resulted in someone stealing the car battery. I go out of the car needing to secure the hood before heading out onto the busy morning traffic on Honoapiilani Highway. When I raised the hood I looked to see if the battery was still there and was grateful to see it in its usual place, however, while I started closing the hood, I noticed something unusual. A new, orange colored wire was attached to the positive battery terminal and that did not seem right. So, propping the hood back open, I took the orange wire between my fingertips and followed it around the engine block to where it disappeared below. Not caring about dirtying my clothes, I got down on my back to see where the orange wire went next. I was suddenly damn glad that I hadn't started the engine. If I had, someone would be picking up pieces of Jack Bryce from all over the parking lot.

I quickly got out from under the car and backed away leaving the keys dangling from the ignition just as I had left them. "Lieutenant Hai Ho please, this is Jack Bryce," I said into my cell phone.

"I'd think you were sleeping longer now that you're not working at *The Onion Express.* If you're calling about whether or not we've gotten Makala, the answer is no."

"That's what I figured when I found a bomb attached to my car a few minutes ago."

"Jesus, Jack! You're kidding aren't you?"

"Nope. No kidding around this time Hai. Someone wired up my Mustang, but botched the job by not getting the hood all of the way closed…luckily for me. Can you send someone to remove this thing? And maybe you could call Tommy and let him know what I found in case someone paid him a visit too?"

"Right. Just hang tight and we'll be right there."

Next, I called Luanne, "Sorry but I'm going to need to reschedule kiddo. I've got some car trouble this morning."

"Are you okay Jack?"

"Perfectly fine but I'm going to have to pick up another rental so I'll call you later. Maybe we can meet for lunch."

"I can get another rental for you Jack. Why don't I have the rental company pick up your car from the condo parking lot and bring you a new one at the same time?"

"That's okay, Luanne. I've already got it all under control from this end. I'll call you in an hour or so to set up a new time to meet."

"I'd better call them for you, Jack. The project still owes you a car for the rest of the week and you might as well let Pua pay for it, seeing how she screwed you over."

"Could you please not say screw in the same breath when you say her name? It freaks me out!" I said laughingly.

"I'll get you another Mustang and I'll call you right back."

"No Luanne. I really just want to rent my own car now. I'm going to have it for the next couple of weeks, and I don't want anymore to do with Pua. But thank you very much for the kind offer."

"Are you going to use the same car rental company and get another convertible?"

"Probably. Veronica and Marie will be here in a few days and I think having a convertible in this beautiful weather is a lot of fun." As I was finishing my conversation with Luanne, my cell phone began to signal that I had another call. I said a quick "call you later" and switched over to the other caller.

"It's Hai, Jack, and I have some bad news."

"Uh oh. Can't get the bomb squad out here for awhile?"

"No Jack. We were too late in calling Tommy." Hai stated straight out.

I digested what Hai had just said, leaving the airway silent for thirty seconds or so, "Too late?"

"Tommy's car blew-up this morning, with him in it. He's dead Jack."

I sat down, hard, on a wheel stop in an empty parking place and lamented on the news. Just yesterday afternoon we advised each other of the need to keep our eyes open. I had been lucky. My friend Tommy had not. The sense of loss was huge, and the impact was being felt from the pit of my stomach to the welling in my eyes."

"Are you there Jack?" Hai asked with a mix of concern and sorrow in his voice. "Just sit tight Jack. I've got people about three minutes away from you. I'm on my way to Tommy's to meet some other FBI agents and to assist in the investigation."

"I'd like to know if the bombs used to kill Tommy and Kainoa match each other and the one currently strapped under my car. My guess is they will."

"Well, when my boys get there they are going to disarm that bomb, and impound your car as evidence. Having your car and that bomb should get us some new leads. I'll talk to you later brudah, but for now you stay low!"

"I've got just a little unfinished business with Luanne and then I'll be back here. I will be okay. Your boys are here now…I gotta go."

It took about five minutes for the Bomb Squad to secure the device and remove it for safe handling. It then took about an hour to give my statement and finally see the Mustang towed away. When that was all done, I wandered slowly out to the beach behind the condominium, where I sat down on the warm sand. There, I watched mostly vacationing families splashing and playing in the warm Pacific waters, and I was saddened that my friends, Tommy and Kainoa, could never again play with their children. In addition, I contemplated my own plight, which did not feel very secure. Of the three people most involved with removing the criminal element from their positions of power only one of us was left. I felt like a walking target, and I decided sitting around and waiting for their next attempt on my life was not what I wanted to do.

CHAPTER 51......
FIRST AND TEN!

I felt I needed to change tactics. Rather than wait around for them to try again, I figured I'd go on the offensive. With Veronica and Marie due in a few days, I wanted to end this.

I arranged my own rental, which was a van. My reasons for the van were several. First, it was non-flashy so as not to attract attention. Second, with Veronica, Marie, and the soccer gear we would need more room. Finally, the likelihood that we would be driving other players (the girls like to ride in each other's cars when going to games or lunch and things) was strong and the extra four seats would be handy.

I called Luanne to arrange the meeting she requested, but there was no answer at the office or on her cell phone.

I called Kappy who had now heard about Tommy and who was worried about me being next. I told him I was plenty worried about me for both of us I asked Kappy to give me the names of all of the workers at *The Onion Express*. I wanted the names of all of the employees who worked there, or had worked there, up until a year before the fire. He said it might take a few hours and we arranged that he would have the information faxed to me at the office of the condominium. It is from the office that landscaping, rentals, and housekeeping are arranged.

With Luanne still not answering, I put Lahaina and the car rental agency behind me and headed back to Kahana to wait for Kappy's fax to arrive. When I got there, to be on the safe side, I parked at a neighboring complex and went into my complex from the beach entrance. It was a little further walk, but I felt it was a lot safer. Besides, I did not want to get in the habit of explaining why the police were impounding my rental cars.

True to form, Kappy delivered, via fax, the requested information, which I took upstairs to digest. As I reviewed the list, I identified and prioritized employees, or their relatives, who I wanted to contact.

It was while I was doing this that there was a knock on the door. I stuffed the faxed papers inside the morning newspaper and quietly approached the front door using the peephole to see who was there. It was Hai. "Let me unlock this Hai," I yelled through the door finally opening it so he could come inside.

"Good job of keeping locked up Jack. You keep doing that okay."

"Sure. How is Tommy's family doing?"

"The FBI is there, taking care of his wife and family. It's a terrible thing that happened to him Jack."

"I don't need the details Hai."

"Good. The FBI is going to want to talk with you very soon. They know I am here now and they are okay with that. They just want you to lay low and stay safe."

"Absolutely Hai. I'm going to stay as safe as I can."

"Why don't I believe that?"

"What's not to believe? Here I am. I'm inside the condominium on the tenth floor. Plenty of groceries and just waiting for you guys to give the all clear."

"I thought you had to meet with Luanne at the construction site."

"I was going to meet her downtown, but I don't have a car now, and she is not answering her phones."

"If you need to go anywhere I'll have an officer give you a ride okay?"

"Sure. As I said, I have plenty of food, great views, and satellite TV. What more could I guy want?"

"I'm not buying any of this bull brudah, but I can't argue with you because it's your life. I know you got something planned...you just be careful."

"I will."

"What?"

"I will be right here keeping safe. What about Makala? Do you even know where he is?"

"The FBI thinks the Los Angeles thing was a decoy. No they think he is still here."

"Did Tommy know that?"

"No. The Bureau just got the info from their Los Angeles office, after Tommy died. Had he known he might have been more careful," Hai said shaking his head from side to side.

As soon as Hai left, I pulled out the fax sheet and my map, and plotted courses to the homes of the two men who died in the fire, Mark Malone and John Chu. For the first time since Kainoa's death, I felt like I had clear direction. I felt like I had the ball and that it was first and ten from the twenty-yard line.

CHAPTER 52........
MALONE AND CHU

It was four o'clock when I arrived at the Malone family home and knocked on the door. "Hello my name is Jack Bryce and I'm..............."

"You're the man who was hired to rebuild *The Onion Express*. I know who you are, won't you please come inside."

I gladly accepted the invitation as it was a very warm afternoon and I welcomed the sanctity of the air-conditioned home. "I was hoping to ask a few questions about your husband's relationship with some of his employees. That is, if you don't mind?"

"What exactly did you want to know Mr. Bryce?" she said seating me in her living room.

"I want to know why your husband was there with John Chu. Did your husband ever talk about the employees?"

"He talked about them all of the time."

"Did he ever talk about John Chu?"

"Oh yes. John started out as a kitchen helper and Mark helped him to become one of the restaurant's top cooks."

"Did your husband ever mention any personnel problems about Mr. Chu?"

"It was no secret that John liked to party. He was a handsome and likeable young man. Quite a ladies man, if you know what I mean."

"Did that cause problems at the restaurant?"

"Well, Mark thought John ....uh maybe I shouldn't say anything."

"Please Mrs. Malone; there really is a need to know."

"Why are you asking these questions?"

"Because this morning another person was murdered and someone also tried to kill me. I want to find out who is behind the fire and deaths at the restaurant, Kainoa Kapuulaa's helicopter explosion, and this morning's murder of Tommy Johnson."

"Tommy was murdered this morning?' I heard about a car bombing but I didn't know it was Tommy!"

"Yes. Tommy and I were working together and this morning someone planted bombs in both of our cars. I got lucky and found the bomb in my car before it detonated. Tommy wasn't so lucky."

"This whole thing is such a mess."

"What do you know about Tommy, and what was going on and what about John Chu?"

"I know that Tommy was a personal friend of Kainoa and that the three of them, had late night meetings about union problems."

"Union problems?"

"Yes, the union leaders were strong arming the employees of *The Onion Express* to join. Mark and Kainoa had no problem with the union itself, but they were concerned some of the leaders were corrupt and stealing from the union."

"What about John Chu?'

"I don't want to cause any trouble for the Kapuulaa family. They have been very good to my children and me."

"Let me guess. Was there something going on between John and Pua Kapuulaa?"

"How did you know that?'

"Just a lucky guess," I responded.

"Kainoa and Mark were very close and Mark wanted to stop John's relationship with Pua before it got out of hand and destroyed the Kapuulaa family."

"Do you think that is what was going on during the night of the fire?"

"Possibly. I know that Mark was looking for the right opportunity to bring it up with John."

"Is there anything else about John Chu, or any of the other employees that could help me?"

"Mark thought that maybe a couple of the employees were doing drugs. He had found evidence of cocaine use behind some supplies in the storeroom of the restaurant. There was a small mirror, a razor blade, and some shortened straws. Mark was very upset and he seemed to think maybe there were some waiters and possibly John involved."

I thanked Mark Malone's widow for the information provided, offered her my condolences for her loss, and expressed my hope to put the responsible parties in jail for a long time.

My next stop was John Chu's home, which was actually his parent's place. I introduced myself to John's father who pulled into the home's driveway just as I was arriving at the curbside. I introduced myself, and like with Mark Malone's wife, John's father already knew who I was.

"John was a good kid until he got involved with the wrong people," his father explained with sour disappointment in his tone.

"Can you explain who the wrong people are?" I asked him.

"People with too much money to burn. You know, fast cars, loose women, lots of parties and drugs."

"John was doing drugs?"

"His mother found drug paraphernalia in his dresser drawer. When we confronted him, he got angry and said he was moving out and going to live with friends who did not criticize his life style. We tried to reason with him that no good could come from what he was doing, but he wouldn't listen. You know how kids are….they know it all." John's father said with disgust.

"Do you know the names of any of these people who John was hanging out with?"

"There were a few phone messages from a man named Blaze. They were mainly invitations to parties."

"Did you say Blaze?"

"Yes. We never got to meet him, but besides the phone messages, John used to talk about him as being powerful and of him giving John opportunities to become an important person."

"What about the drugs?" Do you know who John got them from?"

"His mother and I assumed it was this Blaze person. The drugs, parties and loose women all started about the time we began to hear this Blaze person's name."

I thanked John's father for being frank about his son's relationship, and offered that it sounded like he was good kid who just got caught up with the wrong crowd, which sometimes happens to the best of families.

The whole picture started coming together. I was advancing the ball. I now had a better understanding of what had been going on within the restaurant politics, and I could see how Jude Makala was getting his foot into the Kapuulaa family business. I assumed that Makala was able to get to Pua through John Chu. They probably met at one of Blaze's parties. The bored homemaker with the young stud and the illegal drugs likely provided the perfect venue for Makala to start the relationship with Kainoa's wife. But why burn down the restaurant killing John Chu and Mark Malone? Then it came to me that maybe John Chu had become a liability. Maybe John, losing Pua to Makala, had become a problem, and maybe it was best to get him out of the picture. On the other hand, perhaps a conspiracy was born out of the Jude and Pua relationship to get Pua in charge of Kainoa's family holdings. I had motives now for the fire and deaths of John Chu and Kainoa. Mark Malone was just probably just in the wrong place at the wrong time.

CHAPTER 53...
JUST A DIRTY OLD MAN!

I took my newfound information back home. Again, I parked the van at a different complex than the one where I was staying, and made my way into the condominium from a different direction utilizing the beach. I was avoiding establishing any repetitive routines or habits that could give an enemy an advantage. When I had left the condominium, I had taped a small, nearly invisible thread from the door jam to the door giving me an indication as to whether or not anyone had entered while I was away. The thread was still intact.

"How are you doing Jim?" I said to my still on-duty friend, Lieutenant Jim Alverez, in California.

"Same old stuff Jack. How about yourself? What's new there?"

I spent the next ten minutes updating my police friend and then asked, "What do you think my next step ought to be?"

"Officially I would have to say let the FBI and local police do their job and you try to stay out of their way. Unofficially I would say you had better get this Makala person before he gets you. You got a gun over there?"

"That's what I figured too. However, where do I go to find out where this guy is? And, no, I do not have a gun. Wish I did though."

"It's too bad about Tommy. He might have been able to give you one of his spares. You could ask your dwarf friend but I thing he plays by the book."

"My dwarf friend? His name is Hai Ho. You met him and we had beers together remember?"

"I remember the beers and I remember his name has something to do with Snow White and the seven dwarfs."

"Hi Ho, Hi Ho is the name of a song in the movie you idiot." I teased my good friend.

"Yeah, yeah. How about the father of your friend killed in the helicopter explosion? Maybe he could get you some protection."

"I like that idea. I knew there was a reason for calling you." I teased again.

"Well if he can't or won't do it, you let me know and I'll fly over there and bring you a gun. I don't like the idea of my best friend being in this situation unarmed."

"Thanks. I appreciate the sentiment and I would do the same for you. However, let me try Kainoa's father first. How's the marriage?"

"It's great Jack. What I like best is that we like the same things and we go places together. Last weekend we saw Huey Lewis and the News at the Mountain Winery in Saratoga. Man he puts on a great show. Maybe next time he comes there the four of us could go together. It's a great place to see a concert."

"I'd like that. Let's plan on it. Veronica and I both like their music."

"Any thoughts on how I might dig out this Makala character?"

"You either need to find someone who knows where he is and is willing to tell you, or you got to draw him out in the open with bait."

"I'm guessing I would need to be the live bait."

"How about using the girl? If they have a relationship maybe you could just tail her."

"Not a bad idea buddy. I got a new rental car so it wouldn't be too easy for her to spot me."

"Get yourself some protection before you start digging up the hornet's nest."

"Will do, and give that lady of yours a hug for me. Give her a long, slow, close hug and tell her it's from me." I taunted my friend.

"Get off the phone already will you? You're nothing but a dirty old man!"

CHAPTER 54......
SPECIAL BREED OF MAN

I contacted Kappy and we arranged to meet in the water behind the condominium complex where I surf. He would be alone in his fishing skiff, which would look normal to anyone observing. I'd be just beyond the reef on the surfboard borrowed from Kimo…which is not an uncommon practice for me. The meeting would be early in the morning the next day.

Later that evening two FBI agents came to the condominium, and after carefully checking IDs, I let them inside.

They were all set to start questioning me about working with Tommy, but I beat them to the punch, "How's Tommy's family doing?"

"They are as well as can be expected considering the circumstances," the senior ranking agent replied.

"Have you caught up with Mr. Makala yet?" I pressed.

"Not yet, but we think he is here on this island."

"What about the Los Angeles thing?"

"We now think that was a decoy to make us think he headed for Mexico. What we think now is that he stayed here figuring to remove you and Tommy. He did not want either of you testifying against him. We think he is trying to eliminate both you and Mrs. Pua Kapuulaa now."

The later bit of information caught me off guard and I tried to make sense of it. "Well I'm staying low right here," I replied telling them what they wanted to hear.

For the next forty-five minutes, we went over Tommy and me attending the cockfights, the shooting, and the car bombs, which they concluded, came out of the same lot of material used on Kainoa's helicopter. Before leaving, they gave me their contact information as well as reminding me to call 911 in the event of any kind of emergency and that there would always be a Maui sheriff's deputy within one minute of my location. I offered my gratitude for the nearby protection as I escorted them out the door and down the breezeway.

The next morning, just after the sun cleared the eastern horizon and began to climb the sky, I entered the water and made my way to where I would meet Kappy. When I got there, he was already on the scene and actually setting his nets around the shallow reefs. "Best times of the day to do this are sunrise and sunset," Kappy offered as opening dialogue when I paddled along side him and opposite of the side of where he was setting his net.

"Good morning Kappy. Thanks for doing this."

"It's me thanking you son. You are the one who is doing all the work. Moreover, you are the one who is in danger. I am so sorry for Tommy's family. He was a good and honest man. He was part of our family. I will miss him as I miss my son. Here is the gun you wanted. It is a nine millimeter with a twenty shot clip plus one in the chamber. Here are two extra boxes of shells for you too," he said giving me a small backpack. "Everything is double wrapped in sealed plastic freezer bags so if your back-pack gets wet nothing will happen to the gun or the boxes of ammunition."

"Thanks Kappy. If these guys show up on my door step at least I'll have a chance to fight back."

"We betta go now in case there is someone watching us. You tell me if there is anything else you need okay. I can get you anything you want. Just say the word."

"Thanks again Kappy. Before you go, can you tell me where Pua is?"

"She's at the house on Molokai with the kids. The FBI came by and they told her she might be a target of her boyfriend. She said that was not possible. When I heard her response I smiled a little bit thinking that she deserves it. But I don't want my grand kids mixed up in all of dis crap."

We said our goodbyes and I moved away from the little skiff watching with awe as he set his net like an artist filled with purposeful motion and gracious ease. The old man was a special breed, one that would be hard to find again or to replace.

With the backpack strapped around my shoulders and my chest, I actually caught and rode a few small waves taking my time before heading into the sandy shoreline near the condominium. For some reason, today's ocean waters were filled with an extra amount of kelp and seaweed that seemed to be lurking and waiting to snarl itself around the legs and feet of any beachcombers who dared wade into the tumultuous stuff.

When I returned to the condominium, I unpacked the backpack finding what seemed to be a barely used Browning nine-millimeter automatic pistol, two clips, and two boxes of ammo with fifty rounds in each. Additionally there was an envelope with a note and a bundle of twenty-dollar bills. The note read:

Jack,

No amount of money can ever thank you for what you have done and for what you are doing. The sacrifices made by my son, Tommy, and the others, though deeply saddening, are not wasted. Please use this money as you see fit, whether it be a quest to head for your home on the mainland, or be it used to help destroy those who would stoop to any level for personal gain.

Kappy

A quick count resulted in finding that the old man had bundled ten thousand dollars in twenty-dollar bills. I smiled at what he must have been thinking when he wrote the note and bundled the money. He knew damn well I would use the money to find Jude Makala.

CHAPTER 55........
FINDING JUDE

As I had hoped, Lieutenant Hai Ho was able to provide me with Cigar Face's real name and address from the license numbers he got at the first cockfight that Tommy and I had attended. Hai was very heavy reluctant to give up the information and it took some persuasion before he shared it with me. I had to beg, plead and promise to share any information I got with him before sharing with the FBI. I wasn't sure that was legal, seeing that the whole thing is a Federal Case, but what were they going to do....fire me?

Cigar Face's real name was George Lee, and he conveniently lived in the new housing tract that Jude Makala and his cohorts were building on the other side of the island near Kailua. I left the condominium complex via the beach, watching to see if I had been followed and when I got to the van, I checked it out carefully before turning the key. And no matter how carefully I looked, I cringed each time I started the engine. I would probably cringe for a long time to come.

Cigar Face's house (for me Cigar Face seemed to fit better than George did) was still being landscaped, and where there should have been curtains and drapes I instead saw bed sheets haphazardly hung.

I drove by parking down the street and then walked back to his house. For all I knew Jude could be hiding out inside Cigar face's house.

With the Browning tucked into my pants and under my Hawaiian shirt, I walked up to the front porch and rang the bell. Cigar Face opened the door and I burst inside grabbing him by the shirt at both shoulders. "Hey, what's this? You don't have right to bust in on me in my home."

"You're absolutely right George. And once I leave I think you should call the cops and tell them that one of the gamblers from the cockfights barged in on you. In the meantime who else is here?"

"No one. I live alone."

"Let's take look," I said pushing him in and out of every room and even the garage before we returned to the livingroom where I pushed him down on the couch.

"I know who you are," he said looking me over. "You're the guy they are trying to off. You should be dead by now."

"Thanks for the kind thoughts. What's your relationship with Blaze and Jude Makala?"

"I don't have to tell you anything. You're not a cop!"

"You're right. And I don't have to protect you like a cop does."

"You don't scare me, and you're going to get what's coming to you for shooting Lou and killing the kid. You don't know who you're messing with here."

"Is that a phrase they teach all you guys? Can't you get just a little more original? Here's what I'm going to do. I'm going to visit Blaze down at the county jail, and I am going to tell him how cooperative you've been. In fact, I'm going to tell him how you told the cops where to find him. He should appreciate that."

"That ain't fair man. I just mark the bets and handle the money. I'm not into any of this heavy stuff."

"Well I just brought you into it. I want to know where I can find Jude." I said staring at the little man until wavered.

"I don't know where he is. It's not like we're friends. I deal more with Blaze."

"That's good to know. So where would Blaze say I can find Makala."

"That's Mister Makala to you!"

"Okay, I still want to know where I can find him.

"He'd kill me if I told you where to find him."

"Look. It's likely he's going to kill you anyhow. He's killing everybody who can testify against him. Tell you what. Let's say I can get you some money to escape these islands. Maybe enough money so you find a new life. Here's why you should take me up on this one time offer. You are going to jail. The County has all the evidence they need to lock you up for your part in the cockfights which are highly illegal in this state. They know who you are, what you do, and where you live. Once you're in the slammer it's going to be easy for Jude or Blaze to eliminate you from being a key witness."

"But I won't testify against them. I can keep my mouth shut."

"Maybe you can keep your mouth shut. However, all they are going to know, and I'm personally going to see to this, is that you told the cops where to find them in exchange for a lighter sentence."

"That's not fair man."

"You've already said that. What's it going to be?"

"How do I know you'll keep your word?"

I pulled the stack of twenties Kappy had provided me and let him see the whole pile. I almost laughed at the expression on his face.

"You'd give me all that money and I could leave right now?"

"I could!"

"Jude Makala's on Molokai. He's hiding out with the Kapuulaa widow. They figured that would be the last place for anyone to look."

I was startled by the information. It meant that Kappy and his grandchildren were in danger. They were in the kind of danger needing attention right now.

"Okay. You had better not be lying."

"I'm not lying man. Now give me the money and let me get out of here," Cigar Face pleaded to me.

"You'll get the money as soon as I can prove what you said is true."

"You said you'd give it to me."

"I said I could give it to you. But I've decided you get nothing until I get Makala."

"That's not fair!"

"And strapping razor blades on chicken's legs and taunting them to the point where they kill each other for your profit is fair? I don't think so. Lay down on the floor."

"You going to tie me up?"

"I can't leave you hanging around to warn Jude can I? Now get down on the floor." Cigar Face was reluctant but he lay down and I trussed him up with an extension chord so that I tied his hands and feet together behind his back, and then I gagged him. Next, I picked up the phone and called Hai.

"I got George Lee to tell me where Jude is hiding out. He's all tied up and ready for pick up at his house." I said to Hai. "I promised you I'd tell you first, and I've kept my promise."

"Okay then where is Jude?"

"How about you send someone over here to pick up Cigar Face and then meet me at the pier?"

"Where's Makala?"

"You can go with me to get him but I'm not saying until we get there."

"We'll need some back-up Jack."

"The deal is that it is just you and me. If you want to meet me on the pier, if not, I'll do this on my own."

"I'll be there."

"And don't forget to send someone over here to get 'old Cigar Face (George was grunting with frustration at my every word). We don't want him getting loose and warning Makala before we get there."

CHAPTER 56.......
GOING TO LIVE

The trip to Molokai by boat took less than an hour and by the time we got there, we had a plan roughed out. I would go to Pua's front door and draw Jude outside of the house. Hai, who would be hiding out of sight, would arrest him.

It was a simple plan. We discussed covering the front and back and coaxing him to surrender but then decided that would likely lead to Pua and the kids becoming hostages. Letting him get the drop on me, outside, seemed like the simplest and best plan.

Before heading over to Pua's house, we went by Kappy's and found him in his workshop working on making homemade Marlin lures. I gave him the reason we were there and he was shocked. That Jude Makala could be inside the family compound without his knowledge had him upset. Kappy was extremely concerned for the danger to his grandchildren.

"I brought an extra weapon for you," Hai said lifting a pant leg and revealing a little snub-nosed revolver strapped to his calves.

I lifted the back of my shirt and pulled out the bigger, fully loaded Browning. "Thanks, but I've got one of my own."

Kappy looked at me and gave a quick wink.

Hai went quickly from, "Where'd you get that?" to "Never mind. I don't want to know."

We then had Kappy call the FBI to tell them that Jude Makala was hiding on the property with his daughter-in-law.

The next move was Hai's. By moving around the courtyard, which is between the Kapuulaa family residences, Hai was able to take up a position on the side of Pua's house nearest her front door.

Once he was in place, I went straight through the courtyard to the front door and knocked loudly announcing myself. "Pua, its Jack Bryce. We need to talk about *The Onion Express*."

I heard some movement from inside and waited for what I hoped would be Jude coming to the front door. It was.

Jude opened the door part way showing me he had a gun pointed directly at my belly and wearing a big smile. "If I'd known it was going to be this easy, I'd never have gone to the trouble of a car bomb. Come on in Jack."

I acted surprised. "What are you doing here?"

"What do you think I'm doing here Jack?"

"Trying to take over all of the Kapuulaa family businesses? With them, and families like them out of the way, you could just about run all of these islands."

"Pua said you were pretty dumb. Maybe she was wrong about you. Anyhow, get your ass in here."

"If Pua and the kids are in there, then I'd rather you came outside."

"No way Jack. You probably told that old man over there that you're here. I'm not going out where he can see me. No one knows I'm here and I like it that way. For the final time, get your ass in here," he said motioning me with his gun.

"If I go in there you're going to kill me and no one will know except you and Pua if she is in there. No, if you're going to kill me then do it out here so folks can hear the gunshot."

"Hmm. Seems we got a little stand off here, only I'm the one holding the gun. You are through Jack. Anyway, you look at it you're a dead man. Since no one else is home right now, it will just be our little secret. Are you going to make me come and get you?"

"I'm not going inside Jude." I said standing there with my hands in the back pockets of my jeans.

Jude stepped forward opening the door all the way while peeking to see if anyone were around. Then he stepped out onto the porch within three feet of where I was standing.

"Police! Throw down your gun and put your hands behind your head!" Hai yelled loudly while aiming his gun at Jude.

"Nice move Jack," Jude said with a wink. Then he spoke to Hai, "You shoot me, I shoot him. Seems like a waste. Why don't you just bring me a car and I'll trade Jack for the car!"

"No deal Makala. Drop your weapon or I will shoot you right where you are standing!" Hai declared clearly.

I remained standing with my hands still loosely in my back pockets. "What are you going to do Jude? The Lieutenant is an excellent shot. No one has to die here today."

"I saw Jude start shaking his head from side to side and I knew he wasn't going to surrender. In fact, I figured he was going to take me with him. Breaking the standoff, I dove onto the grassy lawn while pulling out the Browning. The bullet from Jude's gun tore through my shirt, into, and out of the fleshy part of my torso just above my right hip.

Hai fired twice at Jude, who was now moving out toward me to finish me off. I saw Jude wince and lurch from the impact of Hai's second shot, which gave me just enough time to let loose with the Browning. I let go at least five shots from the automatic, and Jude jumped like a puppet on string before collapsing on the lawn next to me.

I kept the big gun trained on him until Hai got there and removed Jude's weapon from his hand.

"You okay brudah?" Hai asked.

"Going to live I think," I said, pulling my hand out from underneath my shirt and showing that it was covered with blood. I looked over at Jude's lifeless body and he seemed almost peaceful.

"Jesus, Jack...Kappy, call for an ambulance. Jack's been hit!" Hai yelled out as loud as he could to the old man.

"Already on it!" Kappy replied across the courtyard.

CHAPTER 57.........MISSING

A helicopter carrying the two FBI agents I had entertained the night before hovered for a minute, and then landed near Kappy's workshop. They had not even gotten out yet when an air ambulance landed in the closer courtyard and two paramedics rushed to the scene. One pushed me back down on the grass and looked at my wound, while the other tired to find signs of life in Jude...and failed.

"You're going to need cleaning and some stitches but it's just a flesh wound. You are going to be all right," said the paramedic attending me.

While it was nice to know that my body would recover, I had some real concerns about what the FBI might do to me let alone Veronica when she hears I was shot again!

"We're going to take him over to the hospital to treat him." The paramedic said to Hai. The two agents who were standing over Jude and me, were looking none too pleased.

When I got out of the emergency clinic, Hai was waiting for me in the lobby. "How'd it go with the Feds?" I asked hobbling towards him and holding my side, which hurt like hell with each step.

"They weren't real happy with the way we handled it, but what are they going to do, arrest us for catching a killer? I'm sure I'll get a nasty letter sent to my Chief for not following protocol, but I can live with that. Shouldn't you be in a wheelchair or something?"

"No wheelchair. I have to learn to move with the pain before my family gets here. What about me?" I asked Hai.

"What about you?"

"What about me and the FBI, or with the local police for that matter?"

"You're a whole different story! We've got you for carrying a concealed weapon; not having a license for your weapon; Not being registered for a weapon: discharging your weapon in public; usurping federal authority and a lot more."

"Usurping federal authority is a criminal charge?" I said playing along with Hai's joke. "Sounds serious!"

"Nah. You're okay brudah. Do you really think anyone is going to charge you? You're a hero! What would the press say? You're okay brudah. No one is going to mess with you."

"What about Pua? Where is she?"

"Well, that's the sad part Jack. We think she is on the run. No one has heard from her, and we don't know where she is. Kappy is frantic over those children. Says he's going to put out a reward for their safe return. For the moment, we have Pua and the kids officially listed as missing.

CHAPTER 58.......NO WORRIES

Veronica and Marie's plane landed on schedule and I was on time to greet them. I had gotten each of them a lei for their arrival. All through the welcoming hugs and kisses, I sucked it up when they touched the wound area that they didn't know was there.

We went straight to the hotel in Kihei and unpacked the girl's things and then we headed out for a nice dinner at a restaurant within walking distance of our hotel. Marie was totally in awe and very excited about being in Maui. I was just happy to be with my family. Holding hands, putting my arm around her and an occasional hug had me thinking, and feeling like I was in heaven.

When Veronica and I finally got to bed in our own room that night she propped herself up on one elbow, searched my face and said, "Want to tell me about it?"

"About what?"

"Want to tell me what's wrong and why you aren't attacking me right now when we haven't seen each other in a long time?"

I reached over putting one arm under and one arm over her and pulling her to me. "I was just making sure Marie had time to fall asleep."

Veronica smiled and slid on top of me, brushing over the wound, I grimaced from the contact.

"Jack?"

"Yes love?" I tried to recover with a big smile.

"What hurts?"

"Not being with you for so long honey."

"Nice one Jack, but I'm not buying. What is going on with you?"

"If I tell you can we still make love?"

"Probably. Let's hear it."

"Well I got his little wound in my side here and…"

Veronica rolled the blankets back and pulled up my shirt. Seeing the bandage she demanded, "What happened?"

"Just a little flesh wound. Doctor says it probably won't leave much of a scar." I said in earnest.

"What happened?"

"I got shot…again," I said with a small frown.

"Are you okay?"

"I'm truly fine. It just went in and out here," I said pointing to where the bullet hole had penetrated and then exited through my side

"So then you're fine?"

"Yep!"

"You're sure?"

"Yep!"

"Then why didn't you tell me before now?"

"Because it's nothing serious and I didn't want it to ruin yours and Marie's arrival."

"You're sure you are up to this?"

I nodded toward my erect manhood, "Silly question don't you think!"

"Well then let's make some love because it's been a long time for me too!"

Despite a few grimaces, we made great and passionate love and then we lay in each other's arms through the night, happy at being close to each other again. We were both happy about not having to sleep alone again. Overall, it was a great night. More importantly, it was a night of no worries.

CHAPTER 59.......
MESSING UP (AGAIN)

I tried to reach Luanne several times throughout the week. I wanted to take care of the unfinished business she had contacted me about, but it was as if she had vanished. Kappy too had noted that she wasn't at work, but he was so involved in the search for Pua and his grandchildren that he couldn't think of much else.

Since the soccer team was not due for a few more days Veronica, Marie and I played tourists. We rented surfboards for all of us, surfed, and barbecued on the beach with Kimo, Paolo and the rest of their family. Paolo and Marie hit it off right away and the two spent all of their time in the water and away from the parents. It was okay by me. It was fun day for both families. We had connected in a way that said the two families would always be friends.

We also rented and rode horses over parts of Mount Haleakala, took Marie to the Seven Pools in Hana and watched her dive from the high rocks. It seemed like there was an entourage of young men following her from diving point to diving point at each of the deep pools. I don't think the boys were there admiring her dives, but she had fun with the attention she was getting. Veronica and I sat watching her and talking about what had gone on in Maui as well as in Boulder Creek for the past several weeks. I told Veronica of my encounters with the now missing Pua Kapuulaa, and I didn't leave out any details. Veronica said she would very much like to meet Pua and I said, "At this point so would the police!" We both laughed and then Veronica punched me in the arm, hard.

"What was that for?"

"For having let Pua see you naked."

"If I had stayed in the shower she'd have just stripped down and joined me." I explained my rationale for getting out and walking past her in the all together.

"I guess your right." Then she hit me again.

"Now what was that for?"

"That was for not latching the front door."

"I guess I messed up on that one."

"Yep."

Chapter 60.......
The Tournament

Things changed when the soccer team finally arrived. There were girls going in and out of our room all of the time. The coaches had multiple team meetings for the girls and meetings for the parents as well. The meetings discussed the rules of the tournament and expectations of needed behavior to help keep the girls focused. We also discussed that the girls had worked hard to earn this trip and we needed to insure, most of all, that they have fun.

The girls had practice twice a day, which was tough on them at first as their bodies adjusted to the Hawaiian climate. The weather was not necessarily hotter than home, but it was definitely more humid and draining. They learned to hydrate themselves, and they were being very cautious not to become overheated, or sick from dehydration. For these girls, teamwork went way beyond the soccer field, and it was Art and Chris who had instilled that in them over the years. It was their teaming and understanding of each other, that made them a highly successful and very competitive team.

When game day finally came, the team felt it was ready for the challenge. Up first for our girls, was a team from Oahu, and the match was a good one. Marie was at center mid, the girl she was playing against was fast, very fast, and Marie had her hands full in keeping up with her. Nonetheless, Marie's skills at trapping and passing the ball taxed her opponent to a point of frustration that caused an error. This gave Marie an opportunity to lay the ball just in front of the left forward who easily pushed it into the corner for a score. The game was close but the Valley girls (a combination of San Lorenzo Valley and Scott's Valley) hung on for a two to one victory.

Back at the hotel, the entire team of parents and girls headed straight for the pool and a well deserved cooling off. Later, the girls ate pizza and pasta while having a team meeting to review the day's game and to plan for the next games. Then they watched a movie in our room, (sixteen girls, in various positions on the floor, chairs, beds and anywhere else they could squeeze together). After the movie, they went to bed early in preparation for the two games scheduled for the next day, one of them being a 7:00 AM start time.

Veronica and I, while the girls watched the movie in our room, remained near the bar in the hotel lobby re-living the day's game as well as games gone by with other parents. It is actually a very fun time with the other parents and Veronica and I are game for most any conversation with the exception of politics. We are both turned off when politics and politicians take over a conversation. When that happens, we tend to excuse ourselves and go for a walk or something. That was the case this time. Some of the folks got into a discussion regarding he pros and cons of the Bush administration. Instead of participating, Veronica and I politely excused ourselves took a walk along the oceanfront and then out to a nearby harbor where we walked amongst the docked boats. Almost anywhere, while in Hawaii, you can find a beautiful place to take a stroll. We got back to our room late and the room was empty except for Marie, who was already soundly sleeping.

The next morning saw everyone in the lobby, ready to travel to the soccer field at 5:45 AM. Once there, parents pulled out juices, fruits, cheeses and some plain bagels that the girls munched on while suiting up, and taping each other before warm-ups and the game.

The morning game pitted us against rivals from Contra Costa County in California. In years gone by, they had provided us with several lessons in humility, but for the past two years our girls owned them, and today was no different. The girls quickly took control of the game and when the score became five nothing our team turned it into a game of keep-away so as not to run the score up and to maintain good sportsmanship by keeping the score low.

After the game, we found a place at the soccer park under some trees where we set up a day camp, and where we waited for the next game, and watched other teams play. In particular, the coaches and some of the parents scouted the local Maui team who also had two wins and no losses. Everyone one said that the Maui team was the team to beat. To win the tournament we knew we would have to take them on. "Good skills, very aggressive and very fast" was the scouting report. Any two of those is enough to win tournaments and championships, but being good at all, three is amazing and very bad news for opponents. The coaches believed we were on a collision course with the Maui team if we were to win the next two games.

The afternoon game was much tougher on the girls than the morning game. The temperature was hot and humid, and the Arizona team we were playing was very good. We had never seen them before so the coaches approached the game with caution. Marie didn't start the second game as the coaches were favoring a strategy of lots of subbing. When her turn came to get into the game the coaches put her in at the left forward position to take advantage of Marie's skilled left foot, and to relieve the starter who needed rest often due to the tempo of the game. At halftime, the score was zero to zero, and by the time we were mid way through the second half the score still hadn't changed. Art and Chris changed up the line-up utilizing the fresh legs of the goalie as a forward, and putting Marie in the goalie position because of her flexibility, training and previous experience playing the goalie position.

After the goalie change was completed, and play had resumed, our girls were moving the ball when a player on the other team got hurt. It was a two-player collision, and the injured player had to be carried off the field by their coaching staff. Our team, in the spirit of good sportsmanship, relinquished the ball to the other team who took quick advantage by making a long pass to the other side of the field where their right forward began to bring the ball in for an unopposed goal shot. I cringed with both excitement and angst for the predicament my daughter now faced as the defending goalie.

Marie, seeing that the player was approaching unopposed, had to either stay back to defend against the shot, or move forward to reduce the other player's shot range. Marie took two bounces on her heels backward toward the goal and then, in a flash, sprinted directly at the approaching player and ball. The action so faked out the advancing player that she slowed her approach while trying to figure out what to do next, which allowed Marie to be on her within seconds to take away any shot. Not only did Marie take away any chance for a shot, but she also took the ball away passing it up the line to our own left forward who took the ball in and scored the only goal of the game.

With that victory, the team won a spot in the semi-finals. They returned to the hotel feeling very up, and very proud of their accomplishments from the long day on the field. Several of the girls,

Marie included, decided to skip the pool and instead headed to a popular beach, about a quarter of a mile away, which was okay with Veronica and me as long as the girls stayed together. According to the girls, they would lay low to conserve energy, and all they were going to do was to watch the local surfer boys. The parents knew better, but we let them go anyhow.

CHAPTER 61.......PANIC

At dinnertime, the team was to eat together, then have a team meeting, with cookies and other treats while prepping for the next game. In order to win the tournament the team would have to conquer another tough opponent in the semi-final match to advance to the title game.

Veronica and I were in our room sharing a bottle of Bonny Doon Big House White and watching a pay per view movie when Chris knocked at the door. "Hey Chris, what's up?" I said holding the door wide open.

"Marie didn't make the team meeting and I needed to make sure she is okay."

"We thought she was there with the rest of the girls. Are you sure you just didn't miss her? Sometimes all of those ponytails look alike."

"No we specifically wanted to talk to her because she has a special role in tomorrow's game strategy."

Veronica and I were becoming alarmed now. "Maybe she fell asleep in another player's room." Veronica offered.

"Well if she's not here, then we need to get a search going with the other girls. I'm sure you're right though, she must be napping somewhere." Chris replied trying to put us at ease.

For the next hour and a half, the whole team turned the hotel upside down looking for Marie with no luck. Veronica and I became more scared with each passing minute. I was to the point now that every hair on the back of my neck was standing at full attention sensing something was drastically wrong.

The girls who had gone to the beach with Marie said she was with them the whole time until she went to use a restroom. They were all playing beach volleyball with some boys they had met. It was during the match that Marie had excused herself to go to the restroom. When she didn't return right away, they figured she had returned to the hotel.

After searching for a while without finding her, I called Hai and reported Marie missing. He arrived at the hotel with three other officers in what seemed a matter of minutes. Veronica and I were very grateful, but very worried. Marie is not the type to disappear. She is outgoing but responsible.

"We'll find her, folks." Hai said to Veronica and me. "My men will interview the girls she was with and turn this place and the area between the beach and the hotel upside down until we find her."

"Thanks Hai. I want to go with you and look too, if you don't mind."

"I'll stay here in case she calls or shows up." Veronica volunteered.

By midnight, there was still no sign of Marie. Hai had even tracked down all of the boys who had been playing volleyball with girls. "Any chance this relates to the Makala case? Could any of his cronies still be around causing trouble?" I asked Hai.

"The only thing we've got happening there is the on-going search for Pua and her children."

"What about Luanne? Anybody heard from her?"

"Not a trace Jack. It's as if she has vanished. Her apartment seems normal; there are no signs of violence or anything. All of her stuff is there, including her luggage, so there is no evidence of her going on a trip or anything. Like Pua and the kids, she has just vanished."

"My gut tells me there is a connection Hai. I think once we find any one of them we'll find all of them. Hopefully, Marie included."

"I hope you are right brudah!"

It was a sleepless night. At six o'clock in the morning, we got a call from the front desk. "We have a message at the desk for you, Mr. Bryce. May we deliver it to you now?"

"Just keep it there and I'll be right down to get it." I partly ran the distance to the desk via hallway and stairs with Veronica right on my heels. When we reached the front desk, the manager and a police officer were waiting for us.

"It's addressed to you, Mr. Bryce. We found the note on the ground in our driveway. It couldn't have been there very long as our staff is in that area often," the manager explained.

The officer suggested I hold the envelope on the edges so as not to smear any fingerprints that may be on it. I followed his suggestion and opened the envelope carefully, keeping the contents private to Veronica and myself.

The note inside was comprised of letters cut from a newspaper and pasted to a piece of plain white paper.

It read:

Yur DaughteR = 500,000 at noon in the MALL. nO policE!

Veronica broke into tears, and I shivered with rage and fear. "It's a ransom note. They want five hundred thousand dollars for Marie." I said to the manager and the officer.

"I'll call it in. Lieutenant Ho will want to know this right away and I'm sure the FBI will need to be notified." the young officer explained.

"Tell whomever you want," I said handing the officer the note. My wife and I will be in our room."

"What do you want do?" I asked Veronica when we got to our room.

"I want to do whatever it takes to get our daughter back!"

"Agreed. Shall we pay the ransom?"

"Never!" Veronica replied.

"Agreed!" I responded

"Any ideas Jack?"

"I have a couple and they don't involve the police or the FBI." I responded searching her eyes for approval and getting it. "We both go to the drop. You go first and you go as any other shopper would to the mall. I don't think anyone here would recognize you, but just in case, you should wear a hat and your sunglasses. I'll make the drop and we'll use cut up paper between real bills. If the person receiving the drop doesn't look real close, it will bide us time for you follow them and see if they lead us to our daughter."

"What if they see the money is phony?"

"Then we take the person doing the pick up hostage in trade for our daughter."

"What if that doesn't work?"

"Then we'll do whatever it is that we have to do to make it work."

"I just want our daughter back."

"Me too. What we can't do now, for Marie's sake, is panic."

"It's too late for that Jack. I'm beyond panic!"

"Me too!"

CHAPTER 62........GOT IT ALL

The FBI and Hai all showed up at our hotel. Now that they knew it was a kidnapping one of the first things they did was to move another team member and her parents from their suite to another one, so that the adjoining suite to our room could be opened up for more room. The area was buzzing with activity and Veronica and I watched for awhile, then we retired to our bedroom to follow through on our own plans of creating the phony money out of newspapers, magazines, and paperbacks.

There was a knock on the door and it was Art and Chris. "Our semi-final game is at noon and the team is torn as to whether or not they should play."

"Play." Veronica and I chided almost simultaneously looking at each other with welling eyes.

"That's what we thought you would say. All of the girls are very upset about this, especially the ones that went to the beach with her. Do you think one of you could say something to the team?"

"Of course we will." Veronica responded. "Where are you holding the meeting?"

"How about meeting us in the parking lot in about ten minutes?" Chris suggested.

276

"We'll be there." I responded seeing them out the bedroom door.

Veronica said, "This is our chance to get out of here without the police."

"Agreed," I said. "Let's put the drop package in Marie's soccer bag. That way we can explain we are going to talk to the team and say we want them to take her bag as if she were there."

We told the police we were going to the team meeting and that we'd be right back.

"Maybe one of us should go with you," one of the FBI agents offered.

"I think it would be better for the team if you weren't there." I said.

"The team is scared enough. I think it is best if it is just Jack and I," Veronica said backing me up.

"No problem, Mrs. Bryce," the agent said backing off and leaving us alone.

In the parking lot we asked the girls to play the noontime game and to do their very best to try to win. We said that is what Marie would do if one of them couldn't make the game. Then we got Art to switch cars, no questions asked and he said of course.

We arrived near the mall an hour before the appointed money drop. Veronica dropped me off two blocks away, while she went in search of a parking spot close to the main entrance. She had to drive around for awhile until someone left, but she wound up with a good spot that would provide quick access to the car if needed. Then she went inside acting as if it were an ordinary shopping day. We were relying on the kidnappers not recognizing Veronica as being my wife.

Taking time to walk the two blocks I stopped for coffee, which I did not really need. Finally, I arrived at the mall's main entry five minutes before the appointed drop time carrying Marie's soccer bag in my right hand. I sat down on a wooden bench in the main foyer and waited.

Almost immediately, a woman with short blonde hair, khaki pants and an oversized Hawaiian shirt sat next to me and peered at me over the top of her flashy sunglasses. "Hi ya Jack!" Pua said crossing her legs and leaning over for a closer look at the sports bag.

"Pua? I didn't recognize you in that wig and those clothes."

"Yep."

"Why my daughter Pua?" I asked still holding tightly onto Marie's soccer bag.

"Because you ruined all of my plans. I hear you killed Jude. Is that true?"

"It was self defense. He shot me first."

"Oooh Jack, you make it sound so exciting. Where did he shoot you? Here? Or how about here?" she said squeezing my thigh and running her hand up the inside of my leg. I hope he didn't shoot you here," she said placing her hand directly over my manhood and squeezing hard enough to make me squirm.

"You're a real piece of work Pua. Where is my daughter?" I said ignoring her touches.

"We'll release her after I get back with the money."

"No Marie, no money." I said menacingly.

"Have it your way then Jack, no Marie." With that, Pua abruptly got up from her place next to me and started walking away.

I let her go about ten steps, hoping that she was bluffing and that she would turn around to come back for the money. She didn't turn around. Quickly I said, "Okay Pua."

"I'm sorry Jack did you say something to me?"

"You win Pua. Here's the money." I said offering the bag for her taking.

"That's better Jack. Now you just stay here for awhile and Marie will be around shortly. Thank you." she said taking the bag and heading out the door.

I watched her walk out of the mall and Veronica was right beside her. I stayed seated trusting in my wife knowing that she would call me from her cell phone. In less than two minutes, Veronica had me on the cellular. "I'm following her on Mokulele Highway back toward Kihei."

"Keep talking honey. I'm grabbing a cab now and I will be right behind you. What kind of a car is she driving?"

"She's in a fairly new, powder blue, convertible Volkswagen bug."

Suddenly it all clicked in. Pua was driving Luanne's car, which probably meant Luanne's and Pua's disappearance were not coincidental. Somehow, the two were connected and always had been. I also remembered that it was Luanne who gotten me to go to my car that had been wired with the bomb. She knew! She was also very insistent about getting me my next rental car. I guessed she wanted to do that to help monitor me, or maybe set me up again.

"I know who Pua's accomplice is. It's Luanne!"

"Your secretary? Why would she be involved?"

"I think Pua is driving her car and I just realized that it was Luanne who set me up to get blown up in the Mustang! Luanne also made the reservation for where we are staying so she knew exactly where to find us." The taxi driver was listening to my conversation with Veronica with great interest.

"Where are you right now Jack?"

I'm passing some burned-out sugar cane fields. Where are you?"

"I know exactly where you are then. You are about three minutes behind me. Wait...she is turning right onto North Kihei Rd. She is slowing down."

'I'm guessing she's trying to see if she is being followed. You should pass her and not look at her while you are going by so she doesn't think you are following her. I'll get the cab driver to speed up and see if we can't catch her."

"Okay honey, just stay on the line. Don't lose me. And do not lose her either!"

"If we do lose our connection, I will call you. Okay?"

"Okay. I've passed her now and I'm coming to the intersection of Highways 31, 380 and 30. Which way should I go?"

"Take the Thirty Road toward Lahaina. I'm guessing that is where she is going. I see her now. We are about five cars behind her. Uh oh… she's turning right onto 380. You had better turn around."

"Okay. I'm making an illegal u-turn across the double yellow line right now."

"Okay babe. You should be all right. We are still a few cars behind her and it looks like she is doubling back toward Kahului."

"Is that you in the blue cab?"

"Yep. You should stay back so she doesn't see your car."

"Okay Jack."

"She's turning left onto Puunene, and now we are only one car behind her."

"I still gotcha."

"You folks some kind of police or something?" the cab driver asked.

"No, it's just a game and thanks for playing along with us. I'll make it worth your while when we're done. Is that okay with you brudah?"

"Sounds good to me. Just so long as you pay the bill."

Just then, Pua pulled off onto a little dirt road and straight into a mobile home park. "This looks like the place babe. I'm going to pay the cab driver and get out. You pick me up okay?"

"Okay honey."

I tipped the driver twenty bucks for "playing the game" and climbed right into Art's car with Veronica. "Let's go get our daughter!"

We drove into the mobile home park looking for the convertible blue bug and it didn't take long to find it. "Do you think they have guns Jack? We don't have a gun do we?"

"No gun pumpkin. The police took it away from me after I shot Jude Makala."

"What are we going to do?"

"We're going to get our daughter back, and we're going to return Kappy's grandchildren to him."

"How are we going to do that?"

"I'm going to knock on the front door while you check the back side of the trailer."

"You're just going to knock on the door?"

"You would rather I broke it down?"

"I don't know Jack. I'll just leave the door to you."

I pointed Veronica to the other side of the doublewide mobile home, while I climbed the five steps that led up to the front porch and the front door, where I could hear some commotion inside.

"How in the hell can you not have checked the money before driving away? That was really stupid Pua!" Luanne blasted Pua inside the mobile home. "He's probably followed you here."

I took that as my cue to knock on the door, and when Luanne opened it, I smiled and said, "You're right on target Luanne! Now may I have my daughter please?"

Luanne tried to bolt away from me, but I grabbed and restrained her even though she was kicking, biting and doing her best to get away. From the backside of the mobile home, I heard Veronica say,

"So you are Pua! I want my daughter!" I dragged Luanne through the kitchen and to the back door on the other side of the mobile home in order to help Veronica.

"So you are Jack's little lady. I have no idea what he could ever see in you. Your little brat is inside. Now get out of my way!" Then she tried to get past Veronica, but Veronica wasn't having it.

"You're not going anywhere!" Veronica said stoically. When Pua tried to move past her again, Veronica popped her with a straight left jab to the nose that sent Pua floundering and staggering for balance. "That's for taking my kid. And this one is for messing with my husband," then she hit Pua again, this time driving her to the ground and bloodying her lower lip.

"Nice punch Babe! I got these two, why don't you go find our daughter?"

Marie was in a tiny bedroom, bound and gagged. When Veronica untied her, she threw her arms around her mom and held her tight.

I got Luanne and Pua to sit on a couch in the family room where we also found Pua's children who had been watching TV until I came in. "Let me guess. Sisters?" I asked them.

"How did you find out Jack?"

"I didn't. I just now guessed and you confirmed it. Pretty good for a dummy like me, heh Pua?" I said, remembering Jude's comment of what Pua had said about me being not too bright.

"You could have been rich beyond your widest dreams Jack. I was yours for the taking, and we could have it all! The ranches, the onion fields, the homes on Molokai, the yacht and *The Onion Express* too!"

"I've already got it all," I said as Veronica and Marie came into the room.

CHAPTER 63...
THAT'S WHY WE'RE HERE!

The police and the FBI arrived to pick up Luanne and Pua, who they handcuffed and took away rather quickly. However, they kept the three of us, plus Pua's children, there for quite awhile. They took statements from each of us, one at a time, so it took a long time.

Kappy arrived just as the FBI was finishing with us. "Nice job brudah. Nice job. I got my grandkids now, and soon I am going to get *The Onion Express* and the rest of the family businesses back. When I do, you can get your job back and finish it the way Kainoa and I wanted it done. You have done so much for my family and the people of deese islands that we can never repay you. You are now a son in my family, and there will always be a place for you in Hawaii. Always!"

"Thanks Kappy. Maybe I could bring a couple of friends back next year and you could take us for more marlin fishing?"

"You say the date and I'll be ready!" Kappy replied. Then we said our goodbyes so that Kappy could take his confused and very upset grandchildren back to their home.

When we finally got back to the hotel, the team was waiting for us, and we got tons of hugs and congratulations on Marie's return. "Who won the game?" I asked Chris as we were happily shaking hands regarding Marie's return.

"It was incredible Jack! We were down three zip at the half. When we came back for the second half, the girls kicked it up to a gear I have never seen before, and they won it four to three in overtime. We're going to the final against the Maui team. The game is tomorrow morning at 10:00 AM. Will Marie be able to play?"

I grabbed Marie and said, "Chris wants to know if you'll be able to play tomorrow?"

"Of course I want to play Daddy. That's why we're here!"

Chris and I looked at each other and I shrugged my shoulders saying, "You heard it. That's why we're here!"

FROM THE AUTHOR
& HIS FAMILY

The beauty and magnificence offered by the Santa Cruz Mountains and California's Central Coast is only surpassed by the people who live there and provide its' protection. From the overpowering and beautiful redwood forests, to the rugged coastal beaches, and the wondrous Monterey Bay, the area offers a vast array of natural treasures for anyone who cares to explore.

It has been our privilege and pleasure to have lived and raised our family in this "Redwood Tall and Mountain Rugged" community for the past twenty-five years. Our friends and cohorts in the area, considered family, and the relationships with our "family", are filled to the brim with heartfelt warmth and appreciation.

With life's inevitable journey comes change, and change is often difficult. Children grow up, families expand, jobs and careers change, and even age constantly challenges us with its new dimensions. Our family is facing those changes now.

As we prepare to move on, our family will never completely disconnect ourselves from its roots so firmly embedded in the Santa

Cruz Mountains. Instead, we will keep our time spent here and all of the people with whom we have shared life's adventures deep within our hearts.

From my family to yours…thank you for your friendship.

Brad

Next:

Please join Jack Bryce as he encounters new mystery and adventure in *Special Delivery*, a thriller set in the heart of the Santa Cruz Mountains.

PROLOGUE

The Wednesday afternoon commute home was typical for the month of July. The temperature was hot, too damned hot, and cars started lining up in the thick traffic at about Camden Avenue for the trek over Highway 17. At Camden, the traffic begins to slow and then by the time one reaches the Highway 85 junction, where the number of lanes diminish, it turns into an agonizing, grueling, torturous, seemingly never-ending stop and go procession of patient and not so patient drivers. All of who are anxious to get home to the Santa Cruz Mountains or the coastal communities where they live.

For Robert Purdy, the scene was familiar. He had recently celebrated his fifteenth year with the microprocessor company he works for in Milpitas. Today, thank God, he at least had a San Francisco Giants baseball game to listen to, keeping him from focusing on the frustrating traffic ahead. The game was a good one, too, with Schmidt pitching, and Bonds and Snow combining for multiple runs. Moreover, it was only the third inning in their game with the New York Mets at Shea Stadium, who had a good team this year but whose pitching was struggling today.

Finally, at around the Cats, a small hillside community and restaurant just above the town of Los Gatos, traffic began to move and the only thing that seemed to have caused the gridlock was a California Highway Patrol vehicle parked near the Cat's entrance. The officer was not investigating a collision, or even citing anyone. Rather, it seemed from Robert's vantage as he drove by, the young officer was just doing paperwork inside of his air-conditioned patrol car and not even paying any attention to the traffic slowly passing by him. Robert smiled to himself thinking about how ridiculous some drivers can be when seeing and slowing just because a police car was parked alongside the road. He suspected, too, that there would be one or two more similar scenarios along the ride home. More backups would probably occur at the Summit and then again somewhere around the Glencanyon Cutoff where the police are known to monitor the traffic on this usually busy and fairly dangerous highway.

The traffic magically cleared, as it does almost everyday, when the speed limit opened up from the posted fifty miles per hour to sixty-five near the town of Scotts Valley. Robert got off at Mount Hermon Road and made his way through the Scotts Valley traffic lights heading toward Felton where, again, he stopped in a long line of cars waiting to merge onto Highway 9 towards the towns of Ben Lomond, Brookdale and Boulder Creek.

It was the middle of the fifth-inning now, and the score was five to one in favor of the Giants as Robert pulled into the mostly hidden U-shaped driveway at his home. The driveway fit nicely into the desert like low maintenance and drought resistant landscaping that he and his wife Helen had designed and installed on their own during the eleven years they had lived in the Glen Arbor Road upscale home.

"I'm home," Robert announced coming through the partially stained glass and solid oak front door. But the only response he received was from their nine-year old cocker spaniel Buffy, who was excitedly waiting at the patio door. "Helen?" Robert queried the quiet and unusually still house without response. After passing through the kitchen where he placed his commuter coffee mug on the breakfast counter, next to a pile of neatly stacked unopened mail, he went down the hallway and toward the master bedroom where he intended to change from his stuffy work clothes into shorts and a t-shirt.

It was when he entered the bedroom that his life was shattered forever. There, on their queen sized, wooden framed four-poster bed laid Helen with her eyes fixed wide open staring blankly at the ceiling. Her mouth was agape and her non-moving lips looked pale and dry. He saw too that her arms were bound, via her wrists, to the posts on either side of their bed. Robert rushed to Helen, whose body lay at an uncomfortable and twisted angle with her neck looking oddly offset. He quickly reached her lifeless body while crying out with never before felt agony and horror, "Helen? Oh my God. Helen!" With tears streaming down his face he held her lifeless form in his arms rocking it gently and moaning, "Please no God, please God, oh, please no."

It was when he returned her still bound upper torso back to the rumpled bed that he noted the strange and ugly purple bruise on his wife's neck and that the house-dress she was wearing was pulled up around her panty-less waist. Too, he noted that the dress was torn at the top exposing one of Helen's breasts, which was badly bruised.

Robert was horrified and sickened by the scene…a scene that he would, unfortunately, mentally replay, repeatedly, for the rest of his life.

Printed in the United States
47930LVS00003B/166-243

9 781425 916268